Jorge Sexer

BERLIN EXPO

1

"Your proposal is unacceptable from every point of view."

Morel opens his mouth to answer, but chooses to remain silent.

"If you had said seven hundred, if you had said eight hundred, I would answer you," declared Keller. "I would answer you that my word has a certain value, as does yours, in case you've forgot it. But the amount you mention ... That's not an offer, that's an insult."

He gets up and disappears into the back room. Morel has never seen him so enraged.

After a few minutes, he is back:

"Mr. Morel, let us better stop here. You give it some thought, and let me know your decision tomorrow. On the basis that the price of *Still Life* is no longer a matter of negotiation."

Let him be angry, let him be furious, thinks Morel; nine hundred marks is still too much for that piece. It was reasonable a few months ago, today the price is below that. A long way below.

He will not return to Paris without the painting. But he wants to have it at the right price.

The day hadn't begun well. He went to the Kranzler, ordered a coffee, and it took the waiter twenty minutes to serve him. And when he finally did, it was without the shadow of an excuse. Is it because he's a stranger? That wasn't a problem in the old days. Not everybody loved France, far from it, but when they heard that he came from Paris, *Stadt der Lichter, Stadt der Liebe* - the city of light, the city of love – he got always a smile.

The café is otherwise as lively as usual, although the clientèle has changed: the old man with a beret and a white beard, offering poems "that the muse Erato has just dictated to him", to praise the beauty of the lady or the nobility of the feelings of her Romeo, has disappeared, as have the gay-lads who had their meeting point in the back room.

Twice during the hour that Morel spends at the Kranzler, youths of the assault troops come into the café ; they walk among the tables, scrutinizing the customers' faces. In the old days, they passed through the street with large deployments of truncheons, but did never actually get in.

It's time. He puts on his hat and leaves the place, passing between the three rows of tables on the terrace. He walks down the Unter den Linden, past the Hotel Adlon, decorated with red swastika flags, and, once at the Brandenburg Gate, he hails a taxi.

"To Savignyplatz."

The vehicle drives for a short while through the Tiergarten – oaks and lime trees are still sparsely clad – then leaves through the side street. The Hotel Palast, with its majestic façade, its colossal pilasters and rounded windows, a huge canopy above the entrance and, of course, two Nazi flags, with their sizes corresponding to the dimensions of the building. After a while, the imposing silhouette of the Gedächtniskirche, the Church of Remembrance, an islet in the middle of the bustling avenue. "The world's most neo-romanesque obstacle to traffic," according to Violetta Brenner.

They are almost at the destination when a policeman barres their way. Behind him, three rows of SA stand at attention.

"My God," sighs Morel. The taxi driver nods. "Does this happen often?" asks Morel. "It happens." "But, for what reason?"

Noticing his foreign accent, the driver watches him briefly on the mirror. "There is surely a reason. But if you prefer to get off here... it's not far."

Grolmanstrasse. The Gallery Kronen. The shop windows covered with black velvet. A landscape and two portraits. On a bronze plaque, the name of the owner: Erwin Keller.

Morel breathes deeply. Discussing prices, bargaining, that's what his trade is all about. But once an agreement has been reached, you must stick to it ; that is one of the principles his father instilled in him.

He pushes the door, it closes behind him with a creaking. Hearing the sound of the hinges, a middle-aged man emerges from the back of the shop. Advanced baldness, the brown hair combed to the sides.

"Glad to see you, Mr. Morel," he utters with a smile. "A coffee?"

Morel accepts and the man disappears through a blue curtain. Morel hears the whistling of the gas let out by a burner, then the small explosion when the fluid comes in contact with a match's flame.

Where is the Schiele, the portrait with the green background? he wonders.

"Was your journey pleasant?" asks Keller from the back room.

"Yes, I changed trains in Leipzig this time."

"Excellent, excellent."

And the street scene by Schmidt-Rottluff for which he was asking a thousand marks? At the exhibition too?

"Come here please," Keller motions him. They take a seat by a small staggering wooden table. The coffee, re-heated, has an acrid taste.

"So?" Morel asks after gulping down a sip. "The *EnKu*?"

Keller looks blankly at him.

"*Entartete Kunst,* the exhibition at the gasometer."

"Oh. It's scheduled to open on Saturday."

"Are they advertising it?"

The other makes a contemptuous gesture.

"I have seen no posters, and I don't even know for sure where that gasometer is."

Morel takes a second sip. He has a hard time trying to hide a grimace.

"So, Mr. Keller, when may I have the picture?"

"As soon as I get it back. The exhibition will last two months, but if you prefer, we can conclude the deal right now."

"No. I'll wait."

The gallery owner, in his fifties, is tall below average. His visit to the hairdresser is three weeks past due, guesses Morel. The wicks are of unequal length, and they have already got loose from the discipline imposed on them this morning, if they were ever combed.

The man is seldom jovial, but at this moment he looks downright glum.

"Your affairs go well?" asks Morel politely.

"I cannot complain."

"But the market is rather dull?"

"Let's not exaggerate. There is some uncertainty, yes."

Uncertainty? ponders Morel. He would call it differently.

"Well, I'm always interested in that piece."

Keller's face lights up.

"But," adds Morel, attentive to the other's reaction, "we'll have to agree on the price."

There. It's been said.

Keller looks at him in amazement.

"But we already have ! Nine hundred marks."

"Things have changed, Erwin."

Keller gets up and heads for the back room.

"I'll tell you exactly when we agreed on it" he mumbles as he rummages through the pages of a thick binder.

"Mr. Keller, there's no need to show me any records. The thing is, the market has evolved since, and nine hundred marks at that date do not amount to nine hundred marks today."

"Oh, no," protests Keller. "If you think prices have gone down, you're wrong."

Morel stares at him, stone-faced. The other looks him in the eye.

"This art is dying, Erwin, Grosz is in New York, so you tell me. What for? To attend an exhibition, to meet his mistress?"

"He was compromised," admits Keller. "But others, like Nolde, are appreciated by the National Socialists. By some of them, at any rate."

"That sounds strange."

Keller looks at him pleased.

"That's what I mean, Gaston: you have a wrong idea of the art market here. Which is normal, living in Paris as you do."

"I'm here often."

"But you cannot keep up with the day to day situation, can you?"

"I subscribe to the *Vossische Zeitung*."

Keller nods, still smiling.

"Yes, yes, Gaston, and that makes you an authority on German art, no doubt. On all things German, I'll grant you that. But, you have to admit that my informations are more up to date. You are surprised when I tell you that Emil Nolde is hold in high esteem by the Nazis. How would you react if I add that he in turn sympathizes with them?"

Morel cannot hide his perplexity.

"You see," the other goes on, " 'expressionist art' doesn't have to be synonymous with 'Bolshevik' or 'anarchist'. I happen to know that Goebbels has a sculpture by Ernst Barlach in his office, in the Ordenspalais. Yes, at the very heart of the culture ministry."

Is he taking him for a ride? He'll have to control this with Violetta Brenner.

"If you lived in Berlin, such things would not surprise you. You would also know, perhaps, that the minister sent a congratulatory telegram to Edvard Munch for his birthday. But the *Vossische Zeitung* may have omitted to mention it ... "

"Are you making fun of me, Erwin? The first of April is still far away."

"Do not underrate the National Socialists," insists Keller. "I have personally attended an exhibition in Spandau a few days ago. Not many works, but well chosen, the very best of Expressionism."

"Did you see anything by Grosz there?" he asks sceptically.

"Grosz works in a different style. And he's a communist. But there were a few things by Hofer, by Barlach. And, mind you, there was nothing clandestine about it. Organized by Cultural Action of Spandau. Red carpet, free *sekt.* "

"Okay Erwin, let's set aside Nolde and Barlach for a moment. I offer you four hundred marks for the Grosz painting, against delivery within two months."

Keller opens his eyes wide. Then they grow smaller. He frowns, his features darken. Finally he utters, pronouncing each word slowly and deliberately:

"Now it is you who are taking me for a ride, Morel."

His contacts with Keller date back four years. He's sorry to see him in this predicament, but he's got his own interests to look after.

Morel was ten years old when his father left Béziers, in the south of France, to cross the Atlantic. As other wine merchants, he was hard hit by the crisis in the southern vineyards. He settled in Buenos Aires and used his contacts in France to import *grands crus*, appreciated by rich Argentinians.

Gaston learned the trade, but he did not want to live in the shadow of his father. In 1925 he was back in France as the representative of *Casa Morel* of Buenos Aires. He was making a good living, but he did not intend to grow old as a wine and liquor salesman. In Buenos Aires he had studied art. One of his classmates at the Academy was the son of *señor* Julio Navarro, the owner of the most important newspaper in South America, and a keen art collector.

Thanks to a loan from Morel Sr., he could open an art gallery. In the first year he suffered losses, until he understood that he had to find his own niche, to exploit the resources that were unique to him. For Gaston Morel had access to more than just two cultures: his mother had grown up in Strasbourg at a time when Alsace was a province in the Kaiser's empire. Thanks to her, Morel speaks, besides French and Spanish, also fluent German.

In Paris, painters from beyond the Rhine were not very well known yet. He grasped the intensity of those artists and, taking advantage of the mark's depreciation, he purchased a number of works of quality. He filled his premises in the Rue Cambacères with German expressionists and neo-objectivists, organized cocktail parties and *soirées*. Navarro, who had friends among newspapers directors all over the world, put him in touch with editors of *Le Matin,* of *Le Temps.*

During his frequent trips to Dresden, Munich, and Berlin, he became also acquainted with Russian art. And his gallery got finally to be known as an introducer of German art, but also - with Fräulein Brenner's help - as a specialist in Russian futurists.

Keller's painting, *Still Life with Three Characters*, by George Grosz, will save the year of Morel's gallery, considering the price that Navarro, an amateur of erotic art, will pay for it. But the deal must be closed without further delay, or the tycoon might change his mind.

And other opportunities will arise: Germany's new masters do not like the avant-garde and they are people who, when something displeases them, don't just frown and go to look elsewhere.

Many collectors will be in a hurry to get rid of a number of great works. As for the state museums, they will be plundered. What are they going to do with those paintings, the Nazis? Burn them? Brutes they may be, but fools they are not.

Only those with acquaintances in the official circles will have access to state property, but then there are the private collectors, anxious to part with objects that have become compromising. This applies to gallery owners like Keller too ; to whom will he sell an infamous painting like *Still Life* if not to him? Even his small Schmidt-Rottluff will have trouble finding a buyer, these days.

In the present circumstances, it would be irresponsible to pay more than four hundred marks for the Grosz. He is sorry for Keller, but in the current financial situation of Galerie Morel, he cannot let a profitable deal go by.

Keller will come to terms.

2

The blue suit? A classic cut, but a bit too shiny, not appropriate for a solemn occasion like tomorrow's lecture at the Library. He will take the dark grey one, in a colour that the red of the tie will brighten up. He's about to hand over the pants to Irene, for her to iron them, when she appears in the door frame.

"What do you think of this dress for tomorrow, Hans?"

All in brown. A skirt that is slightly tight and a waistcoat allowing a glimpse of her figure, without going beyond the limits. The dark brown of the garment provides a good background to the blond of her bun.

"It is perfect, don't change anything. And about your mother, what did the doctor say?"

"Don't remind me. The first specialist sent her to the baths in Karlsbad, remember? Well, the new one says that baths are definitely contraindicated."

Mrs Furtenberg has been suffering from migraines for years, and no doctor has yet found the cause.

He will not beat about the bush tomorrow evening at the Library. The artist, he will say, has a duty to the party and the state, but he is something more than a servant, more than a mere instrument. The artist is a visionary. The State has the right to demand his loyalty, but it must also be attentive to his message ; it is for him, for the artist, to point out the goals of our task, it is he who, with his inspiring index, will indicate us the way, give us a glimpse of the future which we shall then conquer by our political action.

The lecture will be a synthesis of chapter four of his book. "Towards a truly popular art." An art that represents our people, which expresses it wholly. A young, manly art, full of vitality.

"Mr Schattendorf," Oberfrunck reproached him during the Cultural Action Days, "the type of art you promote ..."

"That will be Head of Cultural Action Schattendorf, if you don't mind."

"Honourable Head of Section: this art can never be our Reich's art. It is contaminated with Bolshevism."

"Would you call Adalberth Thiermann a Bolshevik? I know personally that artist, a party member for five years."

"People like Pechstein and Liebermann, all Jacobs, Isaacs and Israels ..."

"Pechstein is as Aryan as you and I, Master Intendant."

"He may not carry the Judaism in his blood, but the germ is deeply rooted in his depraved soul," the other insisted. "Communists, Semites, sodomites, it is not on that basis that German Art will stand. Those doodles insult the artistic taste of the German people, which is decent by definition."

This old roué, speaking of decency, thinks Schattendorf, who knows many juicy details about Intendant Oberfrunck's private life.

"In which way are Barlach's works indecent?"

"Try to show those monstrosities to a normal German, explain to him that those twisted lines represent a woman's body, that that three-eyed face belongs to a healthy human being."

"Have you studied the statues of Worms Cathedral? The proportion of those bodies has little to do with that of an anatomy textbook and, speaking of faces, if you had the round eyes and the flattened nose of those sculptures, you would be in the museum of the faculty of medicine. In a big jar of formaldehyde. "

"Do not compare true works of art with ..."

"And what about the comics that the newspapers publish every day, are they realistic? Yet, people read them. And they don't complain, no, they ask for more."

"Our duty is to raise the cultural level of the people, not to flatter their low instincts."

"Make up your mind, comrade: does the people reject modern art, or does it accept it, and we must then rectify its taste?"

What that ignoramus likes, is Schrader. And Tarnow. Painters that no critics took seriously before. Now, at last, they have their revenge. Now they will sell. Because people like Oberfrunck will buy their bad copies of classical art and order more.

It is not in Eros and Aphrodite we must seek inspiration, but in Expressionism, in the great and tumultuous period born with this redeeming century. It is in that fertile mud that we must bury our roots.

Mud, yes, for one does not reach the light without having passed through darkness. So much confusion in those years. Stammerings, experiments, schools that succeeded one another, pretentious reviews and impotent theorizers. Isms and yet more isms: cubodadaism, simultaneism, purism, neoplasticism, hermetism, eclecticism, paroxysm. Solipsism.

But watch out! It is talented people we are talking about. Alas, talent can be a ballast when it lacks an ideological guide, a fulcrum, when it is nothing but a wheel turning at ever-increasing speed, but always in a vacuum.

A perfect image, he must jot it down for tomorrow evening.

His lecture at the State Art Library will be a pivotal point in his career. Tense but also confident, that's how he feels. Every time he steps up to the podium, clears his throat and adjusts his distance to the microphone, he feels that the stuff he shapes his work with is not clay nor marble ; his material is the audience. Speaking in public is an art, ephemeral but art nevertheless. To convince by argument, but also to persuade by his voice's melody, by the skilful combination of high and low tones, of pianos with fortissimos.

Three days. In three days he will be appointed to the Council of Fine Arts within the Culture Chamber. From that post he will be able to deal the *coup de grace* to the forces of reaction, to confine that insipid, rancid art, from the most prestigious state institutions to sleepy province museums far, far away.

Counsellor of the Reichskulturkammer, directly under the authority of the Minister of Culture and Propaganda. A natural decision. Everything in Schattendorf's career predestines him to that post.

There is only one thing that troubles that certainty: an hour ago he met Mingels, a former colleague at the *National-Zeitung*.

"Hans, congratulations!"

"What for?"

"You're a celebrity, old chap."

"One day I'll become one, but ..."

"There's a portrait of you at the *EnKu*, nothing less!"

He stared at Mingels, baffled.

"The *EnKu*," explained the other, "the exhibition that's going to open at the Kreuzberg gasometer."

"I know what the *EnKu* is but, what have I got to do with it?"

"You didn't know? In one of the paintings there is your portrait. That's what I'm told, at any rate."

He has it from a journalist at *Der Angriff*.

"Aha?" said Schattendorf. "And that painting you mention is by whom?"

"That I don't know. Why? Does it worry you?"

Worried, he? He, Schattendorf, who has a solid background as a critic of art? He, who has the support of Ruprecht Wendtland, of Adolf Furtenberg? Is it he who should be worried?

"If you're interested I can try to find out," said the other.

The *EnKu*. A crappy exhibit in shabby premises. The one he organized at Spandau was of a different calibre.

Should he be worried? If his exhibition at Spandau was at all possible it is because he has strong supports. At the Wilhelmsstrasse, nothing less, at the Ordenspalais more precisely. At the Ministry of Culture. The best proof of that is the fact that Minister Goebbels himself attended the inauguration of the Italian Futurist Exhibition and listened attentively to the great Marinetti's speech.

Dunkels, his rival, can only count on the support of Doctor Rosenberg, whose knowledge about art amount to less than zero.

No, worried he's not. It is just that, well into the last stretch of the race to the Council, any damn detail could assume importance. He needs to know more about that painting. Right now.

19

3

Clausen concludes his "pedagogical talk," as he calls those lectures, and then he leaves the premises, as does Willi, the young boy. Schultze lingers on, he busies himself picking up some tools. He places the pincers in the locker from which he has taken them out in the morning, hangs the hammer between two nails, removes his grey work coat, puts on his brown jacket and hat and, with a *tschüss* to Sasha, he leaves too.

In this workshop, which Schultze calls "the factory", there is a complete set of tools, many of which are never used. Still, Sasha appreciates having them at hand, so that he won't be forced one day to interrupt the work to go fetch them at the central warehouse, half an hour away.

There is also a carpenter's bench with vises, squares, saws, and augers with a wide range of bits. Everything one may need to put together a bedside table as well as a bookcase, although the only things built at the "factory" are picture frames and wooden panels to support lamps.

Sasha wonders sometimes if the gas bell is still there. But he has no way to know, because the building's central enclosure is protected by heavy, padlocked doors, and the ring of corridors surrounding the enclosure has been cleared out before the building was handed over to the cultural authorities.

In the ring's segment intended for the exhibition, three rooms of about thirty square meters each have recently been fixed up, in addition to the "factory" and the "garage." It is in those rooms that Sasha is busy setting up the lighting.

The task did not seem too difficult, and after three days a proud Sasha could show the result to the boss. But Clausen was not satisfied.

"The lighting should make it possible for the visitors to study the works in detail, that's why they come, otherwise they could stay at home and look at reproductions. But mind you, to light and to bedazzle are two different things. It is for you to find the middle way between them, Herr Wassingher. "

Unusual place for an exhibition this gasometer, abandoned when the streets' lighting became powered by electricity. A gigantic circular building, fifty meters in diameter, which could house a circus. And turning it into just that, a circus, is one of the ideas put forward to recycle it, the others being a boxing-stadium or an ice hockey rink. But in the meantime, the old building in yellow and red brick serves as exhibition hall. Here, in Kreuzberg, far from the capital's prestigious avenues, from the Unter den Linden and its museums, from the Westend and its art galleries.

In other newly arranged showrooms, a little farther along the same ring of corridors, the Open Air Photography Show was recently held. And it is in those rooms that the *EDeKA*, the Authentic German Art Exhibition, is being staged.

In the "garage", as they call the warehouse, due to the engine oil stains on the ground before it was cleaned, the items were piled upright, leaning against each other, in six rows. Unlike the showrooms, whose walls are being painted, the garage's walls are full of holes, and the concrete floor, grey and rough, looks always dirty, even after being swept and rubbed. "The factory" is in the same condition, except that there, the tool panels hide the holes of the walls and the work-benches conceal the worst parts of the floor. In addition, there is more sunlight in the factory, thanks to the windows.

Sasha suggested hanging the paintings on the walls instead of piling them on the floor. It would increase the available space in the garage and there would be more room to move around, but above all, it would hide the holes. Clausen stared at him as if he had proposed throwing the pictures in the empty lot next door, which the neighbours used to park their vehicles. But an hour later he came to see him.

"How many objects are we talking about?" he asked.

"If we hang them in two levels, eighty I would say. And after all, why not three levels? That would give ... "

"One hundred and twenty objects," Clausen reckoned. "But that third level will be too high and force you to use the ladder all the time."

"True," Sasha agreed. "But already two levels – eighty objects – would clear half of the floor. Now it's difficult to move between the stacks of paintings."

"I'll give you an answer this afternoon."

The answer came and it was negative: "To hang them on the wall is to expose them unnecessarily to the sunlight. It is not good for an oil painting, even worse for a watercolour."

Sasha resigned himself. After all he only spends a handful of minutes a day at the "garage", the time to fetch an object when Clausen requires it.

Despite being stacked in a way that may seem chaotic, the works are easy to retrieve thanks to the number on the back of their frames, a number recorded on a list that the professor keeps meticulously up to date.

The garage, lit by just three sixty-watt bulbs, is dark, but not cold and, if walls and ceiling have holes, they are not cracked. There is, it is true, a water leak, but only by heavy rain, and the Public Buildings Authority has already found its origin.

Sasha understands why the authorities do not want to invest more money than necessary in repairs: within a few years the whole building will be completely refurbished.

"Months, not years," corrects him Schultze. "Times have changed, Sasha. This is 1934. And you are not in Russia any more."

Sasha approaches the picture which was the subject of Clausen's little lecture. He raises it in order to carry it back to the garage. When he takes it up, his eyes meet the woman's breasts, in the central point of the canvas. She appears entirely devoted to the study of a foreskin belonging to the man on the left, the one with the bourgeois appearance. There is a tiara with feathers on her hair and a cigarette holder between her lips. Her breasts are spread on the red velvet sofa. "The black of her garter belts emphasizes the soft tones of the flesh they are squeezing," as the professor put it. In the lower right corner, a small drawing, just a sketch that reproduces the main subject in smaller scale. Precisely at knee level of the other man, the one behind her, a signature: G. Grosz.

He is right Clausen, the damn picture belongs in *Junggeselle*, it would defend well its place among all those lewd etchings. Or in some of those magazines which the newspaper sellers avoid to display alongside decent ones like *Uhu* or *Die Dame*, but which they will

24

produce from under the counter whenever a customer, with his hat lowered to the eyelashes, requires them in a barely audible voice.

The guy on the left, with his cigar and his unbuttoned fly, bears grey moustaches that make one think of Marshal Hindenburg, finds Sasha. And behind the girl's bare buttocks, the man in blue. Younger than the other, a painter, maybe.

"But, Professor Clausen," Schultze objected, "aside from the technique and all that: do you personally deem such a subject appropriate for a German artist who has had the privilege of studying in our best institutions? "

"I am an art historian, but my role here is more that of an entomologist's. I observe, I study, I classify. Such, and no other, is my relationship to those objects that have been entrusted to us," he finished, pointing his finger to the paintings stacked in the garage.

4

Morel stays always at the Lilienhof, a hotel comfortable but simple. Since he does not receive anyone here - he meets his business acquaintances in bars - he has no use for a fancy address.

Once in his room he lifts the handset. "Westend 2875," he asks. He hears the hold tone: sharp sounds separated by long pauses. No answer.

He goes down to the vestibule and sits down in a brown leather sofa. On a small table, the newspapers of the day. *Vossische Zeitung*, *Berliner Tageblatt*, but also *Le Matin* of the day before yesterday. He browses through them. "Minister Von Neurath signs pact of non-aggression with Poland." "Work for the 1936 Olympic Games soon to start." "First Congress of Soviet Writers." "Non-aryan: interior minister clarifies the meaning of the expression concerning civil servants." "NSDAP uniforms not to be worn in Courts of Justice." "Würtemberg: pupils shall greet their teachers with the Hitler salute." "Lithuanian economy faces problems."

He's alone in the lobby. Behind the counter, the concierge is sorting the mail. Their eyes meet. The clerk smiles at him, without interrupting his work.

There are hotels that are more modern, which offer more services: hairdresser, dyeing, cleaning. There is the Excelsior, with a tunnel which allows passengers to walk from the train at Anhalter Bahnhof straight to the hotel lobby, avoiding the busy traffic of the Askanischer Platz.

The rates at the Lilienhof are more reasonable, but nothing is really expensive in Berlin. No, it is because of the lobby that he prefers it: a room neither large nor small, with beige rugs, dark brown furniture. Cream coloured walls, plants in green ceramic pots, a library filled with the twenty volumes of the Brockhaus encyclopedia.

And an atmosphere. This welcoming atmosphere that Morel calls "north-central European." A smell of wood, of leather, as at a luthier's workshop, a luthier who smokes a mixture of aromatic tobaccos. A thick carpet which cushions noises. An atmosphere that invites to reading, to contemplation, with a pipe in hand and a glass of cognac on the small coffee table beside the armchair.

A Berlin atmosphere, which could be of Vienna too, of Rotterdam or Copenhagen, but which in Paris would be flawed by the acrid smell of Caporal tobacco and in Milan by the bitterness of an espresso ristretto.

The street outside is quiet, though the Kurfürstendamm is only fifty meters off. In this city the noise and the agitation are concentrated to the main thoroughfares. Leave them and you'll retrieve the calm. Trucks, buses, street cars, ignore this street. From time to time, Morel a car is seen through the window. There, a DKW convertible, then an Opel limousine and a ... Morel cannot identify the brand, a Wanderer maybe. Behind it, the bicycle of a girl in long skirt and white sweater. She wears long hair, the cut *à la garçonne* is rarely seen now. Many hair buns these days, or plaited on the neck, in Gretchen style.

He takes up again the copy of the day of the *Vossische Zeitung*. It is a miracle that this newspaper still manages to appear, although its criticism of the government has become much more cautious.

"Minister-President Göring: draconian measures against black jobs." "The Chancellor warns that the law of organization of labour will be applied without the slightest exception." "Kings of Yugoslavia, Romania and Bulgaria meet in Belgrade to discuss situation in Balkan."

"Trust your analysis," stipulates rule number one that his father instilled in Morel. "It may not be correct, but unless proven otherwise, you should stick to it."

The Nazis are sworn enemies of modern art. They hate it because they do not understand it, and not understanding is something they cannot bear. That is why *Still Life with Three Characters* is no longer worth the nine hundred marks agreed last July. It is not worth half of nine hundred marks. And if Keller lets time go by, it will not be worth the third. At that rate, Morel can afford to wait.

And that is precisely what rule number two of the good buyer calls for: give time to time. "Let your business partner marinate," repeated his father, "let him soak, let him imbibe: it will make him tender."

He walks up to the counter and asks for the same number again.

"Bavaria 6233, isn't it?" asks a young concierge, with his hand on the switchboard panel.

"No. Westend 2875."

"I beg for your apology, mein Herr, I have just gone on duty. Give me a second. Now: the phone booth is free, please be so kind as to take a seat in it. "

This time, Violetta takes the call. In the old days she answered with her name, now it's an anonymous "Hello". She recognizes his voice and calms down. A drink? But not at the Jockey. A more discreet place, the same as last time.

"At the Ackerstrasse then?" he is about to say, but stops himself in time.

"Okay, at one o'clock," he confirms.

Morel has time, he'll go on foot. If he cuts across through the Tiergarten, it won't take him half an hour.

He passes the Grolmanstrasse. There's a van parked in front of Kronen. Through the half-open door of the gallery, he perceives Keller discussing with a young fellow with tucked up shirt sleeves and undone tie. He also sees a dozen paintings in the van's box, two of them with geometric shapes and in bright colours.

The door opens. The young man looks suspiciously at Morel as he closes the case of his vehicle. He goes then up to the cabin, shuts the door and starts the van with a bang.

Keller appears in the door frame. He motions to Morel:

"Come in, come in."

"I'm in a hurry, I have an appointment."

"Come in, I'm telling you!"

He offers him a coffee that Morel declines.

In a conciliatory tone, the gallery owner says: "Make me a serious offer, Gaston."

"The situation has changed since our agreement in July, Erwin. We are in 1934 now. Germany has changed, it's not just a change of government, it's not like when Von Papen succeeded Brüning."

"You do not need to remind me."

"There may still be a future for artists like Nolde or Barlach, if what you tell me is true, but your Grosz is finished. We're talking about an exile, far from his roots. A painter who no longer paints. Without a future."

"But you Gaston, you are a first-rate painter, no doubt about it. What horrible tragedies you are painting here ! Personally I think that the change of air will do good to Grosz. Don't worry, he is not the kind to get depressed."

"I often meet émigré actors, writers, and I assure you that ..."

"Writers, actors! But they are handicapped by the language. Painting is a universal language."

"Erwin, I know only one thing universal: money. And believe me, nobody in Berlin will make you an offer for *Still life*, which is not only the work of an exiled communist but which in addition has a lewd subject. You'll have to hide it or burn it.

"Come on, come on, Gaston. It is not forbidden to own works of Grosz or any other artist."

"And of Jewish painters, Liebermann for example?"

"Thus far, no."

Morel sneers: "'Thus far'."

"Grosz is persona non grata, yes, but his works are not banned."

"You wait six months."

"If you are so sure of that, would not it be in your best interest to close the deal at once ?"

That's the heart of the matter. If Morel rushes it, he will not get the best price. If he waits too much, the picture may be confiscated. Or Navarro, his buyer, lose patience.

"By the way," he asks, "how did they hear of the painting? It was not in the shop-window, I imagine."

31

"No, in the back room."

"Which means lots of people have seen it."

"And I wanted them to. Selling art has never been easy, and hiding it doesn't help ..."

"And how was the procedure?"

"Very correct. Very civilized. They came from the Culture Commission and were collecting works for an exhibition that would soon open."

"And then?"

"They signed me a receipt, I packed the picture and they took it with them."

"Did they tell you what sort of exhibition?"

"Only that it was of national interest."

"Civilized people, you say?"

Keller shrugs his shoulders.

"Not all of them are gangsters, you know. Among the high-ranking officials, you'll find cultured people. Did you know that Hitler paints?"

"The floor of his toilet," guesses Morel.

"I've seen a few works by him," corrects him the other. "Well done, in a classic style. No, the chancellor is not a man to burn paintings."

"And the gentleman who has just left in a van, is he one of those civilized Nazis?"

Keller jumps up.

"He has nothing to do with it."

"The van was loaded with paintings," insists Morel. "Is he one of those who go around collecting artworks?"

Keller laughs.

"Not at all, he came to bring me some objects that I had sent for repair.

Morel has a look at the premises ; he spots two pictures leaning against a wall. He takes a closer look at them. They're by Kirchner.

"The one on the right, yes," confirms Keller. "The other is a Pechstein."

Morel whistles.

"I didn't know you carried that kind of stuff."

"They are already sold. As I say, the market is far from dead."

At what price? Morel wonders. Those names are higher ranked than Grosz', but the formats are small. A thousand marks, no more.

He draws a flat silver case from his pocket. He opens it and offers a cigarette to Keller.

"And, speaking of book-burning," says Keller, "do you know that an autodafé took place already in 1820? Progressive students burning reactionary books, that time. And by the way, a few years ago, our Grosz saw some of his lithographs burned in the name of the army's honour. Long before Hitler, mind you."

Morel doesn't know Keller's political opinions. He is not a Nazi, not a Social-Democrat either. A liberal. But even a guy like him is beginning to find positive sides to the regime.

"I know from reliable source," he says, "that there are two Van Gogh in Goebbels' office, and where there are Van Gogh, I would not be surprised to find a Kirchner, and why not a little Rottluff. "

Morel inhales some smoke from his Caporal and studies the expression of his colleague. The man keeps tapping his fingertips on the table and his left eyelid blinks like a worn out bulb.

Rule number three of his father: "When the first drop of sweat flushes on the seller's forehead, it's killing time."

33

"Neither Goebbels nor Göring will be eager to buy *Still Life*," says Morel. "In Paris I can get a few francs for it. Here nobody will give you a groschen."

"Do not imagine that you're my only customer, Mr. Morel. Friedman has made me an offer, just to name one. "

Pierre Friedman is a colleague of Morel.

"He was attacked in the middle of Unter den Linden by SAs who called him a dirty Jew," replies Morel. "The story goes around Paris, he came back with three broken teeth and swears not to put his foot in Germany again."

"I mentioned Friedman just as an example. There are others," mutters Keller. "Grosz is a top name, he still is."

"As you wish, but as soon as you get back *Still Life*, I want to have it. Four hundred marks in hand are better than the thousands that Goebbels or another patron of the arts might give you one day. "

The other shakes his head. But there is already resignation in his gesture.

"Seven hundred," he tries.

"Five hundred, and I'll give you an advance: two hundred and fifty. Right away. On account of our old friendship."

And it is true that he wants to keep a good relationship to Keller. In the coming months, new opportunities are bound to arise.

The gallerist signs a receipt, slides the three banknotes into an envelope and the envelope into a drawer.

Berlin. Potsdamer Platz und Blick in die Leipziger Str.

5

The publisher has sent him the books, but not as many as he had asked for. Schattendorf phones them right away:

"If they are not here at six o'clock in the afternoon, I'll complain to the manager personally."

Tomorrow's lecture will be a great occasion to promote the book. He examines the cover. They did use the image he gave them, by Conny Berg, but the colours are not accurate. Too matte and not clear. The title's typography, on the other hand, looks fine: capitalized sans serif. Massive without being heavy. An impression of strength, of energy. *Culture in our time,* by Hans Schattendorf, Head of Cultural Action.

Someone knocks at the door of the office. It's Peter Litzke.

Newly appointed at his post in Spandau, Schattendorf saw the breeding ground that students represented. He visited the university and was invited to give a lecture. It was there that he met the young Litzke, an art student who, with a classmate, had just founded *Nation und Kultur,* a revue. The political line of the publication was a bit immature, but it was impregnated with Expressionist artistic ideals coupled with a distinct national awareness. He granted them financial support, which enabled the magazine to print a second issue.

"Shall I take those to the Art Library?" asks Peter, pointing at the small pile of books.

Schattendorf hesitates. Is there a safe place to keep them, at the library?

"No. Take them to the local. Tomorrow at six o'clock you'll bring them to the library."

Peter confirms, bows and turns to the door.

Schattendorf is nervous. It's not anxiety, it is tension, inevitable when a challenge approaches, the tension of the bow's string just before the arrow flies away. This lecture, at this precise moment, is different from others he has delivered; this one may be decisive for his appointment to the Council.

He lights a cigarette. What remains to be done? The youths from the magazine will be there to sell the book and distribute a pamphlet that summarizes its central ideas, placing them in today's political context. A few phrases at risk there. "At a time of intensified cultural struggle, it is crucial to clarify the objectives." "The new state which has emerged from the National Revolution must promote an art that is young and vigorous." Those able to read between the lines will recognize who are the real targets of these remarks.

Cultural Action leaders from across the region have been invited, along with other officials. And *Nation und Kultur* will bring about thirty students, Peter has promised. And, by pure formality, an invitation was sent to Dunkels, his major enemy. He will not come, and moreover, he will try to dissuade others from coming.

One last glance at his notes, those notes he always lays on the podium, in front of him: "The role of today's artist." "Individual creator? No, artist engaged in the national movement." "The Middle Age."

To preserve alive the flame of the most genuine German art, of Expressionism, that movement that was so much more than an "ism", which was a true Popular Revolutionary Art. Of course, there have been deviations, dead-ends, but the essence of that movement remains a cry of anguish, an anguish which fosters revolt, a revolt which, in order to become revolutionary, must be politically conscious.

He sits down at his desk, takes a new sheet of paper and rewrites the main arguments. He is reformulating the fourth point, about the "ivory tower", when the phone rings. "Editor Mingels," announces the secretary.

"Hans, it's about your book," Mingels says.

"You are coming to the presentation, aren't you?"

"Don't be mad at me, Hans, but it's going to be difficult. Two reporters are sick here and you know what a mess the department turns into when a few guys are missing."

"It's alright, I understand, but what about the painting?"

"What painting?"

"My portrait, the picture you told me about yesterday."

"Oh, yes. You know, the guy who gave me the information doesn't know much really, just that in one of the paintings at that exhibit there is a character who ... in a word, who looks a lot like you."

"Is it a portrait?"

"No, there are other characters. Like Wendtland. Your friend, isn't it?"

"What are you saying? Wendtland?"

Ruprecht Wendtland is his best ally at the Council of Fine Arts.

"Oh no, I'm saying nothing," answers Mingels. "It's the guy from *Der Angriff* who said it."

And this idiot pretends to the name of journalist.

"Did he also tell you the author of that painting?"

Mingels sounds surprised.

"But, you know that already."

"No."

"Oh, I thought you did. Well, it's Grosz."

Schattendorf hangs up and lights another cigarette, the last one in a pack he's opened the same morning. He tries to keep it at a pack a day, but today it's going to be two.

George Grosz is one of the main targets of his criticism. Because he deserted Expressionism, because his art is negative, nihilistic, desperate, the very opposite of what the nation needs today. And because he does not portray a healthy sexuality, a honest expression of a vital force, but a clandestine sex, an eroticism fit for a whorehouse.

Schattendorf has never concealed the contempt that Grosz, like Dix and other "neo-objectivists" inspired him. They claim to have "transcended" Expressionism, they criticize its so called subjectivity, its "hypersensitivity." He has attacked Grosz many times from his column of the *National-Zeitung*. Well, here is his revenge.

But, who benefits from the crime? Who can be interested in exposing that portrait publicly, associating his name with that of an anti-national painter?

Dunkels. Who else?

He'll send Peter to Kreuzberg to check if Mingels' gossip is true, that's where he will start. Then, he will call Wendtland.

6

The first day of Bang in Berlin would not deserve a detailed description if this gentleman was not destined to play a key role in the genesis of the artwork which several years later would cause such anxiety to Morel, the art dealer, and to Hans Schattendorf, the head of Cultural Action in Spandau.

Bang had taken the train from Copenhagen to Edser and from there a ferry to Rostock. At nine o'clock in the morning, his train stopped with a bump under the glass roof of the Lehrter Bahnhof.

After leaving the station, he could admire the neoclassical silhouette of the Reichstag on the other side of the Spree, with its purple rectangular dome and its four towers, one in each corner of the building. To the right and left, trains were passing over the river, passengers from the suburbs queued up for the bus that would take them to their workplaces in the city centre, or they hurried towards the S-Bahn , the urban railway that connects the Lehrter Bahnhof with other railway nodes of the capital.

Bang had imagined Berlin as a dark city, all brown and black. Large imposing buildings facing small squares, tiny openings in a dense medieval fabric. But he saw nothing medieval here ; the Unter den Linden, wide and luminous, people walking quietly under the trees, sitting on the public benches of the central aisle or sipping coffee at the terraces. An intense traffic, well regulated by policemen with precise gestures.

On a traffic island in the middle of the hustle and bustle of the Friedrichstrasse, a black man of papier-mache. Elegant costume, bow tie and hat, his hands on his waist. With a big smile, he announces the good news: "In Berlin or Paramaribo, I drink nothing but coffee Schibo."

The signs of a policeman force the taxi to stop. From the Friedrichstrasse, a dozen young ladies are approaching while dancing a cancan: an advertising for a show at the *Admirals-Palast*. "It's the *Tiller-girls*," says the driver. "But," objects Bang, "Their sign says *Jackson-girls*." "Psst," answers the driver, shrugging his shoulders, "I can't tell which are which. The city is full of these girls, and there are always new ones coming from London or Leipzig, I cannot care less. But please, *Mädchen*, don't cross the street right now ! Let me pass before, please !"

Trying to find a bar, Bang stumbles upon a café, not far from his hotel, at the Wittenbergplatz. The menu of *Café Schimmel* offers a wide range of drinks: Moka coffee, Fachinger mineral water, Tarragona wine, Vermouth of Cadiz, Elixir of Antwerp. But it is hot in Berlin this October of 1925. He chooses neither an Arak grog or a Goldwasser from Danzig:

"Ein Bier, bitte."

The brillantined waiter moves away with a nod.

Bang pulls out a cigar and takes out a match from its small box, when someone asks him for a light. The guy, who is part of a group of young men dressed in a rather eccentric manner and who are engaged in a lively discussion at the back of the room, examines the matchbox. "They are not German," he decides. "No, Danish," replies Bang.

"What a coincidence, we are just discussing Knut Hamsun. I maintain that all Expressionist literature stems from Hamsun."

He has a protruding dimple chin. His black hair is divided into two equal parts by a meticulously traced line. Unlike his friends, he is dressed in a quite conventional way: a well cut jacket, a tie neither too large nor too thin.

Bang accepts the invitation of the young fellow to join their table.

"Here is Paul Wiegener, this one is Heinz Brehme, and over there, the presumptuous young man who dares oppose my theory: Harry Shadow. Friends: I have the pleasure to introduce to you this gentleman, just arrived from Hamsun's Copenhagen. "

The aforementioned Harry is the only one in the group not to wear glasses. Twenty years old, long chestnut hair, dressed with careful negligence. A fairly worn-out Prince of Wales costume, a violet velvet waistcoat and a very large black silk tie with a loose bow attached to the shirt by a golden brooch. A chain with a pocket watch at its end, and a tweed cap, complete his outfit.

"Allow me to point out, Dieter," he says, taking a pipe out of his mouth, "that among Hamsun's all merits you won't find that of being a Dane. If you said Norwegian, I would take your theses more seriously. "

"Bang", introduces himself the newcomer.

"That's not a name, that's an onomatopoeia," comments Shadow.

"It's my last name."

"What about the first one?"

"Nobody calls me by my first name."

Shadow whistled. Out of derision or admiration.

"Harry is a remarkably promising artist, with a future that can only be described as colossal," says Dieter. "But literature is hardly his field."

"I don't seem to be completely illiterate," retorts the other, "since a collection of my poems is going to be published."

"Is this a joke?" exclaims Dieter.

"I do joke on occasion, but not at this moment. *Der Sturm* has accepted a selection of my works. "

"Are you talking about the publishing house or the magazine?"

Harry makes an ample gesture.

"I'm talking about *Der Sturm*, review, gallery, publishing house. I'm talking about Herwarth Walden," he explains to Bang.

"Herwarth?" repeats Bang.

"Walden," completes Dieter. "His gallery is on the Potsdamerstrasse, a few minutes away. But Harry, answer me, are you speaking of a book or of a few poems?"

"Well, I'm just going to the gallery to discuss it. There are different possibilities."

"And the one does not exclude the other," exclaims Heinz ironically.

"Exactly what I was about to say," Harry says.

"This sentence will make him famous if his poems don't do the trick," Dieter laughs. "'The one does not exclude the other', will be engraved in bronze letters on his tombstone."

Paul, addressing Bang:

"Harry writes things of great value, besides being a painter."

Dieter: "And his greatest admirer, after Mr. Shadow himself, is right here." He points to Paul.

"Why shouldn't I be?" replies Paul. "Harry is the greatest Expressionist poet at the moment. Trakl is dead, Becher still writes, but he is no longer an expressionist."

"And what about Benn?"

"Trakl has already killed himself and Benn's suicide will be announced in the newspapers any day."

"So," says Bang, addressing Shadow, "you are not only a painter, but also a writer."

"And a director, and an actor," adds Dieter.

"Like all of us, actually." That's Heinz Brehme.

"But, can one be so many things?" asks Bang sceptically.

"The means of expression fertilize each other," explains Brehme. "No one can limit himself as before, we are not like the Liebermanns or the Slevogt who put a plate marked 'painter' on their door. We are artists, that's all."

"We are creators, period," says Paul.

"We are, we are ..." mimics Harry Shadow. "We are what we become. Stop putting labels on everything."

"Yet ...," Paul insists.

"No labels, period".

A vehement discussion bursts out, Heinz raising his voice and Paul trying desperately to make himself heard.

"We are pioneers, if we are anything at all. Gold diggers, like Chaplin in *The Rush*," settles Harry Shadow. "We break moulds every day, unrelentingly, continuously, that and no other is our job. In case the subject interests you, Herr Bang."

Bang, who has lost the thread of what's being debated, retains nevertheless that the guy called Harry is the group's leader, with

45

Dieter as the mosquito that prevents him from taking a nap on his laurels.

Harry gets up, he's got to go see Walden. But before leaving he pulls out a few magazines from a leather briefcase. He picks one of them and hands it to Bang.

"Here you can read some of my pieces."

The title of the review, in characters between expressionists and art deco, is *Der Bruch*, The Break.

With a chivalrous gesture, Harry bows and takes leave.

"Hey ho!" cries Dieter. "You forget to pay your coffee."

Harry digs in his right pocket, then in the left and finally in his waistcoat.

"Sorry, no small change. Tomorrow."

Dieter makes an ironical gesture.

"Tomorrow, always tomorrow. With modest means and step by step, our friend is building up a debt that inspires respect."

"But he's going to collect a nice sum for one of his watercolours. A rich guy, an industrialist."

"Wilton again?" asks Heinz. "How much?"

Bang notes that these intellectuals spend as much time discussing philosophical matters as counting marks, pfennigs and groschen.

Lying in bed in his hotel room, he browses through Harry's magazine. On the cover, an engraving signed Ottakar Kirsch pictures a sun seen through a window. The window is broken into a thousand pieces. Articles, poems, including one of editor Shadow himself: *Necropsy.*

The eyes, her eyes,
Lying in the metal grating of the drain

46

Shattered with light, saturated with darkness
And in her lungs?
Xylyl bromide, phosgene, mustard gas.
Never has it been more beautiful, more desirable
Our true homeland,
Death.

"Bullshit!" decides Bang. But the next day he returns to the café. In the section closest to the entrance there are twenty tables, he counts mechanically. If the Schimmel was a theatre, this part would be the scene. To reach the "parterre", the rear sector, separated from the other by a bronze balustrade, one has to climb three steps, which the waiters curse each time they trip over them.

The "philosophers' table", as waiters call it, at the back of the café, is now occupied by Paul, Heinz and a third one: Geza, a journalist.

"And the others?" wonders Bang.

"They will soon be here. But you, what do you do? Are you a journalist?"

Bang had owned a bar in Copenhagen, just half a dozen tables. He did fine, but he did not get along with his partner. He sold him his share and left for Berlin. The few thousand Danish crowns he got, expressed in German currency, assumed considerable proportions.

Heinz looks at him surprised.

"Interesting," he comments. "You know, we're going to open a bar too, we've found a place at Fasanenstrasse, it's a dairy shop, but it's going to be closed, the problem is the rent: seven hundred eggs."

"With Wilton's allowance, no problem," says Paul.

The man known as Wilton is an art-loving industrialist from the Rhineland. At first it was not to them he wanted to grant his patronage, but to Waltraud Brenner, an artist better known as Violetta. But she declined the offer. Harry, on the other hand, got to know about it, invited Wilton to *Der Bruch* and convinced him to support the magazine, which was also an artistic endeavour after all. But then the editors decided to use that aid to finance the bar project instead. They have no doubt that Wilton would approve, if his opinion was ever required.

Nobody knows his real name, but it is said to include a "von" in it. When he comes to Berlin, he spends much time visiting art galleries. He became infatuated with Violetta's paintings and told her he would be honoured if she was kind enough to accept a monthly fee from him. They are not uncommon in Berlin, those rich people eager to sponsor artists or writers, but Violetta, who had heard of Wilton's womanizer reputation, politely refused.

"A bar, you say? That's hard work," warns Bang. "If you think it's about drinking beer and discussing art, forget it."

"Would you like to manage it?" asks Heinz. "Or are you here as a tourist?"

With a strong foreign accent, Geza asks:

"Like those they take on the open buses of the Elite Tour to see the Brandenburg Gate, the Tiergarten, Potsdam and its peerless baroque palace?"

"Can't you see he's not a tourist?" Paul said. "Bang is an intelligent person and tourism is by definition a silly activity."

"And useless," adds Heinz. "In your village you will reach the universal, Tolstoy knew it already."

"Tolstoy had never been a tourist guide. But I was," mentions Geza.

"And, mind you," explains Paul to Bang, "Geza was guiding tourists when he was newly arrived from Budapest, when he did not know the difference between Alexanderplatz and Potsdamerplatz."

"True. I took once a group of Englishmen to Alex that were supposed to go to Grunewald. Another time, another group missed their train because of me: I had mixed up Anhalt Station with Lehrter's."

"That's why you got fired, didn't you?"

"Not at all: I offered them a free boat ride on the Spree and a few hours later they were aboard the next train, happy as a clam. No, the reason I was fired was because the Finns are hopeless at Hungarian. "

Convinced that the two Finnish-Ugric languages were mutually understandable, Geza proposed himself as a guide for a Finnish group. But he discovered that, apart from some twenty words, these languages were as close to each other as Spanish to Czech.

"So you'll help us with our bar?" asks Heinz.

"I have other plans."

"Berlin is the future, Berlin is the heart of Europe. Why go back to Copenhagen?" pleads Dieter.

"Who's said anything about going back? I came to Berlin to open a bar myself."

"Open a cabaret instead," suggests Geza.

"As if there were not enough cabarets," says Heinz.

"I mean something different, something creative," Geza replies.

"There are cabarets and cabarets," says Harry Shadow, who has just arrived. "Last night I was at *Schall und Rauch*, on the Bellevuestrasse. Tucholsky, Spoliansky, talented people. I'm going there tonight as well.

"I don't know a thing about cabarets," replied Bang, annoyed. "I came to Berlin to open a bar."

7

Sasha Wassingher arrives at work earlier than usual. At the entrance of the EDeKA, the other exhibition of the gasometer, there is much bustle. A truck is parked in front of the door and parcels are being discharged. They are tall, two meters by four the smallest, all carefully packed. The employees unload them under the supervision of a man dressed in a grey overall, underneath which the reverses of a brown jacket and a tie can be seen.

Once unloaded, each parcel is handed over to other employees who lay it at the entrance of the building with great care.

One of them makes a friendly gesture to Sasha.

"You work at the EnKu, don't you?" he asks.

"Yes."

"Come on then, you're also staff after all. Want to take a look?"

The rooms seem deeper than those where Sasha works, although both exhibitions will take place in the same circular building. Perhaps because the walls are painted in ivory white and not in dark colours.

"Herr Kersten, the pieces marked H3, where are they going?" asks someone.

The man in tie, in a bad mood: "To room three, where else?"

The premises of the two exhibitions are not contiguous, they are separated by a section of the building to which there is no access, a segment of thirty yards.

The employees have gone back to the truck. Sasha is alone. In the main hall there is nothing to be seen yet. He ventures to the second. Here there are several paintings, not yet unpacked except for two of them, leaning against a wall.

The first represents an alpine valley. A medieval church on a height overlooking a river. It would go well above our sofa, he thinks, where they have nothing except a calendar of the *Alte Leipziger* insurance company. It would go well with their room's colour.

The second picture depicts a village festival. About fifty people sitting around a table full of good things – cakes, trays of roasted meat, cold dishes – dancing or engaged in lively conversation. In the foreground a little girl with blond tresses helps herself from a basket full of fruit. No one around her notices, busy as they are discussing, eating or serving themselves from the bottles lined up on the table. Her mother, who is seen from the back, is arranging her hair, dishevelled by the dance. She is as blonde as her daughter and dressed in the same white dress.

It's summer, judging by the clothes, and the sun is ready to set. A Bavarian landscape, or Austrian. At the bottom, a platform. On the stage, dominating the whole, among red standards with the swastika, a Hitler portrait. In the lower part of the frame, which is decorated with gilded mouldings, a small bronze plaque with the work's title: *The Joy is Back.*

Sasha cannot quit staring at the picture. The little girl on one side, the old men on the other, all around the same table, like a family. It reminds him of something. It's strange, but he's moved. If he had to speak, his voice would break. He too was born in a village like that one. He thinks of his childhood in Russia, of his mother, far away in Tonkoschurovka.

"Who are you? I did not ask for reinforcements as far as I know." The dry voice snatches him from his contemplation. It's the guy in tie. Herr Kersten.

"Excuse me, I work here too, but in the other exhibition."

"In that case, let me point out that you are just now, not in the other exhibition but in this one. Go back to work, that is why you are paid."

Sasha follows the curved wall of the building until the other entrance. Some workers are busy fixing a large red sign over it: *EnKu. Entartete Kunstausstellung.* Irregular typography letters, some of them twice the size of the others, none of them aligned. It could have been the poster of a funny movie.

"Do it discreetly," had Schattendorf instructed Peter Litzke. "Never mention my name. You come from the Department of Heritage, from Chief Intendant Oberfrunck, Karl-Dietrich Oberfrunck."

He looked worried at the young man. He would have preferred to go himself, but could not take the risk.

"Speak in a tone of command, like an inspector, not like a student. Like someone who's got the right to ask questions."

Discretion, repeats Peter to himself. When he approaches the room, he reads a sign above the door: "Art should appeal to our feelings, but this art makes us ashamed."

He looks through the first window. Nobody there. Through the second window, he sees a blond young man in a grey overall, a screwdriver in his hand. He knocks twice on the window and enters, without waiting. The young man looks at him surprised. A few meters away, a girl sitting in a stool is checking something in a binder.

Without looking at her, in the harshest tone of command he is capable of, he addresses the guy:

"I come from the Department of Prussian Heritage to inspect three of the works. They are by George Grosz. Please bring them to me."

Sasha hesitates. He answers:

"It's Professor Clausen who takes care of that."

Peter scans the room. A large number of paintings are piled, some with the canvas turned towards the walls. He recognizes one oil, a Kirchner he's seen at the Moritzburg Museum.

"Is that how you take care of works of art?" he exclaims with an indignation he doesn't need to feign.

Sasha looks desperately to the front office, Clausen must be back from one moment to the other. He's gone to the EDeKA, to find out when the painters are coming to finish their work here.

"I have more important things to do than wait for that professor," barks Peter. "Bring me everything you have from Grosz. Now !"

"But, is it a gallery you come from?" asks Sasha.

"Are you deaf? I told you that I come from Heritage."

Sasha hasn't the vaguest idea of what that institution may be. If only Schultze was there...

He stammers that he is so sorry, that unfortunately, that for the time being ... That's when Peter notices his accent.

"Are you a Pole?"

"No."

"But you're not German. How come you are working here?"

Because Clausen hired me, thinks Sasha. Because the local ministry delegation is closing its eyes.

"This is very serious," exclaims Peter. "If this comes to the attention of Intendant Oberfrunck, he will take action. But I am not here to check work permits, that is the task of the police. You have wasted enough of my time already. Bring here immediately all the Grosz you have! "

Clausen is furious.

"Who gave you the right to let strangers into the premises?" he scolds Sasha when he hears of the visit. He takes a notebook and writes: "Intendant Oberfrunck, Department of Heritage." Then he dials Commissioner Dunkels' number.

"Oberfrunck? From Heritage, are you sure?" asks the Commissioner.

Clausen hangs up. "He's raging," he tells Sasha. "And for once I can understand him. Never let anyone in again. If I'm not here, call the Hildebrandsstrasse and ask for Dunkels."

Then, with the help of Leni, the secretary, he starts preparing the documents for the inventory, as every Monday. He holds a blue notebook in his hand: a list of all the objects in the gasometer. Each page is divided into columns: author, year, title, number, technique (A watercolour, G engraving, Ö oil), origin, estimated value in reichsmarks (RM).

76. Macke, 1910, In the Zoo, Ö, Moritzburg Museum, 3,000 RM
77. Schmidt-Rottluff, 1918, Blue Woman, A, Potsdam Pavilion, 4,000 RM
78. Grosz, 1927, Still Life with 3 Characters, Ö, Galerie Kronen, 1.400 RM
79. Klee, 1922, Rising Sun, A, Pinakothek Oranienburg, 7,000 RM

All in all two hundred items, each with its number in black ink on the back of the canvas. Clausen has selected fifty out of them to be exhibited.

"Mr. Schultze: you will return the unselected items. You have my permission to request transport and you will personally attend to each devolution."

"Personally? But that will take me days," protests Schultze, who has just arrived.

"These are objects valued at thousands of marks. They have to be returned in good and due form."

Schultze swears in a low voice. Clausen pretends not to hear it.

"Leni!" he calls. "Please bring the books."

The secretary arrives with the requested documents. Clausen gives Schultze a pad of receipts with the heading of the Ministry.

"As you see, Mr. Schultze, the receipts are in five copies, all of which must be duly filled out and signed. And now, gentlemen, let us proceed to the inventory."

"Of the selected objects, you mean?" presumes Schultze.

"Of all objects, as usual. As long as they are here, the preservation of the whole stock is our responsibility."

There is something of a ceremony to it: Clausen enumerates the works, Schultze, the young boy or Sasha, depending on which row the object is stored in, fetches it and poses it in front of Clausen, who, notebook in hand, makes sure that author and title agree with his records. Finally, the work is carried back to the "garage."

"107. Kandinsky: Sunset on the Danube."

Schultze presents a canvas framed in grey wood to Clausen. Impossible to guess what sunset the title refers to, thinks Sasha, who sees only large spots, blue and green. In one of the lectures that

Clausen holds for them once a week, he defined the style of that painting as "figurative on the verge to abstraction." The purpose of those talks is not clear; they could do their job without them. But then, Clausen is a professor. At Breslau University.

The professor grabs the board with both hands, turns it over and makes sure that the number 107 is on the back. He returns it again and checks title and author engraved on a small plate. With a nod, he authorizes Schultze to return the object to the "garage".

"108. Oskar Schlemmer: Three figures in a garden."

The boy nearly drops the picture, with a heavy metal frame. Three heads, one in profile view, hieratic, the other in full frontal, the third one seen from behind. They are like puppets, thinks Sasha. A disturbing sight.

"109. Max Ernst, Ariadne and her daughters. "

Sasha brings the requested piece: a female figure with thick red hair and bare breasts. Behind her, against a background of purple curtains, two other characters of ambiguous sex.

"Daughters? Her sons rather," sneers Schultze, pointing to their breasts that barely protrude on the surface of the torso.

Clausen, without a smile, checks the entry in his notebook against the text on the picture's frame.

"Daughters," he maintains. "Ariadne and her daughters. Proceed, Mr. Wassingher."

"120. Felixmüller. Ancient silence. "

Schultze disappears into the garage and returns with item number 120, a watercolour.

"Felixmüller?" Clausen repeats, looking at it. "But he's figurative, that painter." No recognizable shape in this picture, only a series of squares in continuous tone.

"It's not possible," he mumbles, staring at the notebook, then at the canvas, then at the notebook again.

Schultze winks at Sasha. The order that Clausen always insists on is not so rigorous after all.

"Oh, I see," exclaims the professor, opening a large red folder with copies of the delivery receipts. "It's Felix Muehler and not Conrad Felixmüller." He corrects the notebook with a pencil. Once in his office, he will cover the wrong part of the name with white enamel and letter the correct one over it.

"We have already made dozens of inventories and it is only now that he realizes it," whispers Schultze in Sasha's ear,

"Anyway, the picture could not have disappeared, the numbers do match," says Sasha.

"And who cares? Does it matter if it's Felix, Müller or Bloody Russovich?" growls Schultze. "I bet you ten marks that when people come to see them they won't give a damn who among all those parasites who signed these pieces of crap."

That is probably true, considers Sasha, who nevertheless understands Clausen's zeal. The man is not a member of the party. He has to be careful.

"Come on, I'll show you something," says Schultze with a mischievous smile, once the inventory is finished. He leads Sasha to a small room adjacent to the workshop. Behind a water hose, there is a wooden square object leaning against the wall.

Schultze lifts it. It's a painting. A watercolour depicting two thin young girls by a river. The signature looks something like Bernatzki.

"That name says nothing to me," Sasha said.

"It's just another kike. And you know why you don't recognize the name? Well, quite simply because it is not in the professor's notebook. No delivery receipt matches it. Isn't it great? That's Clausen's fine system for you"

"It's strange," says Sasha. "It cannot be among the fifty that have been selected, so much is clear."

"No, but it's not even among the original two hundred. There's simply no receipt mentioning any Bernachik."

"No, you're right, and that's why it has never been labelled," mutters Sasha thoughtfully. "But, if we have no receipt, to whom will it be returned?"

Schultze grins.

"Do you know the Lohmühlenbrücke on the Landwehr Kanal? Well, it's from that bridge that I will proceed to return this extremely great and significant work of art. And no one will need to sign any receipt. Efficient and practical, isn't it?"

"But... " Sasha protests.

"The bloody thing's got to disappear. Clausen is going to accuse us, he will say that it was me who received it or you who forgot to write it up. We'll get in trouble, you and me. No, we don't need this piece of junk here, I'll take it with me tonight."

"But the caretaker..."

"The caretaker leaves at six o'clock, and in any case he's half eyeless half blind. I'll stay here till six-thirty, I have to file all the receipt pads that Clausen has poured over me, you know, " finishes Schultze with a wink.

Almost without thinking, mechanically, Sasha whispers:

"How much can it be worth?"

"It's not worth a groschen, even if it's evaluated to a thousand eggs. If I saw this junk on the side walk I wouldn't even bend over to pick it up. You want to take it home maybe? "

59

Lena, Sasha's girlfriend, would love it. It is her kind of art: dark colours, twilight, two strange figures seen from the back, staring at the lake. But it would be a theft. Of course, all these things will one day end up in the public dump, but for the time being, they have a legitimate owner.

8

At his office at the Hildebrandsstrasse, Commissioner Dunkels keeps a file with the names of all those he deals with. He has three secretaries at his disposal, but this file he updates himself personally.

But no need to search any records in order to find out who Karl-Dietrich Oberfrunck is. This person has already caused him trouble. He is an intendant, but the post he covets is that of commissioner. He does not forgive Dunkels for having been appointed in his place. And now he sends one of his henchmen to the EnKu.

Dunkels knows he has more enemies than friends in the movement. Without the protection of Dr. Rosenberg, he would never have reached the position that he holds now, not to speak of being nominated to the Council of Fine Arts.

Another character whose file card he does not need to check is Curt Hagener. Journalist, says his card. "With qualities of bloodhound," it could had added.

The *Schlosskeller*. A bar which Hagener uses as his office, on a side street of the Unter den Linden. There he is, leaning on the counter, blue suit and red tie, like a dandy of the old days. Dunkels wonders how long it will take before someone reminds him that the era of decadence is over, that the appearance expected of a journalist at the service of the Movement is different.

"What will you have?" asks Hagener.

"Same as you."

"Chris," he asks the bartender, "an Old Fashioned."

How much does a reporter earn at the *Deutsche Tribüne?* wonders the commissioner. True, Hagener has long experience, but still, how does he manage to pay for his Wilmersdorf apartment, his Daimler-Benz of the latest model and his dinners at the Metropol?

"What is it?" asks Dunkels with a grimace after taking a sip of his cocktail.

"Angostura, orange juice, and good whiskey, of course. Not Scotch, American."

Dunkels pushes back his glass, and orders an Alt Heidelberg. Then he starts searching in the rich archives that the memory of the journalist constitutes. He shows him the photo that Professor Clausen gave him. Hagener places the image under one of the lamps over the counter.

"The one on the left looks like Hindenburg," he says.

The photography is small, all in different shades of black and grey.

"Couldn't you get a better focused one?" asks Hagener.

"Come with me to the gasometer and have a look at the original".

"No, need, This one will do. And yes, I have already seen this painting."

"Where?"

"Give me a minute."

Then he notices the text at the foot of the picture. *Still Life with Three Characters.* Oil on canvas. George Grosz, 1927.

"A Grosz," he says in a low voice, as if providing that information to himself.

Dunkels taps the counter impatiently.

"What I would like to know," he says, "is why this painting interests Oberfrunck. He's sent someone to the gasometer to make inquiries about it."

Hagener takes a sip from his tumbler.

"You know," he tells with a smile, "this cocktail was invented a long time ago in Kentucky, But in our days, to fool the prohibition, they had the idea, very shrewd if you ask me, to replace the bourbon by ..."

Noticing Dunkels' impatient look, he stops himself.

"If I were you," he advises, "I'd go and see the owner."

"That's Gallery Kronen"

"Erwin Keller. Well, he must know the background of that painting."

"I'll do that, don't worry, I just wanted to have a word with you first."

"Well, sorry to disappoint you, but I'm not Delphi oracle. Excuse me, Dunkels, but I have to make a call."

There is a telephone at the other end of the counter. But Hagener bypasses it and proceeds to a red padded door. He goes through it and closes it behind him.

The guy is too important to use the same phone as everyone, mutters Dunkels to himself. He finishes his beer and orders a second one.

The artist Ruprecht Wendtland, a friend of Schattendorf, started painting in the folkloric style that Germans call *völkisch*, but tried later to adapt it to the new trends. His works have a touch that some call spiritual, influenced by the Russian painters of the late nineteenth. If we add to this a zest of Kandinsky and a tiny drop of Chagall, the secret of his unique style stands unveiled. It goes without saying that Wendtland, ultra-conservative and physically impossible to distinguish from a Prussian officer – something of a Marshall Hindenburg look-alike-- would never recognize any kinship with Chagall or Kandinsky.

Schattendorf loathes that style, but their artistic differences arise curiosity and even sympathy in Wendtland. It is true that he is grateful to Schattendorf for having taken up his defence when an art critic attacked him so savagely in the *National-Zeitung*.

Wendtland acts as if the gulf separating their aesthetic ideals was but a thin crack that could easily be sealed. In his inner self he seems able to reconcile his traditionalist vision with the iconoclastic ideas of the other. When a fundamental dissension is impossible to brush aside, he observes a contrite silence, only to recover his usual good mood a minute later, blaming the incident on the originality of his friend, on his eccentric side.

"Mediocrity personified," is Schattendorf's opinion of him. But a strategically important support because, as a member of the Chamber, he backs his candidacy, being at the same time firmly anchored in the traditional camp. Such supports are worth gold for him, who's always accused of avant-gardism.

The bar of Hotel Palast. In front of Wendtland, a mug of beer. Schattendorf stirs furiously up a cup of black coffee in which he has previously poured neither cream nor sugar.

A caricature of him? That makes Wendtland smile.

"You can laugh," Schattendorf says, "but I'm running for a position in the council. To appear in a Grosz painting will hurt me."

"O, let's not exaggerate."

"And that's precisely the goal. It is no coincidence."

"But who is going to visit that exhibition? And even if someone notices any resemblance ..."

"Thousands of people will see it. First they will laugh at the scene, no doubt ridiculous, like everything that guy paints, but then they will start asking questions. Why he, the Head of Culture Schattendorf? He must have known Grosz. Perhaps they moved in the same circles... "

"Look, Hans, I can go have a look, if it makes you feel better."

"Thank you. Can you do it this afternoon?"

"Sorry, I'm leaving for Braunschweig in an hour. The new museum, you know. But the day after tomorrow, no problem."

"After tomorrow it will be too late."

"Hans, I wonder if you are not overrating Dunkels' importance. You're the favourite for the Council, not him."

Rudolf Dunkels. Graduate in Philosophy and Political Science. Too mediocre to make a career in that field, he jumped at the opportunity when he was offered a post as cultural editor. He spent a few weeks visiting museums, one after the other, taking notes, as the diligent student he is. And after having concocted a number of dull articles, taken directly from the Great Thesaurus of German Artists, he is now at the Inspection of Culture.

"How do you explain that such an incompetent manages to make a career in the world of art?" Schattendorf asks. "It is the knowledge, the skills, that should make the difference. That's exactly what the Führer said in his speech before yesterday."

"The Führer cannot be everywhere, and Dunkels is, whatever your opinion, ideologically unassailable, a true patriot."

"A worthy son of Rosenberg," growls Schattendorf.

65

"But Hans! Alfred Rosenberg is a great thinker. He has made an invaluable contribution to the national ideology."

"Listen, Ruprecht, I am going to explain to you the artistic ideals of people like him: they go into ecstasies before sweat-soaked but nevertheless neatly dressed labourers, before damsels with cheeks fresh as a rosebush. The essences of Germanity, Odin, the Valkyries, Wagner's whole tetralogy with brush strokes instead of chords. The apotheosis of dust."

Wendtland laughs heartily.

"You have the gift of speech, Hans, no one can deny that," he says. "But all the same ..."

"Have you seen anything more obscene than Ziegler's *Judgement of Paris*? Three goddesses in different degrees of nudity, the first exhibiting her charms with a provocative smile before a Paris with his eyes tantalized by the divinity's tits. The other two are waiting for their turn, seizing the opportunity to display their butts in front of the client, sorry, the spectator. The whole scene could perfectly take place not at the top of Olympus, but in a whorehouse, the *Grüne Trompete* of the Linienstrasse more specifically. There is a mural in that brothel that could have been painted and signed by Ziegler himself. "

Wendtland bursts out laughing, not without casting a worried glance around him.

"I understand your point of view," he says. "But Ziegler is a favourite of the Führer, you know. You should be more cautious, some might misunderstand you. Our comrades are not very knowledgeable about art."

"That's why we have to struggle to show them the way."

"But you have to be careful, Hans."

"And I'm not alone. I've already introduced the lads from *Nation und Kultur* to you."

"And I also know that the minister's views are close to yours, but Doctor Rosenberg is strong, even more than Minister Goebbels in my opinion. If you expose yourself too much, you could ruin your political career."

They say that the Führer is against Expressionism. But if that is true, Schattendorf is convinced that the reason is simple: he has not had time to consider the issue in depth, absorbed as he has always been by the political struggle. Schattendorf dreams of an interview with him, of an opportunity to develop his ideas. His arguments cannot but be finally accepted by such a superior mind.

"That pseudo art, neo-deceased, neo-petrified," would Schattendorf argue, "can never express the soul of our German people, so rich in deep feelings, because it is an art of curators, no, of taxidermists. Frozen, sterile. No, *mein Führer*, art must go to the people, not to be 'exhibited', 'admired' by them, but to inspire them, to inseminate them, to penetrate down to the innermost folds of their being."

Late in his life found Schattendorf his mission: promoter, no, instigator of art. Art is forms and colours; he would endow it with a voice, he would express what neither brushes nor paint tubes can. He would open paths for it, he would fight for art. He would convince.

He would explain to the Führer that those swirling, swaying brush strokes, seemingly exaggeratedly applied, those jagged lines, those bold colours, were meant to convey the extreme emotions of an artist reacting to the anxieties of our modern world. An emotion that was but the initial phase of a revolutionary awakening.

He is sure that the Nation's Leader, an artist's soul, will endorse this creed: the message of Expressionism and that of National Socialism are but one.

In order to achieve this, he must be something more than Head of Cultural Action in one of the districts of the capital. He must sit at the Council. With the support of Wendtland and of Adolf Furtenberg, his father-in-law, that will soon be a reality.

That's why he must identify the threat which Grosz' painting represents. And make it disappear, without further delay.

9

Sasha needs a saw. He goes to fetch it. He passes in front of the "garage" and sees that one of the non selected items has fallen down. He raises it and puts it back in its row. The objects being all of different size, the stacks in which they are piled look chaotic. Without Clausen's inventory, that would be a jungle.

At that moment he spots Macke sneaking into the garage.

"But where do you come from?" he exclaims. He runs after him, but Macke is faster; in two leaps he is at the top of the pile in the back of the garage and looks at him defiantly.

"Get out!" he tries, but Macke doesn't flinch. It follows every movement of Sasha with its yellow eyes.

It's a white cat, except for head and tail, which are black. He lives in the upper part of the gasometer and feeds on whatever he finds in the garbage cans of the neighbourhood. Schultze used to play with him and Sasha gave him the remains of his lunch, but one day Clausen surprised Schultze offering a bowl of milk to the cat and he flew into a fury ; animals are strictly forbidden in the premises. So, Macke got banned.

Sasha succeeds in attracting the outlaw with a piece of ham and urges him to leave the premises by the same window by which he entered. Fortunately, the feline visit will go unnoticed for Clausen; he won't be back until eleven.

It was Schultze who named the cat. On one occasion, young Willi, who had come to fetch a water-colour from Hofer, surprised the pussy in flagrant urination on *Lake Constance*, an oil by August Macke. Since then, the cat, formerly known as Miaou, Fuzzi or Mushi-Mushi, boasted the same surname as a prominent member of the *Blue Rider* movement.

"A hell of an art critic, our Macke," said Schultze.

Sasha glances at the yellowish walls. They are more than three meters high, which gives the enclosure a volume that partly compensates the absence of windows. Holes can be seen at regular intervals, probably pierced on the walls to place iron beams, subsequently withdrawn. He proposed using those holes to secure shelves on the walls. Simple ones, just plain planks of wood, since it would be, like everything else here, a temporary solution. But it would have made it possible to store the objects more systematically.

They would have been useful, those shelves, at the time of the flood. It was soon after Sasha's arrival at the EnKu: it had rained two days in a row and one morning when he arrived, he discovered a leak in the garage ceiling. The water had run out for hours and a puddle had formed, small but large enough to affect a dozen works.

Clausen turned pale when he heard of the incident. Usually he didn't go into the garage, but that day he inspected it carefully. The drawings and watercolours, protected by glass, had not suffered at all, and the oils had resisted well the water. But there were two gouaches that showed stains of humidity in their mounts. In one of them, painted by a certain Feininger and belonging to the Kaiser Friedrich

Museum in Magdeburg, the water had attacked even the painted part of the canvas.

Clausen required the services of a restorer of the *Kronprinzenpalais*, the Museum of the Crown Prince's Palace. The gouache had not yet been returned, and that matter was the subject of a good deal of Clausen's telephone calls.

"But, do you believe anyone will notice?" wondered Sasha. At most it would be a stain of moisture, and that picture was full of stains or spots, it seemed to him.

"I do notice, and that's enough," Clausen declared.

From there on, he ordered to protect the floor of the garage, as well as the objects, with tarpaulins. It made their work more complicate but, after a week, as the weather remained dry and the threat of rain seemed minimal, they stopped doing it. Clausen pretended not to notice, realizing the impracticality of his measure.

Nobody knows if the gasometer has had any purpose since it was put out of use. Sasha asked Clausen once if he could take a look at the old engine room. But the professor did not see the use of finding out whatever there was in the central part of the building, provided it was not rats.

On one of the condemned gates there was an acronym. B.C.G.C. British Continental Gas Company, a German-British firm, explained Schultze. The locks are not new, but they are not old and rusty either, noted Sasha. Surely someone operates them from time to time, someone activates the mechanisms that make the doors rotate on their hinges. To remove some machines? Definitely not to maintain them.

Schultze doesn't know either what the function of the building has been in the last twenty years. Of course there was the war and then

71

revolution, chaos, inflation, crises; other decisions to be made in Berlin, more urgent than the function of the old gasometer.

Clausen calls him. How many bulbs do they need to order and of what power? He has already asked him that the day before and Sasha promised to make a list. He has a rough idea, but an exact figure is needed.

Thirty should be enough, but, what if it is not? Better to ask for fifty. What the hell ! I'll ask for seventy, basta. Finally he settles on sixty-eight, it sounds more precise.

"One more thing," adds Clausen. "Herr Dunkels demands a survey of the classified items, according to a number of criteria."

"But," thinks Sasha aloud, "there are only two days left for ..."

"For the inauguration, yes, I know that just as you do. Fräulein Leni, too, knows it, don't you, Leni? But this fact, however undeniable, fails to call the attention of the Commissioner."

Rudolf Dunkels, Commissioner of Culture, is Clausen's immediate superior, a member of the party and of the cultural machinery of Alfred Rosenberg – the regime's ideologist – called the *Amt-Rosenberg*, "the Rosenberg organization", with its premises on Margarethenstrasse.

The inventory they had just completed was only intended to verify the stock. The task before them, a classification, is more tedious.

"The works are classified already," says Clausen. "Expressionists in the main gallery, neo-objectivists in hall two and the rest - abstracts and other - in the third one."

But the formal aspects are of no interest to the Commissioner; what he now requires is a classification by subject. Five types: Degradation of the German Woman, Semitic Ideals, Bolshevik-Anti patriotic Painting, Negroid Art-Racial Degradation and finally

Absurdism-Irrationality.

But for now it is lunchtime. Sasha brought his usual snack: a cheese sandwich, a sausage, two apples. He always takes his lunch sitting on the public bench near the Fichtestrasse, in the park behind the vacant lot.

When he finishes his second apple, he sees Schultze approaching.

"Sa-sha," he pronounces, detaching both syllables, savouring each consonant. "Alexander Wassingher, nice name. There is a good sound to it, I mean. Russian from the Volga, right?"

"Yes, but my ancestors came from the Rhineland."

"There are Germans all over Europe. We have always been a great nation, but now we have finally taken the path of true greatness. Now the world will respect us. It will have to. "

Sasha nods, giving another bite to his apple.

"And your mother?" asks Schultze suddenly. "German too?"
Sasha has the answer ready:

"Yes, everybody in our village are Germans."

"And, what is her last name?"

"Redmann."

"Redmann," Schultze repeats. "It could be from Thuringia, but there was also a Redmann who played center-forward at Holstein Kiel, and by the way, think about it, there was a Redmann shopkeeper in my neighbourhood of Stuttgart. Isaac Redmann."

Schultze watches Sasha as he deals the final bite to the apple and then throws the kernel into the air. It lands on the grass, ten yards from the bench.

"Don't get me wrong," says Schultze. "You are a good Aryan, no doubt about it."

He had always wanted to be an engineer, Sasha, he had never had the doubts of other young people of his age. And the Soviet State seemed to support his vocation. Once the revolution consolidated, it was time to build the new society. Housing, factories, bridges. Other times, new times. Philosophers were needed, yes, and an artist here and there too, but above all engineers, battalions of engineers, hordes of engineers.

He entered the Saratov Technical School without difficulty, but realized soon that behind the beautiful neoclassical marble façade, the drawing boards were simple dining tables and that for each teacher there were five hundred students.

The third year, the curriculum was changed. The recently adopted Central Educational Plan emphasized the practical needs of the region. Two hundred machines for the dairy industry had to be ready and installed in 1928. The School would concentrate on that project, so the students would have to make a pause in their training to perform routine tasks at the orders of engineers from Kharkov. They would become soldiers in the battle of industrialization.

A year ago Alexey, a comrade, had left the country. He had received a fictional invitation from an imaginary parent in Germany, which allowed him to apply for a passport. The exit visa for thirty days had cost him two hundred roubles. Alexey had never returned, but through his mother, Sasha knew that things went well for him.

If Alexey could, why not me? he thought. After all, he had a relative in Germany, a really existing uncle, living in Leipzig. In addition, Sasha's last name was German. His ancestors had settled on the banks of the Volga at the time of Catherine the Great. The Czarina, herself German, had invited her ex-compatriots to come to develop agriculture in the south-east of Russia.

He had written to his uncle, and one day, when he had already given up hope for an answer, he was summoned to the post office. The only letters he received came from his home town of Tonkoschurovka, one hundred and fifty versts from Saratov, and these letters, invariably from his mother, went directly to the student residence.

He had to show his documents and sign three different receipts before the employee set back all the stamps on their support, rose from his stool and disappeared into the building's depths. When Sasha saw the envelope, with an unusual looking green stamp, he knew at once that the letter did not come from Tonkoschurovka.

In the chaos of the first years of revolution, his uncle had chosen exile. He had opened a luggage store in Leipzig, near the railway station, a flourishing business for a few years, until the last economic crisis pushed it to the verge of bankruptcy. He could not offer Sasha a place, but he had found something for him in Berlin.

"Go ahead," his mother told him. "You are young, here you have no future."

His brother, a party member, looked at him with contempt. To abandon the socialist fatherland by pure personal ambition! What dignified future could there be for a Soviet citizen in the capitalist camp? But he did nothing to stop him. Moreover, it was thanks to his brother's acquaintances that Sasha could, showing the precious letter with the green stamp, obtain his exit visa.

The job in Berlin, in a small rubber valves factory, was poorly paid, but the working hours allowed him to attend the courses of the Technical University, Europe's best renowned. He managed to complete the first year, but then the factory was bought by a competitor, who sacked half of the staff, including Sasha.

But in the meantime he had obtained documents which gave his stay in Germany an air of legality, so that he could register at the employment office. Not being a member of an union, he was not entitled to unemployment benefits, but the office gave him the occasional job that allowed him to survive and continue his studies.

One day, it must have been in 1929, a friend gave him a hint: in Babelsberg, the big movie studios, they needed an electrician.

He presented himself to the reception and, after a few minutes, a grey-haired gentleman came. When Sasha heard his name, he was awe-struck.

In Saratov he went often to the cinema. It was the only art that interested him, and for fifteen kopecks he could view the films of Pudovkin, Eisenstein, Dziga Vertov, but also foreign productions, especially German. Thanks to the late shows of the cinema October, at the Sadovaya Street, he got to know well the work of Fritz Lang, Murnau, Pabst. That's why Arnold Braillowski's name was so familiar to him. He was one of the most famous directors of photography.

The interview took place by the reception, at the entrance of one of several hangars which together constituted Babelsberg, the European Hollywood. In front of them paraded sweat-drenched ballet dancers on their way to the locker rooms. One of them, who had a limp, was leaning against a wall, rubbing her calf. When she saw a huge moving platform approaching, she was off like a shot. The operator manoeuvring the platform, with a camera on it, succeeded at the last moment in dodging a white horse, held by the bridle by a centurion in purple tunic and a gilded helmet adorned with a red plume.

"Where have you worked?" asked Braillowski calmly, as if what was going on around them was just routine.

"Well, I have worked in the industry. A factory of rubber for valves. And also in the manufacture of spare parts for official institutions."

"Spare parts?"

"Buttons. For uniforms . But I have also worked in a theatre: the Luxor of Uhlandstrasse."

"With the lighting?"

"No, at the ticket office."

"I see. However, what I am interested in is your experience in the cinematographic field, in film production more precisely."

Sasha hesitated.

"In the production of films per se I was not involved in a direct manner, but I know everything about electricity, I am a student at the Technische ..."

"Yes but, you see, this is not a button factory. I need an electrician, yes, but an electrician with experience in ... all this," he made a gesture that embraced the reflectors mounted on footbridges ten meters high, projectors on tripods, a panel with hundreds of switches of various sizes and colours, and cables, cables and more cables, stretched throughout the hangar walls or meandering on the ground.

"Herr Braillowski: I know how a lamp works, I can fix it when it stops working, and what I do not know, I will learn in a few hours. Electricity is the same in a film set or in my mother's kitchen. "

Braillowski was looking around, trying to find an excuse to put an end to the interview, noticed a desperate Sasha.

"It's true that I have never worked in a studio," he added, "but I do love the cinema."

"That's fine," commented the other with a courteous smile. "Really fine. It proves that you are a man of good taste, but for the time being I have nothing to offer you. Call me in a few months and we'll see."

He went away. Sasha stood there, gloomy, not knowing what to do, seeing his dream, scarcely born, already broken.

But now it is 1934. And here he is, Sasha. In Kreuzberg, far, very far from the studios of Babelsberg. The classification Clausen talks about will be boring, he fears. He and the boy are in charge of fetching all the objects, helped by Leni.

All Klees and Kandinskys were meant for Room Two. But now, these pieces have to be classified differently. Being abstract, this art is neither specifically anti-German nor necessarily Judaic. They are to be placed in the room of Absurdism, which they will share with works which, while figurative, are so denatured, so bizarre that they provoke scandal or derision. Kirchner, Marc, Ernst.

A painter like Grosz, explains Clausen, with his war cripples disdainfully looked upon by officers with monocle, would in principle be predestined to the Bolshevik-pacifist room. But the only work they have of him cannot be placed there: it represents neither military nor workers. It cannot be classed as absurdist either; ridiculous, satirical, if anything. In any case it is clear that the different degrees of nudity of the three characters hurt the moral sense of any decent German, and that the female is a prostitute. Reason enough, Clausen sums up, to place the object in hall two, with others offending German women's honour. That is, if Hildebrandsstrasse does not change its mind and deselects the Grosz at the last minute; with Commissioner Dunkels, anything is possible.

The new classification will therefore demand a complete reorganization. In the main hall: the Jewish and Bolshevik sections. In the second, the wild-negroid and absurd-ridiculous paintings. The bawdy subjects can then be reserved for the last room, the smallest and the worst lit.

Wild-Negroid painting will be here synonymous with Emil Nolde. The guy must have travelled to Africa or Oceania; his pictures are full of dark-skinned characters with big lips. The Jewish section is going to be a little sparse. Jews are not rare among the names represented, but their works are either Bolshevik or depraved. What remains then for the specifically Semitic, for art that can be labelled purely and simply Judaic? Only two Chagall and one Nussbaum. Hildebrandsstrasse will find it too exiguous.

"But for God 's sake, if he wants a Jewish section, let him send me some works by Jews, he's the one who requisitioned the objects, not me," exclaims Clausen, in a fit of impotence.

And of rage, because he is forced to reconsider his selection, to add another five or six paintings. The quantity, fifty, had he decided himself, considering the number of rooms and their size.

"Let's see," he says, adopting a pragmatic attitude, "which Jews do we have in stock? Bloch, is he Jewish? "

Sasha has no idea.

"Leni, call Dunkels and ask which administration can advise in a reliable way about the ethnic status of the individuals represented here. Regarding Chagall, it seems clear: his pictures are full of candelabra and rabbis, but the others ... "

"Oppenheim sounds Jewish to me," says Sasha.

"No assumptions, please," warns Clausen, "there are Jews named Rosenberg. It would be a gross mistake to call a German painter Jewish."

"This is not serious," he adds. "What I agreed to take care of was an exhibition at the Kronprinzenpalais, a retrospective of German art of the present century. I asked for a six-month leave at the university. My daughter lives in Berlin and for my wife it was an opportunity to come closer to her. But once here, I learn that the exhibition will not take place in the palace, but in an industrial building located in a peripheral neighbourhood. "

Clausen makes a pause. Normally steadfast and full of energy, now he looks tired.

Sasha has met his daughter. It was thanks to her that he was hired for the exhibition; she is a friend of Lena.

A truck stops in front of the entrance. Clausen hurries to the door, but Willi is already out. He beckons the driver over to the other exhibition. The truck starts again.

It takes a few seconds for Clausen to retrieve the thread of his speech.

"At first I did not understand. Degenerate art? Finally, I realized. You see, Wassingher, authentic art, is based on learning and toil. The stuff we have here," he makes a gesture towards the garage, "are experiments, fashionable amusements that don't belong in a museum. Expressionists, cubists, nothing but a bluff. They aren't capable of producing a decent drawing, that's why they use those jagged, distorted lines, that crude, rapid brushwork, those jarring colours. Beauty? Truth? They couldn't care less about those values. And it was precisely that kind of things they entrusted me with. "

"But, couldn't you ...?" begins Sasha.

"It was too late to refuse," interrupts him the other. "But one thing is certain: once the exhibition is over, I'll go home. I'm tired of this town, of this unhealthy climate. I cannot even stand the air. It must be all the mercury. "

"I heard," says Sasha just to say something, "that it is precisely the mercury in the air that explains the liveliness of the Berliners."

"I count the hours to return to Breslau," continues the professor, "to resume work, because we do work there. Seriously."

"And speaking of work," he exclaims, tearing himself away from his depressive mood, "have you been able to reach the Commissioner, Leni?"

10

This is Morel's first visit to Berlin since January 1933. He's been in Francfort, in Munich, but not in the capital, not since then.

Berlin is the opposite of a harmonious city; it is made up of oppositions and dissonances. The effervescence of Alexanderplatz against the calm of the residential districts. The bucolic Tiergarten and, close by, the feverish movement of Potsdamerplatz, the largest traffic node in Europe.

The city is both cosmopolitan and provincial. Cosmopolitan? Actually, there are not so many foreigners here, two out of a hundred, no more. Russians fugitives from communism, but also Poles, Czechs, Hungarians, Swiss, British, Swedes, people from all the Balkans. Some attracted by the sexual offer, plentiful and diversified, as well as by the depreciated mark.

Cosmopolitan all the same, less by its population than by the circulation of ideas: this city adopts quickly the latest trend, whether it comes from Paris, Chicago or Moscow. Berlin fears, above all, not to be up to date with the latest fashion. A little snobbish our dear Berliners, perhaps because their city, an upstart among European capitals, lacks the traditions of Paris or Rome.

German cities with tradition are Munich, Cologne, Augsburg, and also Vienna. Ex-sieges of the Holy Roman Empire, of the Aulic

Council, the Imperial Diet. Berlin has not been an important capital for long: most palaces and ministries, museums and faculties, were built after the city became the centre of the German Empire. Before that, it was only the capital of the Prussian kings.

That is precisely why she is so impatient to become something today. To become, if possible, everything.

His visits to Berlin are an adrenaline injection. The rhythm of the city transmits to him, and he feels that tension, a positive tension, still weeks after being back in Paris.

He quickly realized that to make connections in the world of art he had to spend time in Berlin's cabarets - *Le Chat Noir, Katakombe, KuKa* - and in bars like the *Jockey.* He made some excellent deals late at night, between a Gimlet and a Side-car. Today he can congratulate himself of a good network. It was thanks to it that he managed to make his small gallery one of the most up-to-date in Russian and German art. And then, there was of course Fräulein Brenner's invaluable advice.

Her own things are not easy to sell. She is a realistic painter, but not really a New Objectivist in the style of Grosz; there is something peculiar and disturbing in her paintings. Landscapes with no characters, as if the inside of the bar in her oil *The sparrow* had been painted early in the morning before any waiters or customers arrived, when only the artist is there, in front of her easel, preserving all this desolation for posterity.

When seeing her works, one imagines her tormented, depressed. But Violetta is a vital woman, full of energy. She is self-taught, and her first steps in art she took on the other side of the easel, as a model.

"Well," she replies when he questions her about her style, "I reproduce things, you see. I have a ... like a kind of respect for what I see, I do not dare to ... I mean: what the expressionists did fascinates me, but that's not for me. "

"Why not?"

"I'm not schooled. I got to prove that I can paint, I can't allow myself those thick, kind of clumsy strokes ... And then, I don't want to ... That would not be me. Because I'm fussy with details, you see? I like details. And I love to draw. "

How old is she? Not to reveal it is one of her rare touches of vanity. She does not follow the fashion, she was never dressed "à la garçonne", never in short skirts.

"Hello Gaston," she says, joining him at the bar on the Ackersstrasse.

"What a mysterious air! A true femme fatale," he greets her.

She is wearing dark glasses and on her head a scarf, instead of her eternal beret. As he does every time he sees her after a long absence, he notices that Violetta is less tall than he remembers her.

"You still have your workshop at the Invalidenstrasse?" he asks.

"Not any more. I would like to find something further away, more discreet. And you, always on the hunt?"

"That's why I'm here."

"You do not ask me if I have something to sell."

"I do ask you."

"No, nothing. But, we could talk about a watercolour by Jawlensky."

"If it's the one I saw at your atelier, blue with yellow and red lines and circles, I'm interested."

"You know, you have so much Soviet stuff by now that you should organize an exhibit in your gallery."

"With your help then?"

85

"Why not?"

"I'm also looking for Rodchenkos," Morel says. "It's for an industrialist, he only likes collages, he bought me things from Heartfield."

"Forget Rodtchenko. The things he does these days are bogus, dishonest. If he ever falls out with Stalin, Goebbels could well hire him."

"You are severe, the man is still a serious artist."

She makes an obscene gesture with her index finger.

"Well, and now seriously, how do you make a living these days?" asks Morel.

"Seriously: I've never had a job, I've never been a clerk, a secretary or a hairdresser."

"But you have a rent to pay, unless one of your lovers lodges you for love's sake. And by the way, we have not talked about your sexual life for a long time."

She leans forward on the table, supporting the chin in her hand, and smiling, her first smile since she arrived:

"And what about yours? You've already met your local sweetheart I guess."

Nina Bovrik, she means.

"No diversions, please! I have come to Berlin for your sake, and this time I will not accept any excuses."

"You came to Berlin to buy cheap to sell expensive. And you did not answer me, what about Nina Bovrik. Could you be jealous, by any chance?"

He stares at her without understanding.

"Ah, sorry," she says. "I thought you knew she's back with Vittorio."

86

Nina is an artist, she comes from Kiev.

"If she feels like having an affair with her legitimate husband, well, I've always been tolerant," he says.

"Tolerant but bourgeois, you like to amass, to accumulate. You never give up anything."

"You're wrong. I'm open-minded and have nothing against polyandry. I'm almost a Berliner, in that way."

She laughs, a laugh with a hint of bitterness.

"A Berliner of bygone days, you mean."

"Anyway, I was not talking about politics," he interrupts her, "but about your love life."

She casts a worried look at the front door.

"What is it?" wonders Morel.

She does not answer.

"No, don't look," she asks him when he turns around.

After a few moments, she seems reassured.

"I thought I recognized someone. What were you saying?" she says, staring at him, but with her thoughts elsewhere.

"Are you okay, Violetta? You want us to leave?"

"Don't worry. Ah, yes, we were talking about Madame Bovrik."

"No, we were talking about you, about all the fun you have in bed."

She smiles. Always that smile.

Morel flirts with all women, even with Greta Stuhler, a sculptress who is past eighty. Not doing it would be considered rude on the part of a Frenchman.

With la Brenner it's different.

Every time she resists his advances, he tells himself: maybe she has a migraine, a depression, maybe it's not the right moment. But next time, ah, next time ...

The next times follow one another, but he doesn't give up. Because he cannot get it: they understand each other well, share the same interests, the same tastes. He is not repulsive, she is an emancipated female, a Berlin woman after all.

He does not abandon the hope that if they begin their rendezvous with Rodtchenko, dawn does not surprise them still debating Soviet constructivism.

No, he does not give up the idea of reaching that region of Violetta for him unexplored. By avoiding his advances, she refuses him something he needs. Need it? Yes, desperately. Why? He does not know.

There are few customers, this is a café that lives out of breakfasts and of workers stopping for a quick *pilsener* before going home. For both things it is too early.

The bistro is small and dark, barely twenty minutes' walk from the Unter den Linden, but light years from that renowned avenue's fashionable terraces. But the Ackerstrasse was close to Violetta's atelier, and she never liked trendy bars. A sort of inverted snobbishness attracted her to shady joints in the vicinity of Alexanderplatz or the Stettiner Bahnhof, in some backstreet with an iron bridge crossing over it, blackened by the locomotives' soot. Or near the river, not the noble Spree that surrounds Museum Island, no, the other Spree, the one with rusty ship hulls and banks dirty with industrial waste.

The bar owner, a fellow with a broad, reddish neck, is running a cloth over the counter. When his eyes meet Violetta's, he gives her a discreet nod.

She seems flattered by the cordial gesture of the man, who does not seem to be prodigal with them. She smiles, and when she meets Morel's eyes, her smile turns into a delighted laugh, revealing her teeth, slightly uneven, but resplendent white.

Her skin is pale, something that was fashionable some years ago, but which today brings to mind dissipation and sleepless nights. These days, it's better to have pink cheeks and the hair in a bun.

She has a beautiful mane, almost black, with red reflections. Redheads are said to have bad character and she sure got a strong temperament. "It's my mother, my Hungarian side," she explains. But now she's in a pleasant mood. And calmer than before.

"And you, Gaston? Things seem to go fine with you. You travel around Germany, a few days in Berlin, then a trip to ... "

"Trips? I'm here to work."

"I see: you take the temperature of the cultural climate, and then you go back to France, to your nice and quiet life."

"I do not know what your idea is of a gallery owner's everyday life, but ..."

"I know that life well, I also had a gallery once. Does it surprise you? "

"On the contrary, I can well picture you as an art dealer."

"Would you accept me as a partner?"

"If you move to Paris."

"Don't tell me that twice."

"Come, by all means, and we'll arrange that Soviet exhibition you were talking about."

She laughs. She has never been to France.

"I could leave Germany but I could never leave Berlin. And then, why travel? To live here is like living in a railway station, with people coming in and out all the time. Besides, travelling is a pastime and I don't let time pass: I use it. "

"And what do you figure I do? I've just closed an affair: I bought a Grosz. Later today, I'll visit another Baumgarten to discuss an El Lissitsky, then I'll meet Konrad Berg, the new talent, you know. You are offering me a Jawlensky yourself. I'm into business, you see, business and cultural exchanges. "

"Exchanging culture for money."

Morel shrugs.

"Everything I earn, and it's less than you imagine, I reinvest in art. As a coming partner of the gallery Morel & Brenner ..."

"Brenner & Morel," she corrects him.

"... you ought to have a more exact idea of our business. And don't' forget: in the long run, art trade benefits the artists. You know what? I buy right now three of your future works. Straight away. "

Violetta stares at him and her look is now neither mocking nor provocative; it is sad. She lowers her head, fixes her eyes on the table's surface, on the ashtray with the text *Pschorr* in red letters, on the two empty cups of coffee.

He has always thought she was about thirty: at this moment she looks older.

"I cannot paint any more."

To paint is of course a suspect activity these days, if you don't belong to the Art Chamber, and oil is an indiscreet material; neighbours can smell it. But couldn't she do watercolours?

"That's not what I mean. Painting has become a kind of ghetto to me, I suffocate."

He looks at her, puzzled.

"I was not an artist, you know, I was actually ... I was a swimmer, you see, like a fish. One day I emerged in an art gallery, the next day I worked in my atelier, another day at a friend's studio, some other time I came up to the surface as a model, next day I sang at a cabaret. I have even been a film actress."

And it is true. Only once, as the maid of Gerda Maurus, who played a Russian agent in a thriller by... Pabst?

The rest is true too. Violetta has a poignant voice, expressive more than beautiful. When she climbed onto the stage of the Katakombe or the Blue Mouse, all noise stopped. She stared at the floor, serious, concentrated, as if she did not see the audience, as if she wasn't even aware of it. She began to articulate some words, in a low, hoarse voice, which, supported by some piano chords, shifted gradually from recitation to song.

"If I cannot do a little bit of everything, I can do nothing. I can barely breath, that is the truth, Gaston. And now, well, I wonder if I am not at the end of the road. Am I still alive, Gaston? Be honest with me. "

"If I give credit to my eyes, I would say that you are indeed alive" he tries to joke.

"Thank you!" she says, and her relief, genuine, unaffected, stupefies Morel. "Because sometimes - I know it sounds weird -, sometimes I wonder if I ... if I still belong here."

To the realm of the living, she means.

In the corner of her right eye, a pearl is just about to free itself; in a second it will roll down her cheek.

He takes her hand, she lets him caress it.

"There are those who leave," he suggests.

She shakes her head.

"I can help you come to France."

"I don't speak French and I would never adapt, and then ..."

"You would adapt in three months, and then you would be able to swim freely again."

"And then... But I'm not a fish, Gaston! Do I have fins maybe? I swim, alright, but I am terrestrial. An animal, yes, but a Berlin animal."

Berlin is like a train station, says Violetta, and yet there are those who take root in this city where people are all the time arriving and leaving, this city of buses and trams, traffic signals and railway viaducts. There are those who grow roots in this soil grey and hard, as if it was not bitumen but nutritious humus.

It was not for nothing that Violetta was once called the muse of Moabit. She was not born here, but what could be more typical for a Berliner than having a provincial background? Like Bert Brecht, from Augsburg. Like Claire Waldoff, famous for her abrasive voice and her song texts in crude Berlin slang, who is born, not in a district like Wedding or Friedrichshain, but in the Ruhr, five hundred kilometres from here.

Waltraud Brenner, Violetta, came to the world in Munich, and until the age of fourteen she had not set foot on Unter den Linden. When she heard the nonchalant accent of the Berliners, she, with her singing Bavarian, felt like a little peasant. She tried to assimilate the local melody, to jump a few consonants, to pretend that some final vowels did not exist.

"And your Harry?" he changes abruptly the subject.

She crushes her cigarette against the metallic bottom of the ashtray, then she looks him in the eyes, just a fraction of a second before she turns her regard towards the enamelled sign on the wall - "*Smoke North State*" – then to the picture with a tavern scene, then to the street.

"Is he still in Berlin?"

She turns her gaze towards the boss and mimics with her lips the phrase *"ein Bier bitte."* "And one for me," adds Morel. The boss arrives with two bottles of *Pschorr*.

"He's in Berlin," she answers at last.

Morel finds it astonishing that so few people seriously consider leaving the country. Those who are not directly threatened are trying to make arrangements, to find compromises, hoping that things will get better. "They cannot get worse, right?"

"Once you're in Berlin," she replies, "you're not going anywhere. We're at the top, from here all the paths lead down."

Violetta has heard of the exhibition at the gasometer, but it is from him she learns its name: *Entartete Kunst.* Degenerate Art. The term makes her laugh.

"Well, I'd be delighted to lend them my paintings. I've always been a bit degenerate."

She adores that kind of joke. It was not for nothing that Anita Berber was her friend.

"She was attractive, of course, but not my type," explains Violetta. "Besides, there was something sinister about her. Still, Anita was an open, sincere person. That's what killed her in the end."

"I thought tuberculosis did."

It annoys Morel that she refers to her sex life in this ambiguous, crooked way. To muddy the waters, he tells himself. To make him stray from his course. He decides that this time she will not escape, that he will not leave Berlin without having screwed her. Not to discover any secrets, not to know the deep reason of the desolate landscapes she paints, of her relationship with that Harry. No. To free himself of an obsession. Bad thing an obsession, even worse than love.

"I'd love to see my paintings in that gasometer," she says. "Maybe I'll send them to Goebbels."

"Your things are not depraved enough, and anyway, the idea of the exhibition was not his. Our good doctor has a weakness for avant-garde art, didn't you know? "

She laughs at him.

"Gaston, next time you need information, ask me, please. I could have given you this world exclusivity five years ago."

"Well, enlighten me then. Have pity on my naivety."

"Seriously, I don't see how you can make any good business deals if you ignore that kind of stuff. What else do you not know? That Goebbels has been a novelist, not to mention a dramatist?"

Morel admits his shortcomings.

"Not really a Schiller, mind you" she explains, "but the man has had literary ambitions, and in this band of thugs, in this kingdom of the blind, no one can dispute him the crown."

"Not even Rosenberg?"

"Another intellectual giant. Yes, Rosenberg is his great rival. Imagine, what a clash of titans!"

She enjoys her superiority. He submits himself willingly, because there is something in her teasing smile that indicates a change. She delights in her power, he guesses, she feels strong behind her ramparts. Strong enough to lower the drawbridge at some stage?

Perhaps this very day? In his room at the Lilienhof? But how to suggest it without making her run away?

A lunch. At the *Eckhaus*.

"In my situation I cannot refuse an invitation to eat," she replies. "It's just that I'm very busy. I got a job in a framing studio, you see."

"At what time do you finish?"

"Around six."

"A dinner then."

The *Eckhaus*, a few meters from his hotel, would be a little too obvious for a dinner, he decides.

"You choose where," he adds.

She hesitates, seems about to propose something, then changes her mind. She reflects with her gaze lost at the back of the room. Finally, slowly and somewhat mechanically, she says:

"There's a Russian restaurant near Nollendorfplatz."

Not far from his hotel either. And that, she cannot ignore.

At the office of the Director of Cultural Action of Spandau. The premises have been previously used by the Prussian delegation to the Public Ministry of the Reich, which, following the concentration of functions in the new Ministry of Justice, had to move away.

It is a three-storey house in neoclassical style, surrounded by a beautiful garden. The upper floor is still partly occupied by the Ministry, but Cultural Action has the ground floor and the first floor, eleven offices in all. For the moment it is enough, because the staff consists of only eight people, but Schattendorf has already asked for reinforcements, a series of concerts in the garden has been scheduled for this spring, and the music section is understaffed.

Music has never interested him much, but he understood that the public of this district loves concerts. By giving them a drop of Mozart and a few pills of Strauss, he hopes to make them gulp down a good portion of modern art.

Rosenberg advocates a reorganisation of the Reich's entire cultural administration, which, starting 1935, would involve the absorption of all Local Cultural Actions by a single entity controlled directly by him, by his own *Amt-Rosenberg*. But the Ministry is reluctant to change an organization that has not yet had the time to prove itself.

The phone rings: it's Peter Litzke.

"I saw the painting," he says. "It's an orgiastic scene. A brothel I mean. Realistic style, a woman, two guys. And, yes, one of them looks a lot like you."

"Give me more details," Schattendorf asks.

A woman on all fours on a velvet bench, explains Peter. The other bloke, a bourgeois, with a moustache and a sparse skull.

"And how am I dressed?"

"In blue overall, like a worker. Or an artist, because there is a photographic camera in your hand. You stand on the other side of the woman, to the right."

Schattendorf turns pale. In a barely audible voice, he asks:

"Does the bourgeois resemble Hindenburg?"

Peter thinks for a second.

"As a matter of fact he does. He has the same handlebar moustache, but no uniform. Do you recognize the picture? "

Schattendorf doesn't answer.

11

Seven thirty. Berlin has woken up and eaten breakfast. A seemingly unending procession of white- and blue-collar workers is coming out of the subway or hastening to the S-Bahn station.

Sasha stops for two minutes on his way to his work at the gasometer, to admire the view from the bridge over the Spree, while lighting a *Juno*. He studies the different hats. Caps predominate in this neighbourhood, caps with a narrow visor or a wide and lustrous one like those of coachmen or station-bearers. On occasion a bowler, or a panama, a tropical island in an ocean of dark felt. And then the secretaries, typists, standard operators, with their blue, green, pink headgear, touches of colour in the gray male stream.

He throws the cigarette butt on the side walk and crosses the bridge too. On the other side of the river, a circle of onlookers. A man in a brown suit and cap, standing behind a folding table, catches the attention of passers-by with a stentor's voice. "On behalf of the well-renowned house *Krüger und Söhne*, for the very first time in the Reich's capital." But what is he selling? Sasha sees neither a kitchen knife nor a wallet with a special pocket for identity documents and photos of the beloved ones, the perfect accessory for both ladies and gentlemen.

Folded on his right arm there is a jacket that he proceeds to soil with black ink. In his left hand, a small cardboard box. He lays the jacket on the table, opens the box and dilutes its contents - a white powder - in a glass of water. He closes the glass' opening with the palm of his hand and shakes it vigorously. Then he applies the mixture to the jacket.

Miraculously, the ink stain disappears. "A miracle? Nothing of the sort, dear and highly respected audience, merely the strictly scientific effect of this amazing product that I have the pleasure and the honour to make available to you in absolute exclusivity and in representation of the firm *Krüger und Söhne*, flagship of the German chemical industry, a product whose formula is a carefully guarded secret. No miracle, ladies and gentlemen, but what can truly and without any exaggeration whatsoever be called miraculous, is its price! Barely a mark twenty the box, a special promotion valid only for today."

Sasha is about to cross the avenue running parallel to the bridge when he sees a street car of the line thirty-two coming. Two other pedestrians approach the track as well. "Watch out!" he shouts. The men look at him but they do not stop their walk, it is rather the tramway that reduces its speed, to stop completely at barely two meters from the pedestrians. Imperturbable, they pass in front of the vehicle without deigning to look at it.

How could they know that the tram would stop? There is no ordinary stop here. No, but they have seen many times that at this point the driver is forced to brake, leave the steering wheel and jump off the vehicle to switch tracks with his iron pole.

He is fascinated by this casualness, by this metropolitan self-assurance, by the elegance of people's movements, deftly eluding other pedestrians, judiciously evaluating speeds and obstacles in order to avoid stopping, to avoid breaking that rule of the big city: the law of perpetual motion.

"Today is the big party, huh, Wassingher?"

Sasha, just arrived, looks puzzled at Schultze.

"*Sekt*, salmon sandwiches. We'll have a great time," says the other.

This afternoon is the unofficial inauguration of the other, parallel event at the gasometer, the EDeKA, the Authentic German Art Exhibition.

"Rosenberg will be there, Commissioner Dunkels too, the Gauleiter, the Regional Head of Youth, maybe even Dr. Goebbels," says Schultze.

"And Hitler?"

Schultze smiles.

"The Führer has more important things to do. Although, being himself an artist, it's not impossible."

He has not considered that possibility. The idea further increases his expectations.

"But are we invited too?" asks Sasha.

"Of course, both exhibitions are two faces of the same medal, that is what they explained to me when I started here."

As for the EnKu, with two days left to the opening, the lighting is still not ready. The last-minute changes imposed by the Commissioner have upset the plans. It was necessary to order new lamps, which were promptly delivered, but of a power different to the required. In order for them to be replaced, they had to be returned first.

At a quarter to four, the professor warns them:

101

"In less than two days we are opening and, as you are well aware of, we are late. As if it was not enough, at five o'clock we will be forced to make a pause to pay a visit to the other exhibition. We will show up there, that will be all. Twenty minutes, no more. "

Schultze cannot hide his frustration.

"Herr Schultze, how many objects remain in the warehouse?" asks Clausen.

He means the non selected works, those that have to be returned to their owners.

"I would say ... about fifty," replies Schultze, pursing his lips.

"About fifty you say. But what I want to know is whether they are forty-eight, fifty-one or maybe forty-nine."

"Forty-six," replies Schultze without hesitation.

There are more, Sasha is certain of that.

"Did we not agree that you would return twenty yesterday and another ten this morning?"

"You are absolutely right, Dr. Clausen, but Propaganda and Cultural Action did not send me the truck requested, but a smaller one. Here's the copy of the requisition form, if you want to see it."

Clausen takes the paper that the other tends to him and examines it.

"It is enough to drive one mad," he explodes. "Well, we'll have to speed up the pace, it will soon be four o'clock, and until six you can go on delivering in the vehicle they've been good enough to provide us with."

"But," Schultze protests, "the museums close at five."

"Well, then let us concentrate on other owners. The galleries do not close until seven and, for what regards the private collectors, they will be delighted to recover their property even if you knock on their door in the middle of the night . "

"But," Schultze mumbles, "at five o'clock is the pre-inauguration of the EDeKA."

Clausen looks at him severely.

"We do not have time for those things, Mr. Schultze. Wassingher and I will pay them a perfunctory visit. As for you, your priority are the returns. "

Schultze becomes livid. His lips tremble, his gaze turns to the professor, then to Sasha. But he doesn't utter a word.

Clausen resumes his task without looking at him. Schultze stands at attention, clicks his heels and leaves.

Unlike the EnKu, whose premises have no windows, the EDeKA has been assigned, in addition to the ground floor, an upper storey with sufficient natural light.

Downstairs are the entrance and the front office, with stylish furniture and a red carpet which stretches out onto the wide staircase leading to the upper floor. Fixed on the steps with bars and bronze rods, carpets cover the lavish reception and the staircase, but also the floor of the rooms above.

It is a striking contrast between the neglected exterior of the old industrial building and the sumptuous style once inside. What cost the most, Clausen *dixit*, is the new staircase, which replaced the old spiral one. To put it in place it was necessary to tear down a wall. But under the thick crimson cloth, the stair steps are plain wooden boards. And the majestic staircase, which would suit a five meters high hall, seems out of place here.

A tall guy, with his fine reddish hair combed with a stripe in the middle, comes to meet them. He is in uniform: brown pants, ochre jacket, black tie, a military cap in his hand. The man, in his thirties, greets Clausen ceremoniously.

"My assistant, Mr. Wassingher," introduces the professor Sasha.

The other nods.

"Dr. Dunkels, Culture Commissioner of the Capital Region," says Clausen.

The commissioner takes the professor by the arm and leads him to a false plaster column next to a rococo writing table. Sasha goes quietly up to the first floor. Few people in the rooms, almost all in uniform, some with jackets like Dunkels', others in brown shirts, one or two clad in black from head to toe. He tries to identify some personality, but in the end, the only one he would be able to recognize is Dr. Goebbels, by his fast and irregular pace he has seen in the newsreels.

In a corner of the main room, a stack of prints, forty pages of glossy paper: the catalogue. On its cover: some symbols: an eagle, a lighted torch and a Greek helmet. The eagle carries a swastika crowned with laurels between its claws. In golden letters on beige background, "Juni 1934" and "EDeKA", the initials of the *Echte Deutsche Kunstausstellung*.

He studies the works on display, starting from the left. The first one represents a SA in brown uniform with his cap attached to the jaw by a leather band. The visor of the cap throws a shadow that hides his eyes, but the prominent chin, his arched lips in a bellicose gesture and his posture - leaning forward, a chair in his hand - stress his unshakeable determination. We are in the middle of a bar brawl, so common when Nazis and communists disputed the control of the city, tavern by tavern. In the background, some diffuse silhouettes, a riotous crowd: the enemy. A very well executed work, judges Sasha, although the SA he has seen in real life are far from having such a noble aspect.

The next picture is by someone called Schmutzler. Three girls walking on a country road, their gaze ahead and upward, a confident smile on their lips. Two of them are singing, the third one accompanies them on the accordion. The middle one, her pretty face lit by the sun, is the very image of vitality, of joy.

This is real art, thinks Sasha. First-class art, accomplished by top range craftsmen, a Ziegler, a Hommel, true masters, trained at the best schools. But what have they given to the professor? All the weird creations, twisted faces, green torsos and violet fields, all that is extravagant and sickly. A freak show, a cabinet of horrors.

In the second hall, the painting he saw last time he was here. But it is now hung on the opposite wall, with a more intense natural light: *The Joy is Back*. He discovers details that had escaped him the previous time: sitting in front of the little girl and her mother, two old men, farmers maybe, engaged in a jovial discussion, glasses of wine in hand. At the next table, a man of venerable beard eats calmly, looking down at his plate. The characters on the platform seem to be preparing a ceremony. To commemorate an event. An inauguration? Of the house to the right of the painting, perhaps, painted in bright colours and with a wooden veranda.

Joy seems to be one of the great subjects of EDeKA, and what more appropriate subject for art? thinks Sasha. If art serves a purpose it must be to strengthen the morale of the people, to propose models that induce admiration, not mockery or contempt.

105

He feels the same emotion as the first time. This is not Nazi painting, he feels, this is real painting, period. An accomplished art, not childish sketches, not grotesque buffooneries.

On the lower edge of the golden frame, below the plate with the title, a smaller one with the name of the author has been fixed. *The Joy is Back* is a work of Eberhard Novak. He leafs through the catalogue. On page seven there is a reproduction of the painting and a presentation of its author: born in Bohemia in 1892, art school in Vienna, exhibitions in Linz and Zwickau.

How much can it cost? He always thought that if he ever won the lottery he would buy himself a car, a Standard or even a Steyr. He dreamed of moving to a more comfortable apartment, of making a trip to Switzerland, to Austria. But not of buying paintings.

These colours, this theme, remind him of something. His native village, to be sure, but also of something else, of a picture seen some place. But where? He never visits art exhibitions. It is Clausen who, between a scolding and a rebuke, taught him the little he knows of painting. He had never seen so many watercolours, oils, drawings, in ink or charcoal, as he has at the gasometer.

He goes through his recollections searching the once seen picture, but as soon as he reaches the spot of his memory where it is recorded, the image, at first so clear, gradually vanishes, as a screen can fade in a film. Three seconds later it has disappeared without trace, as if it had never existed.

But here is the professor, tapping him on the shoulder: "Time to go back to work."

And indeed, there is work to be done. The lighting of room number two, intended for Negroid art, is difficult to put in place. In his first attempt, Sasha distributed 100-watt lamps regularly on the upper part of the walls, but that left the nether half too dark. They have to be lowered to a height of three meters. Alas, the lighting panels are difficult to fasten: they weigh over ten kilos each. When in the end he succeeds, with the help of Willi, he realizes that the illumination has become too uniform, the pictures look now flat, dull.

At last he finds the solution: to alternate panels of different intensities. And they should not be aligned so regularly ; as it is, they illuminate the displayed objects with the same intensity as the hall's entrance, where there is nothing on show.

About nine o'clock, Schultze comes in, a bottle of beer in his hand. Smiling, he announces to Sasha:

"Mission accomplished, all objects returned. Most of them anyway."

"Well, we have two days left, and a small delay should not matter that much," says Sasha.

Schultze puts the bottle's neck to his lips. His Adam's apple quivers three, four times, then he tosses the bottle away, but so awkwardly that it stumbles on some documents on the table. Sasha does not succeed in catching it, but fortunately the bottle was empty.

Schultze bursts out laughing and gives him a strong pat on the back. He pulls another Beck's out of his bag, pops off the cap by knocking it against the edge of the table and hands the bottle to Sasha.

"I like you, you know, you're a good chap. If all the Jews were like you, Germany would not have any problems."

"But ..." stammers Sasha.

"Yes," Schultze interrupts him, "I know that not all Jews are thieves and exploiters, but look at it for a moment from the Führer's point of view: he cannot put his own people at risk. Some innocents will pay for the sinners, it is inevitable, it is a law of history. And after all you hadn't so many scruples when it came to exploiting us, had you? Still, Wassingher, you're my chum. I'm generous, I'm German. Here, take another sip."

"But," insists Sasha, "why do you say I'm a Jew?"

Schultze smiles.

"I am old in the Movement, I know how to recognize you people. During all these centuries they lived abroad, those Volga Germans mixed with who knows which races. Slavs of course, but with Jews too."

"I have never heard of any Jewish ancestor."

"Show me your certificate of aryanity then. If you work here you should have it."

"Nobody asked me for that, and anyway I could never get my parents' birth certificates, the communists will never give them to me."

At that moment, Clausen arrives.

"Mr. Schultze, I have just got a call from the Potsdam Pavilion wondering when we will give them back *Red Twilight*. By Frantiszek Riegel. Our man has already returned it, I replied. No, nobody did, they answered. Have you anything to say, Mr. Schultze? Don't tell me that canvas is still in the van!"

Schultze replies, without blinking and in an impudent tone that the beer accentuates:

"There's nothing left in the van, everything has been delivered. He lied to you that bloke."

Clausen opens the rear door of the vehicle. He sees a few pieces of wrapping paper and two empty jute bags, nothing more.

"If you think you can make fun of me, you are wrong. I do not know what you have done with that object, but if it's not here tomorrow morning at the latest, I will denounce you."

Schultze looks at him with an insolent smile.

"Do as you like. I have also some information for the authorities. I have written down all your remarks during your talks: that this painting has pictorial values, that that one doesn't lack some merit. But the fact that they are degenerations painted by Bolsheviks, doesn't worry you. "

"I did the job I was entrusted with. That is hardly your case."

"Professor Clausen, make no mistake. You don't know who I am."

From the inner pocket of his jacket, Schultze takes a red booklet with a swastika and "NSDAP", the acronym of the party, on its cover.

"It was not you, Professor, who hired me. Commissioner Dunkels did, by recommendation of the Kreuzberg Section of the party. I don't owe you any explanations. And if you persist in harassing me, I will tell everything I know of the funny business that goes on here."

"Funny business?"

"Objects that are not to be found on the inventory list. Objects with wrong author."

"We go through the inventory regularly, you know very well that."

"Oh yes, but the inventory, the blue notebook, is your private property, no one else has access to it. And you change the prices of the works."

"I have modified some, yes, because they were obviously wrong. Who can believe that an object coming from a museum, from a private collector, can be worth just twenty marks, as was the case for a Chagall? "

"You increase some, but others have been lowered."

"Never."

Schultze looks at him sceptically.

"And as for that *Red Twilight*, or blue, I've never seen it. Are you sure that it's in your notebook?"

"Of course."

"With which price?"

Clausen takes a look at the inventory.

"Six hundred marks."

Schultze whistles.

"A neat little sum, isn't it? Maybe it has been returned by someone else and not necessarily to the Potsdam Pavilion?"

Clausen gets livid.

"Do you accuse me of diverting objects?"

Schultze does not answer, and he makes no great effort to conceal a smile.

"That's unacceptable," exclaims Clausen. "What evidence do you have? Say it right away or get out. I do not want to see you here any more!"

Schultze stares at him, and his smile turns imperceptibly into a grimace of contempt, then of fury. He yells:

"In this exhibition, organized to warn our people of the Semitic threat, in this display of degenerate and judeo-communist art, there are members of the staff whose Aryanity is not proven. "

Clausen seems overwhelmed.

"I don't see what you're talking about."

Sasha looks down. The professor did mention that certificate of aryanity the first time he came to the gasometer, but the subject was never brought up again.

Schultze: "If I report to the Section Kreuzberg that objects which are State property are disappearing and that in addition non-Aryans have been employed, you will be in trouble, professor."

Clausen glares at him furiously. He picks up a file and leaves the room. Schultze remains there, looking triumphant.

12

"I have nothing for you for the time being," had Braillowski, chief photographer of Babelsberg, said that day of 1929 which seems so distant today. And after having said it, he had left with long strides. Sasha stood there, dispirited, unable to react. No one noticed his presence, neither the technicians running behind the directors, nor the make-up artists trying to call the attention of the actresses, all of them jumping over the electric wires.

But, can that one be Greta Garbo? he asked himself. No, she looks more like Brigitte Helm.

It was as if he was nailed to the ground, fascinated by the spectacle. And cursing himself for having missed the opportunity to become a part of it all and for being forced to return to the buttons or to the valves, to bury himself in an anonymous factory of insipid products.

"I love the cinema," what a pathetic phrase! "Cinema is my passion, my all-consuming interest !" should he have said.

The painful realization that he had spoiled this unique opportunity, that he had been turned down by the great Arnold Braillowski, revolted him: why hadn't he told him that he had seen all his films, why hadn't he grabbed the occasion to provide further details, to impress him with his cinematographic erudition?

His temporary job at the button factory had come to an end, but they had promised to call him if they ever needed him. The work, apparently simple, required nonetheless a few days to learn to operate properly the metal press and avoid material waste. The buttons, struck with the coat of arms of the city, were for the police uniforms. Thousands of copper buttons per day: large ones for the jackets, middle-sized for the sleeves, small for the pockets.

There was another button maker in Wiedenau. Perhaps he could go there, show them his letter of recommendation. As he wondered which bus could take him to Wiedenau, he saw Braillowski again, hurrying towards the reception desk.

"But, are you still here?" he said, noting Sasha.

Instinctively, scarcely aware of what he was uttering, Sasha mumbled:

"I have seen *The Brothers Karamazov.*"

The other looked nonplussed at him.

"I have seen *The crime of Professor Wiener.* I have seen everything you photographed."

"Oh, I see," said the other embarrassed, "but as I have already told you ..."

"And *Nebuchadnezzar,* and *Sadness of the Faubourg.* True works of art."

Braillowski looked at him with curiosity. No one used the word "art" in Babelsberg. After the films were finished, they were discussed in the newspapers, in specialized magazines like *Der Film* or *Kino-Magazin.* He considered himself something of an artist, in a way, but his job consisted primarily in solving practical problems.

He was in a hurry, but decided nevertheless to spend one of his precious minutes on the young fellow with the foreign accent.

"You're interested in our art, aren't you? The seventh, as the press calls it. In that case you must like Florian Maartens. Let's see if you know what movie I did with him."

Maartens was a little known Austrian director, but Sasha recalled a film, the only one he had seen of him: *Sacrilege*. He remembered it because he had seen it in the company of a girl with whom he afterwards had had a fierce argument: she thought the film "incorrigibly bourgeois", while he was impressed by the strongly contrasted close-ups and by the innovative montage. Pure formalism, she argued, the antithesis of what a proletarian film should be.

What the hell, what do I have to lose? he decided.

"*Sacrilege*," he said.

"You mean *Ramses*, maybe?" suggested Braillowski.

Ramses, a commercial blockbuster, was not Maartens' work. Thiele's or Waschneck's perhaps, but never Maartens', who had only made two or three films in Germany.

"No, *Sacrilege*. Maartens would never have done a thing like *Ramses*"

Annoyed, Braillowski retorted:

"What's the matter with *Ramses*? The purists criticized it, yes, people who have no idea of what cinema is about, who believe you shoot a film like you paint a picture. *Ramses* was an excellent job. If you only knew the technical difficulties we had to overcome."

"I didn't mean to ..." Sasha apologized. He didn't know that his interlocutor had been involved in that film too.

Braillowski scrutinized him from head to foot. At last, shrugging his shoulders, he declared:

"Let's get this right: having or not having seen my movies is scarcely relevant, but you seem to be a nice guy. Go see Mr. Bauer at the central warehouse, they need always people there. A temporary job, mind you, a week or so."

A success. An incredible triumph. A job in Babelsberg!

The daily routine at the warehouse: to help carry a Louis XV console for a film about madame Pompadour, to stack Prussian uniforms in a cart for a production on Frederick the Great, to push a rolling cabinet with sequinned dresses across the stage for a cabaret scene.

The week became a month and the month a trimester. But in the fourth month he left the warehouse for the studios, to work, not with cables and switches as he expected, but with the sound.

The Americans had cleared the way for sound film and the Germans were forced to follow or else miss the train. It was a new technique that had been developed in speed, on the fly. In the beginning, all the scenes were shot in a soundproof room to eliminate the camera noise, but that limited the actor's mobility. Eventually someone came up with the idea of the mobile microphone, that is, to fix a microphone at the end of a long rod, "the pole", a gadget that allowed its operator to follow closely the actors' and actresses' all movements.

Sasha was twenty-three years old, and instead of drawing power plants or milking machines, he was busy assessing the speed at which Wera Engels, Fritz Rasp or Lil Dagover moved across the studio, in order to follow them with his mic, without stumbling on any wire and making sure that neither the camera nor its shadow sneaked into the frame.

Like so many emigrants he had been forced to modify his plans, to adapt them to a changing and chaotic reality. But destiny does things

116

well sometimes: Sasha was now learning the trade of a boom-operator, a speciality few people had heard of and still less mastered.

And a job for which Sasha developed an interest bordering passion. If Babelsberg had still been a possibility for him, he would not care about Schultze's threats. He would gladly leave the gasometer, the professor and his little lectures, the degenerate as well as the genuinely German works. But he could not. Only pure Aryans were allowed to work in the cinema since the Nazis seized power.

The Schlosskeller is Curt Hagener's favourite bar, but only "à l'heure bleue", as he puts it. For the evening he prefers more lively places. In the old days he favoured the Jockey or the Café Braun. Now he can be seen several times a week at the Red Top.

The first of the place's three rooms is also the largest. In the back, a door that opens onto two more intimate rooms. In a corner, a piano. A dozen tables with white tablecloths, a few stools at the counter. The walls are covered with paintings and photographs. In a conspicuous place, the portrait of a bearded fellow of an austere appearance that belies the bar's atmosphere: the gentleman had been the owner of the pharmacy that was there before the Red Top took over the premises.

A guy in black tail and prominent eyebrows bows at the audience, sits down at the piano, and plays the first notes of a sentimental tune: *Wenn wieder Frühling ist*. But then he interrupts himself and attacks instead the chords, slow and sensual, of *Georgia on my mind*. So, with a resigned gesture, he goes back to the original melody, one of those that evoke tropical paradises in the moonlight, "with you," "always with you."

Hagener has seen the great Marlene here, accompanied at this very piano by Friedrich Hollaender, who usually played at the Jockey.

"Hey, Curt," someone taps him on the shoulder.

"Hello, Johan ! Have a seat ! What will you have?"

But his interlocutor is not alone. A young lady is waiting for him.

"Sit down, just a moment. You've worked for a while with Oberfrunck, haven't you? If I tell you he's interested in a painting by Grosz, what would you say?"

The man makes a gesture to his companion and sits down on the edge of a chair.

"Interested in what way?"

"It appears that he sent someone to inspect a painting at the expo of the gasometer. A Grosz."

"The gasometer, huh? No, that rings no bell."

"But he does buy art?"

"Yes, but, something by Grosz?"

"The picture has a theme that is ... raunchy."

Johan grins as he gets up.

"In that case," he says, "and speaking of Oberfrunck, I'd exclude nothing."

Hagener remains alone at his table. He orders a Red Russian. Where can he have seen that picture? The woman on a stool, feathers on her head, a guy behind, and another, a look-alike Hindenburg, in front of her. The Kronen Gallery? But he has not set foot there more than twice in his life.

And above all, why the heck is this damn Dunkels bothering him? Dunkels hates Oberfrunck, Oberfrunck hates Dunkels, and dozens of people hate both of them. In what way is all this bickering Hagener's business? Why does Dunkels have to annoy him every time he can't deal with things on his own?

Still, he cannot drive that cursed picture out of his head.

There are people who make drawings while they think, others who mutter aloud the sketches of ideas that come to their mind. Hagener neither writes nor speaks, he does not hum or tap on the counter with his finger either. He just thinks, he does nothing but think, and while that thinking goes on, one could swear one hears a sort of rattling, as if Hagener's brain was made up not of neurons but of tiny metal gears.

At last, he snares his prey, he finds the answer to the riddle that has been haunting him for hours. But he does not cry *eureka*, he does not burst into cries of joy. He just pronounces, slowly and in a low voice, three words: *Der Blaue Maus.* Bang's cabaret.

13

In Berlin, Bang realized after a few days in the capital, everyone was talking about opening bars, cafés, music halls. "Something like the *Plaza*, but smaller and focusing on what is really the core idea." "A little like the *KDK*, if you see what I mean, with a more subtle style but not a bit less corrosive."

But the projects remained projects and the new *Katakombs, Grössenwahn* or *Café Zielka* rarely passed from brilliant idea to reality in brick and stucco.

That evening of 1925, his first in Berlin, he had accepted Harry's invitation to the cabaret *Schall und Rauch*. The beer was excellent, he thought, but the show - poets reciting the fruits of their imagination, political satire declaimed by well-known intellectuals – was not Bang's cup of tea.

"What do you think?" asked Harry, leaning at the counter.

"The music is not bad."

The cabaret had engaged a genuine american-jazz ensemble.

"How much would you say they make?" wondered Bang.

Harry approached one of the black musicians and succeeded in finding out it, in spite of his bad English and the other's sketchy German. Bang recorded the information in the small notebook he had bought and where he wrote down prices, rents and wages.

But to open a bar he needed someone who spoke German better than him and who knew the scene. This someone was Geza Nemes, a resourceful chap, an habitué of all kinds of night joints and an expert in the art of obtaining information, whatever the subject. Geza, journalist and tourist-guide *manqué,* had acted for a year as press secretary for a large theatrical group, twelve months of forging relations, of making acquaintance with theatre critics, editors, advertising agencies.

Unfortunately, the group's accountant had concluded that all those endeavours cost more than they yielded. Geza, in spite of his efficiency, had to swap his tastefully furnished office in the premises of the *Volksbühne* theatre, for the more spartan waiting room of the employment office of central Berlin.

"I hire you," Bang said. "But remember, the day I don't need you any more, you're fired."

As far as Bang could see, the cabarets were all the same. A counter and a small stage with some tables around. A singer with pleasant looks, her voice being less important, a comedian who climbed to the platform and told a few jokes, political or otherwise, and a master of ceremonies to pull everything together, exchanging jokes with the comedian, commenting the performance of the singer in a more or less suggestive way. And beer, of course, gallons of beer.

Counting the number of customers, studying their alcoholic preferences and multiplying the total of orders by their unit price, Bang confirmed his conviction that the best business was not a cabaret but an ordinary bar.

Geza begged to differ.

"Well *mein Freund,*" said Bang. "Who prevents you from opening a cabaret yourself? After all, that's what you and your chums from

122

the Schimmel are doing at that dairy shop in the Westend. As for me, I'll stick to my field. It worked in Copenhagen and it will work here, at least I'm sure of that. "

"You shouldn't," retorted Geza. "There are thousands of bars here. To convince the public to come, you'll have to offer them something more than just booze."

"Okey, it'll be a bar with a girl singing."

"And where will she sing? You'll need a stage. A singer, a stage, a counter, that's what we call 'a cabaret' down here."

They were precisely at one such place at the time, on a study visit. It was poorly lit, the public was composed of men, some women who had had too much to drink and a handful of prostitutes. The music, between Charleston-music and Argentinian tango, made one appreciate the value of silence. The master of ceremonies was half drunk.

"And it is something like this that you want me to open?" asked Bang.

"No, my friend," said Geza. "This joint is at *Hundegustav* level."

Hundegustav, *Dog-Gustav*, was a hangout near the Stettiner Bahnhof, where all sorts of asocial characters mingled. But also fine people seeking thrill; some obtained it by inhaling cocaine, others went slumming to Hundegustav's. There, they could enjoy a beer while watching the call-girls with their pimps, the burglars talking business with the pickpockets, or the Africans joking in Berlin slang with an accent from Togoland, while at the same time admiring the tango dancers sporting newsboy cap and a scarf around the neck, a kind of Parisian apaches, East Berlin-style.

Gustav, the boss, had worked at the dog pound, hence the name of his establishment. It was said that it was at the pound he had taken a liking to dog meat, and that for his birthdays he treated himself to a Doberman fillet or a juicy Schnauzer chop.

"What you're going to open," Geza explained, "is not a cheap joint like this or a smokescreen for a brothel like the *Grüne Trompete*, but a cabaret of quality. The artists, I will find them for you. We'll need also someone to recite poems, satirical poems which throw a light on current events, you see?"

It was Geza who found the premises on the Jägerstrasse, in the heart of Friedrichstadt. The rent was high but the place was in good condition, no reforms needed. All that remained was to find a name. In the Friedrichstrasse there was the Black Cat, a legendary cabaret. A few yards away, another establishment had opened which, to taunt the cat, called itself The White Mouse. Bang's cabaret was the third tetrapod of the neighbourhood. The new mouse would be neither white nor black. *Der Blaue Maus,* The Blue Mouse.

It was during the inauguration party that Bang made the acquaintance of Violetta Brenner, Harry's companion, who rarely came to the Schimmel.

"You know, this woman is not only irresistible, she is also a first-rate singer," Dieter introduced her.

"No, no," she said while sipping her beer, "when I sing I sing, when I booze I booze."

But when Fredi, the young Czech pianist, let hear a few chords from a Claire Waldoff hit, Violetta could not help herself from humming along.

Hannelore, Hannelor
the prettiest babe of Halesches Tor...

The humming grew into lyrics, the voice got in tune with the piano, and the chatter died gradually down among the audience. It was the début appearance of the Muse of Moabit at Der Blaue Maus.

Thanks to Bang's firm management and the creativity of Geza, who every other night brought along an unknown genius newly arrived from Bremen or Bucharest, the Mouse made itself a clientèle. Berliners were known for their partying appetite. On summer weekends, everybody went to the lakes to swim, or to take a walk in the Grunewald forest. But when the night came, woods and lakes became peaceful again and it was the restaurants and the cabarets that assumed the main role.

The inhabitants of the capital demanded entertainment and did their best to enjoy themselves in a frantic but at the same time conscientious manner, taking advantage of every opportunity to have a good time, just as – at work – they employed each hour in the most rational manner.

And it was not difficult to be entertained: the revues of Erik Charell had little to envy to those of the Folies Bergères, and the erotic performances went often beyond anything Parisian scenes dared to show. But if the Blaue Maus was making itself known among these party-lovers, the competitors were legion. They had to find their niche.

The "artistic dance" – naked girls who moved rhythmically behind a transparent veil - had become commonplace. The telephones to flirt from table to table required an installation that only big establishments like the *Residenz* could afford. A character like Jolly the Starving Artist who, locked up in his cage, night after night, growing skinnier and skinnier, gazed impassively at the customers stuffing themselves, the *Hackepeter* restaurant had it already. Parrots fluttering through the room, a black panther squatting on the counter, beer that was not pumped from a drawer, but that flew in a basin illuminated by golden spotlights: none of this impressed the public any more.

Geza would willingly have hired Baker, but with Josephine's fee, the Blaue Maus *would* only be able to afford two or three of her hip wiggles. It is true that some friends provided free attractions: Violetta showed up occasionally with Anita Berber, an artist of sulphurous reputation, and even if Anita didn't dance naked on the counter, even if she didn't imbibe her favourite appetizer - white rose petals frozen in a mixture of chloroform and ether - her sheer presence distilled some pearls of glamour on the establishment.

"We have to find something," repeated Geza all the time. "We have to be different."

"Tell me how," Dieter asked. "You're the inventive one."

"Fredi: how were you dressed when you came today?"

Fredi Körner, the pianist who had been promoted to master of ceremonies, looked puzzled at him.

"Well, in black trousers, blue jacket and hat."

"Yes. And that's how you'll get on stage tonight."

"'Come as you are'," would be the slogan of Blaue Maus. "Come exactly as you are, even just out of the tub if that's the case."

A success ! Their most resounding since the opening ! But innovations come of age quickly in Berlin; the sensations of April are ancient history in May.

More! Better! Fresher ! demands the public. Let us behold the never seen, we want to hear the unheard of! Berlin, where extravagance is never enough and where excess is barely sufficient.

Geza was indeed the inventive one, but the idea of the "poet-express" came from Dieter. Someone from the audience would give him a word around which he composed a four-lines poem. The word could allude to current affairs as "bankruptcy" or it could be philosophical as "angst", but, more commonly, it was one of the terms that designate parts of the body below the belt. Dieter took pride in coupling "thunderstruck" with "fuck" and "politik" with "dick" and, building upon a salacious first verse, he rhymed heroically through the whole strophe to cast finally anchor by an unexpectedly elegant conclusion.

He discovered he had a gift for rhyming. Being an expressionist poet, he had always disdained rhyme. And that's the purpose a cabaret should serve: to break taboos and overcome prejudices. But at the Maus, even traditional monologues had their place, sometimes performed by the same Dieter, other times by Fredi and occasionally by Harry Shadow, poet, painter and editor.

Because also Harry revealed an unsuspected talent at Bang's cabaret: that of speaking in public. But Dieter's monologues were funnier. Until then he had been regarded as a poet, but above all as the manager of the artistic-literary enterprise Der Bruch. A serious and responsible lad, despite all his witticisms. Less impetuous, less iconoclastic, he had always lived in Harry's shadow, all the time teasing him, bur more like an impertinent little brother than like a rival. But Heinz Brehme had once said, "People underestimate Dieter. Harry dazzles, he's a magnificent firework, but Dieter's flame burns longer."

For Violetta, Dieter had always been nothing but Harry's friend. Now she discovered that the man, usually lunar, could also glow with a light of his own, like a star.

"But who the hell needs long burning fires?" said Anita. "Do you like to watch a chimney fire for hours and hours, until you have red cheeks and sore eyes? No, I hate things that stay for ever, that never finish. Give me every time a nice firework that delights me and then blows up and disappears for ever. Puff! "

The new Dieter disturbed Violetta. She had had affairs parallel to Harry, but they were – and so she wanted them - evanescent. Stars? Falling ones in that case.

With Dieter it was different. How? In which way? She never wanted to talk about it. It was one of the secrets of the Muse of Moabit.

Bang, without being secretive, was nevertheless not a man to display his emotions. Still, everyone could see that he was satisfied with his business. Always behind the counter lining up glasses or pouring a *pilsener*, a watchful eye to detect a customer with an empty glass or another one waiting to pay. It was his portly figure that was the Blaue Maus' symbol, more than the concept of the Come-As-You-Are cabaret or the custom-made express poetry.

His sociability didn't go much further than shaking hands with the regulars. And then, he left that to Fredi, who was the new master of ceremonies. The former one had gone too far with his jokes about the dancers. His insinuation that the girls' profession included something more than just dancing, displeased Bang, who threw him out.

"But they are whores!" he defended himself.

"For you, they are young ladies," corrected Bang.

It was true that the boundary between dancing for a fee and accepting a cash compensation for more intimate services was not always clear cut. Some dancers were not always insensitive to the charm of certain wallets. But it was not allowed to discuss those transactions in the premises, let alone to provide such services there. That was Frau Schramme's department.

When leaving the Maus, if one took to the right, there was first a drug store, then a hatter's shop, and right after that, the unassuming parlour under the *Paradiso* sign, where Frau Gudrun Schramme run her business. Being neighbours, it was natural that Bang made her acquaintance. While a tad chubby, she was nevertheless an attractive woman, so that it was no wonder that their relationship evolved from good neighbourship into friendship of the most intimate kind. A discreet man, Bang never appeared with her in public. But one summer Sunday, Dieter came to the Schimmel with the scoop: he had seen them both together, rowing on the Havelsee.

It is true that in addition to the sentimental bond, they had also common commercial interests, because their establishments complemented each other: the Paradiso provided the kind of services that the cabaret was not in a position to offer. Thus, the Blaue Maus could retain its reputation as a place for good and somewhat clean entertainment. A guide of the Berlin night described the Maus, overdoing it a bit, as "the favourite hangout of Reverend Schmidt."

One day, Bang asked Geza if he knew any artist who would like to expose at the Maus.

"I didn't know you were interested, otherwise I would have suggested it myself," said Geza.

Bang shrugged.

"It could attract customers."

Discreet in his private life, he was it also in his tastes. The rough appearance of the pub-owner caring only for the cash movements, concealed a soul sensitive to art. As a child, he often flipped through a volume of art prints which, through the hazards of life, had ended up in the sparsely populated bookshelf of the family. Afterwards, the opportunity to cultivate his mind had seldom arisen.

For nothing in the world would he have admitted it, but there were paintings that moved him, and his tastes were not confined to landscapes or still lifes; he loved Chagall, and even an art as controversial as that of George Grosz.

Secretly and for a large sum, he had acquired a series of ink drawings of that artist and hung some of them in places so secluded that few customers paid attention to them. And one day he decided to devote a portion of the surplus cash to art sponsoring. That's how the Argus Prize was born, awarded to the most corrosive and satirical creation.

He had never explained the name's meaning. Someone remembered that in Greek mythology, Argus was a giant with hundred eyes. And indeed, Bang, always behind the counter, keeping an eye on everything going on, could be compared to such a many-eyed entity.

But that was not the reason.

14

"What right do you have to criticize Harry?"

Her black eyes fulminate. It is there, in her eyes, that Violetta's rage is concentrated. Her lips, clenched, tense, are not about to reopen, feels Morel, other than to let out new recriminations.

And yet the evening had begun well. Morel was not in a hurry, since the art critic of the *Vossische* had cancelled his appointment. The Russian restaurant is in the Augsburgerstrasse, so he allowed himself a walk along Leipzig Street, then he crossed the Landwehrkanal by the cosy bridge of the Köthenerstrasse, which runs parallel to the more spartan U-Bahn viaduct, an example of modern architecture with its black iron arches.

The canal, a haven of peace in the city bustle. A barcass passes under the bridge, slow and phlegmatic as if it were moving not on water but on syrup. On the other bank, on the Halesches Ufer, another boat - also flat, but with a high chimney - slumbers, attached to the dock.

Suddenly, a gust of wind. The blinds of the shops of the Tauentzienstrasse shake, threatening to fly away, carrying with them their metal frames, and then twirl in the air at the whirl of the gusts, like disembowelled Zeppelins. A lady crosses the street quickly, quickly, keeping both hands on her elegant bow hat to hold it in place.

It is raining. Those who have an umbrella open it, others seek refuge: the marquise of a cinema, the colonnades of a church, a tram, any tram, why not the 199 towards Marienfelde? Two girls who have just come out of a *konditorei* grimace and return to the shop with the sign *Warme Küche* on the door.

The pavements, opaque asphalt just a while ago, shine now like jet. The street lamps turn on, dyeing the rain with light. The city becomes more intimate, more secret. The downpour lends to the banks of the canal - who would have guessed it? - a whiff of Venice.

A red awning with golden letters on it: *Maximov*. The head waiter comes to meet him. A table for two, asks Morel. Not that one, I prefer some other by the wall. Would you like an aperitif, sir? Yes, a Dubonnet. Terribly sorry *mein Herr,* can I offer you a Cinzano instead? No, bring me a Madeira.

This morning he received a telegram from Navarro's secretary. He is an impatient guy, when he has decided something, he wants it at once. He terrorizes his employees, doesn't give his suppliers a moment of peace.

Morel answered. The picture, he explained, has become an icon of resistance to Nazism. He will have to wait a little longer, but in exchange, his friends will have something to admire that is more than a simple licentious image. A publisher of mass newspapers which are far from cultural, Navarro is himself an avid collector of art, especially erotic. And he does not skimp on expenses.

Morel does not believe he will cancel the deal. Not really.

His Parisian gallery has made a name for itself, it is frequented by everyone interested in the European avant-garde, but it remains a small venture. The average sales allow the gallery to survive, but if its owner is to survive too, a juicy deal is essential every now and then. And 1934, there is only one deal in sight: the sale of Grosz's *Still Life* to the South American press tycoon.

Suddenly, he sees people around him looking up at the entrance of the restaurant. Breathless, trying to put order in her wet hair: Violetta.

"Excuse me Gaston ! The thing is, when it rains the traffic turns chaotic. It took half an hour for my bus to make it from Alex to Potsdamerstrasse."

"And what were you doing at the Alexanderplatz?" asks Morel, but so the waitress comes in: "What would you like, madam?" She could be Russian, with her little white embroidered apron, if her accent wasn't, according to Violetta, from Prenzlauer Berg. On the wall, a large tapestry with conifers and berries. Rural landscapes, St. Basil's Cathedral, the Neva in Leningrad and, in a corner, an icon of Virgin Mary.

There is an orchestra integrated mostly by violinists, almost all bald. They play vigorously while staring at the audience with a cold, indifferent gaze, as if the agile fingers and the impassive eyes did not belong to the same body.

The public: elegant ladies and middle-aged men of aristocratic appearance with well-groomed moustaches. Morel hears one of them addressing his neighbour as "general." Exiles.

"There are more Russians here in Charlottenburg than in Nizhny Novgorod. Charlottengrad, that's how Harry called this neighbourhood," says Violetta.

Harry? thinks Morel; everybody calls it so.

"Violetta," he asks as they take a sip of "Ivan the Terrible," a mixture of vodka, blackberry liqueur and ground black pepper, "do you know Goldenberg? The art dealer I mean."

"I do," she replies.

"He has a superb house, facing the Tiergarten," he goes on.

It could have been Hyde Park, though with a different flavor, perhaps because this panorama so harmonious - a park like a forest, an avenue of linden trees lit by lamps of amber light and traversed by horse-drawn limousines - is so close to the red Berlin. One never quite forgot the proximity of the explosive, proletarian Wedding district, even while enjoying a glass of champagne in the balcony. It was this contrast that made the beauty of this view fragile, perishable.

Violetta draws a puff of her cigarette, notices that the ash at the end of it is growing dangerously, pulls the porcelain ashtray towards her, and, with a slight tap, knocks the grey powder off. Then she exhales a cloud that her lips, by tightening the opening of the mouth, thin down to a slender volute.

"It was precisely in one of those superb homes facing the Garten that I first met Harry."

Again that Harry, thinks Morel, who tries to redirect the conversation to Goldenberg, the gallerist. But Violetta continues:

"It was a spring party, and I came with Anita. People asked her to sing and she looked at them as if they had asked her to croak, or to pull rabbits out of a hat. It was not that she was drunk, she just looked that way sometimes, as if she had just landed on earth from another solar system.

"But her eyes were well focused when she spotted Harry, who was dressed more elegantly than the others, even if his clothes were a little

136

worn. Velvet vest, gold chain, and a small fine moustache which made him look older than he was.

"It was she who approached him. Hardly a feat for her to attract his attention: men came running to her at her slightest sign. But she quickly lost interest and fell asleep on the couch. He turned to me. He told me he was a painter. I asked him to show me his work."

"You can be straight to the point when you want," says Morel.

"In short: a week later he was leaving his shabby room in the East End to settle in my flat."

Things were going well for Violetta. For some time she had done a cabaret act with Anita and it had given her a certain reputation. Cabaret was her first career, and it was precisely after appearing at *Das Schiff* that a friend of hers, a journalist at the *Volks-Zeitung*, named her "The Muse of Moabit."

"But I do not live there any more," she objected. She had just moved to a more fashionable neighbourhood.

"If you want me to call you 'The Muse of Aschaffenburger Strasse', I'll do it, but it is less catchy."

She did modelling too and, after having observed painters work, she decided to take the paintbrush in her hands. She learned by herself, watching, listening to advice.

"In what style did Shadow paint?" wonders Morel.

"A little Kirchner, a little Rottluff. Maybe something of Schiele."

"Nobody would say that of you. Whether they like it or not, what you do is different."

"Someone accused me of imitating De Chirico."

"An idiot. Who can never have really looked at Chirico. Nor at your work. But Shadow was eclectic, you say."

"One of his favourite phrases was: one does not exclude the other."

137

"He had no self confidence then."

"I did not say that. He was a real artist, and also an intellectual. A sharp tongue and a sharp pen. He's been compared to Tucholsky, you know. And he wrote in Herwarth Walden's magazine, along with Mann, with Marinetti."

Moving to her place had been a godsend for Shadow. The apartment was large and he could even work there, since Violetta had her own studio on the Invalidenstrasse, in one of the rear apartment blocks of some "rental barracks," as those poor-quality apartment buildings were called. For her it was also convenient to have someone to share the rent of her beautiful five-room flat overlooking the dome of the Church of Remembrance, even if Shadow only managed to pay his part half of the time.

"The silly boy. He was talented but had no discipline, he got up late and started his day with the feeling of having wasted the morning, which prevented him from making the most of the afternoon. As for the evening, everyone knows that it is not made for work, especially when you live in the heart of Berlin's night life. "

"There is something there that doesn't make sense. A real artist, as you call him, may well have a chaotic private life, but he does work. Artists may have lots of vices, but only one is incurable: working to exhaustion. They can't help creating."

"The artists I know are all different. Artists? There is no such thing, artists are just a bunch of special cases."

"But you for example ..."

"Me? I am Violetta. He was Harry."

A few blocks from their place lay the Romanisches Café, a meeting place for artists and eggheads. Closer still was the Schimmel, an elegant café, a tad too much so for Harry's taste, but with the advantage of not being infested with intellectuals, as he put it. He found that the rear area, after the large pots with philodendrons, being too close to the toilet, was ignored by the chic part of the clientèle. One of the tables in that section, the eighteen, became his base of operations.

It was at the Schimmel that he had his coffee at eleven o'clock, and it was also there that he sat down to chat with his friends by eight o'clock in the evening, discussions punctuated by a brief foray to the Romanisches, the Jockey or Der Sturm gallery to have a beer with Walden.

But one day Violetta discovered that it was not at the Schimmel he had his rendezvous with Lotte, a *Morgenpost* journalist. What's more, it was through her, through Violetta, that he had met that Lotte.

"Ah, what a surprise," comments Morel.

Violetta, who was leafing through her memories with a certain distance sprinkled with nostalgia, if not with fondness, stops short.

"It doesn't surprise you?" she asks, staring at him.

"No. I mean ..."

"Yes, tell me what you mean, please."

It is clear to him that unless she obtains a satisfactory answer she will say nothing more.

"That is to say," he tries to explain, "judging from the little I know of him, he doesn't strike me as particularly confidence-inspiring."

"Ah," she reacts in a tone that is no longer tense but neutral. "It is a moral judgement then."

"Me a moralist? But ..."

"Yes, that's exactly what you are, Gaston, at least when it comes to others. But you would be well advised not to blame people you scarcely know."

139

"Well, I didn't mean to upset you, I promise not to interrupt you again."

"You won't, because I will not discuss the subject any more. I didn't even want to talk about Harry, it was you who asked me."

I have done nothing of the sort, thinks Morel, but prefers to keep silent.

The mood at their table has cooled off, but the atmosphere in the restaurant gets warmer: the audience, stirred by the nostalgic Russian music, takes up the songs in chorus. Two middle-aged men kiss each other, without releasing their glasses. In the vehemence of the hug, one of them spills some vodka on the shoulder of his friend, who was calling him "general." He bursts into tears, moved by the recollections which the violin's complaint must evoke in him, while the other tries to rest his glass on the table, and in so doing knocks over a goblet of wine ; a reddish spot grows rapidly on the white tablecloth and then starts dripping on the carpet. A boy with a tray of caviare in his hand works his way between the two men, followed by another waiter bringing a bottle of Armenian brandy.

Morel understands why she chose this restaurant; the ones on the Kurfürstendamm, which the political police keeps an eye on, she's well advised to keep away from. Maximov, on the other hand, has never been a hangout of the Left.

The waitress brings the bill. Morel slips a ten-mark note under the little golden tray's clip.

"How about a drink in a quiet place?" he tries.

"No, for me it's time to go home."

"It's barely nine o'clock."

"If you want you can follow me to my house."

140

"*To* her house," he ponders. But she does not suggest a cup of coffee once there. Is it entirely out of the question?

They take the Augsburgerstrasse and then turn north west towards Charlottenburg. The shortest route to Spandauer Damm, where she lives, is the Kantstrasse, but she avoids the main streets. Therefore she makes no objection when he turns southwards. That way, they will soon pass by his hotel.

But for the moment they are in front of Hotel Nollendorf, where he stayed first time he came to Berlin, on the same floor as Eddie North, a black jazz-man who played the violin at the *Elysée* of the Fritschestrasse. "You see, here is the place where ..." begins Morel, eager to tell her about all the glasses he emptied with Eddie at the Nollendorf's bar. But she pays no attention. Instead, she explodes:

"You're an incorrigible bourgeois, Gaston! You imagine I was mad at Harry because he slept with Lotte. What really bothered me was his dishonesty, the fact he did it behind my back. Besides, I had also my affairs.

"You have always been faithful, haven't you?" she continues. "Faithfulness is not a virtue, you know. It is just lack of imagination. To have strong desires, to push life's limits to the utmost, without measuring, without respecting every rule, every demarcation, should that be a sin? A transgression that should be punished?"

He had never imagined that his little remark would trigger such a reaction.

By Nina Bovrik, Morel knows that there has been something between Violetta and a certain Dieter, one of Shadow's friends. "Not a one night stand," had Nina said. "Something more serious."

Violetta's reaction caught him off guard, but it confirmed something: Harry is not a relic from the past yet.

15

And speaking of Violetta's affairs, there had been more than Dieter; there had been Vittorio too, 1925 or 1926.

Vittorio Carraro, a futurist artist, had come to Germany shortly after the war. He had gained a certain fame in Berlin, where the Italian avant-gardism was in vogue. Without being part of Der Bruch, he was for a while a regular at the table eighteen of the Schimmel, where he was esteemed for his good humour and his wit, although he – being in his forties - didn't belong to the same generation as the others.

Vittorio became their guardian angel and he worked miracles, as an angel should. One day, the house that printed Der Bruch went bankrupt. The number thirteen of the review, despite being ready for press, could not appear.

"I know the people who make *Elixir*, their printer is not expensive," said Vittorio.

"*Elixir*, really?" Harry reacted. "That elitist pamphlet which only publishes aesthetic poems à la Stefan George?"

But next day, Vittorio gave them their *imprimatur*. Number thirteen appeared, no more than two weeks late and with a better graphic quality than before.

The Italian solved every problem with a smile and a slap in the back. He moved around the café as if he were at home. Already after his second visit he called the boss by his name, and never omitted to shake hands and exchange a few words with him. The waiters greeted him with a smile when he arrived, always elegant, never without his bowler hat, and a cane in his hand with a mother-of-pearl knob, figuring a jaguar head. He cruised across the place, neither fast nor sluggishly, taking the time to study the audience, with a self-assurance that made his short height pass unnoticed.

Geza Nemes, who was to become Bang's right-hand man, had just lost his job at a regional newspaper.

"I'll have to go back to Budapest," he moaned.

Vittorio came back to the table, a glass in his hand, after a bit of chat with one of the waiters. He did not confine himself, like the others, to the usual coffee or beer, but browsed through the drink menu, trying them all, from the *Balzam* of Riga to the *Carlsbad Becherovka*.

"Geza, I know someone in the team Reinhardt. The *Deutsche Theater*, you know."

"Geza is a journalist, not an actor," Dieter remarked.

"The fact is," continued Vittorio, "that the Reinhardt crowd realized that in a modern enterprise, and that's what they are by now, contacts with the press must be managed in a professional way. And a young talent like Geza, with his international experience, would fill marvellously that vacuum. "

Max Reinhardt was a theatre director and impresario, the most important one.

"You will spend your time dining with all the critics, with Kerr, with Jhering," said Dieter enthusiastically.

"And you could invite us," suggested Paul. "I've always wanted to eat at the Metropol."

"Do as you like, but personally, for dining with theatre critics, I would choose the Majestic, "says Dieter.

"Well, as long as it's not at Aschinger, I'll take it."

"As for me, I accept in advance and without reservation any invitation, Aschinger not excepted. Their pea soup is not bad at all, especially in this cold weather. Did you know that it was Ostwald who invented the formula for that soup? "

"Poor thing, do you believe everything you hear?" laughed Paul. "Wilhelm Ostwald, the Nobel Prize of chemistry would have invented the formula for a soup? Soups, unlike syrups for coughing and mixtures against hot-piss are cooked according to recipes, not chemical formulas."

Vittorio intervened:

"The Majestic is not bad, but when it comes to Italian cuisine I recommend the Metropol, they have a chef from Verona, and his Venetian style cuttlefish risotto is celestial. Much, much better than the *Osteria Toscana*, where the cook comes from Osnabrück. "

Vittorio had a refined taste, and the money to cater for it. His paintings sold well, but in addition he came from a wealthy family of Trieste.

On those evenings of January, the meetings of the circle stretched until late in the night. It was not until the waiters had cleared all the tables and the cleaning ladies were already there with their buckets and brooms, that the editorial staff of Der Bruch resigned themselves to leave the Schimmel and head for the entrance of the U-Bahn station Wittenbergplatz, trying not to slip on the ice on the side walk. At the Schimmel it was warm and bright, while in the attics they inhabited, the snow threatened to slip through the windows' cracks, and not even five blankets were enough to protect them from the cold spell

145

which, according to the weather forecast of the *Funk-Stunde,* originated in the Novosibirsk region.

"I'll make a call tomorrow," Vittorio told Geza. "Come to my studio at eleven, and don't forget your job certificates."

That's how Geza, thanks to Carraro's rich network, was appointed Secretary of Press Relations of the theatre group, and made friends with the second of Jules Marx, boss of the *Scala,* as well as with some members of the team Erik Charell, the king of the operetta.

The Schimmel, at this long-gone epoch when Hitler was just an Austrian clown and Göring a patient in a clinic for morphine addicts, was the meeting place of the Der Bruch band ; none of them had neither the space nor the comfort to entertain. The café was their office, they could even make and receive telephone calls there. And then, they preferred a place in the midst of the hustle and bustle of the city. Recently redecorated in a style that Paul called "art deco", but which according to Heinz was late "art-nouveau" and which Harry defined as "composite of cocktail bar and Balkan tavern," the establishment had two sections at different levels, encompassed by a balustrade. The large columns, dividing the space into smaller parts, made it appear larger.

Each section had its clientèle. The lower level, closest to the entrance, was the favourite of elegant ladies as well as of newcomers. The regulars chose "the parterre": it was more quiet for chatting and, from there, they dominated the whole place.

The table eighteen, where Harry and his gang sat, was known among the waiters as "the philosophers' table." There was also "the professors' table", just on the railing. The only one of that group who was actually a professor was an old gentleman who had once taught history in high school. But there was also a certain Gregorius, who

146

called himself a professor, with "experimental astrology" as his speciality. Another regular at the table was a retired colonel with monarchist ideas.

Gregorius had devised a Germanic zodiac, with Thor, Odin and Wotan instead of lions, fishes or rams. Thanks to the colonel, whose brother published a local newspaper, he wrote an astrology column every week.

The professors' table was not chosen at random: at the beginning, they sat at another one, by the wall, but, after careful measurements and estimates of the lines of force and the energy currents circulating through the place, Gregorius determined the ideal position. It should be slightly offset from the geographic middle of the café. The new table was not on the exact spot, so that Gregorius always moved it a meter and a half, a manoeuvre that met the opposition of the waiters and, on occasion, the irritation of neighbouring customers.

Wilton, the patron of the arts, had long talks with Gregorius whenever he came to the café. It was rumoured that he had had his astral chart established, a chart which, according to Gregorius, took into account not only the position of planets and stars, but also the "historical coordinates" and the "normalized genetic frequencies". He had set up a detailed table of those frequencies at his "astral laboratory." According to the same gossip, Wilton made no important decision without checking with the astrologer, and it was in fact to meet him, and not to tour the art galleries, that he visited Berlin.

But while the *Der Bruch* gang spent much time at the café, they had little contact with the staff. Not due to class prejudice, but because they did not feel really welcome at the place, the reason being that, chronically broke, they left no tip. Harry had made a virtue out of that necessity: "Tipping makes the client a feudal lord and turns the waiter into a serf."

Vittorio was the only one who exchanged with the personnel. Since he was not, strictly speaking, part of the group, he felt free to flutter about the place as Dieter put it. He came every other night, arrived by nine and set out again soon after ten. For the Romanisches Café.

He came to the Schimmel because he liked the company of the young people of Der Bruch, but in order to enrich his social network, the Romanisches was irreplaceable.

The only names they knew were those of the two servers assigned to their table: Max, who went on duty at five, and Marko, who replaced him two days a week, "Max and Moritz", as Heinz called them, alluding to a children's tale. But they had never paid attention to another waiter, a young man with short hair combed with a ray in the middle and who, born Konrad, answered to the name of Conny.

Vittorio knew where Marko lived and how many children Max had (three from two different wives). But when he, intrigued by Konrad's meticulous appearance, by his shyness, questioned him about his private life, he only got monosyllables for an answer. But in the end, the cordiality of Vittorio overcame the young man's reserve.

He had worked as salesman in a clothing store, but the establishment had recruited a new sales manager who applied methods developed in the United States, which consisted of measuring each employee's performance and "efficiency-rate" hour-by-hour.

The result of his evaluations was conclusive: Conny was not up to modern sale standards. So, he was forced to live on meagre unemployment benefirs for several months, until he started at the Schimmel, where he earned significantly less than at his previous job.

"What do you do when you are not here? Do you go to the Wannsee to swim?" asked Vittorio. "To dance at the Pavilion?"

The young man shook his head with an embarrassed smile.

"Do you take the train to go fishing at the Müggelsee then?" "To play football? Ah, I know: you go to Hoppegarten, it is at the horse-races you spend your pourboires."

In the end Carraro's stubbornness paid off: what Conny did with the few marks he had left after paying the rent and buying his potatoes and his sausages was not to get drunk. It was not to the brothel he went, but to the art supply shop at the Hardenbergstrasse, where he purchased paper, pencils, coal. Conny liked to draw.

"Ah, *anche tu sei pittore*!" exclaimed Vittorio, delighted. An artist in the black and white uniform of Café Schimmel! "Tomorrow you'll show me your work. And I admit no excuses!"

Next evening Conny handed him eight drawings wrapped in a copy of the *Lokal-Anzeiger*. Conny had not been to any academy and it showed. But it was not the failing technique that attracted Vittorio's attention; it was the subjects.

He was no outdoor painter. The characters were always lonely, sometimes seen from the front, at others in profile, often with their eyes closed. And they were lying down. Asleep? Sick? Dead?

Der Bruch's reactions were disparate.

"There is something gloomy there" said Dieter.

"Very violent, a silent, sinister brand of violence" Heinz added.

Poor technique, disturbing atmosphere, were other reactions. A strictly personal art that owed nothing to the outside world. Pure obsessive introspection. The painting of a madman, diagnosed Paul, or of a zombie.

"Caligari's zombie," said Heinz. "The one who draws this stuff does not sleep in a bed but in a coffin."

And there was in fact a kinship between the drawings and expressionist film sceneries. Expressionism in painting was out of fashion, and Konrad was hardly aware of its existence. But he loved cinema and had seen *Nosferatu, The Golem,* and – indeed – *Caligari,* not one but several times.

"So," Vittorio summed up, "what are we going to do with this material?"

"We? Is that our business?" Paul rebuked him.

"Der Bruch," Vittorio reminded him, "'a magazine whose mission is to promote a young and revolutionary art'. I'm sure I have read that on the title page".

"But, is it art we are talking about?"

"Strange question," answered Carraro. "If you do not feel the power in these drawings, what are all your years at the academy worth?"

Harry and Dieter approached an avant-garde gallerist. The exhibition didn't have much repercussion, but it did receive a couple of positive reviews and Conny managed to sell six drawings that reaped him as much as a week's wages as a waiter.

A new printer for the magazine, a job for Geza, and now this new young artist: Konrad Berg.

Vittorio, the one by whom dreams materialize and the long-term jobless find secure and lasting employment. Vittorio, the guardian angel of the table eighteen.

But an angel can fall. An angel can become a demon.

Yes, it was at Bang's place that I saw it, concludes Curt Hagener, 1927 or 1928.

How could he have forgotten it? When leaving the toilet of the Blaue Maus, it was impossible to miss. The scene, comical, absurd, was forever associated with Ronny in his memory; it was there, in front of that picture which now puzzles Dunkels, that he had met the boy for the first time.

It was not the best that Grosz had done. Shocking for the prim and proper, yes, but otherwise ridiculous and quite incoherent as satires go. But then, it was Bang's choice. That kind of thing probably tickled his Lutheran conscience. It was his way of revolting.

He, Hagener, had other ways, and Ronny was one of them. A boy beautiful as an ephebe. Beautiful like the young giant outfought by Athena, had he told the boy in a fit of rapture while they admired together the Pergamon marbles. Or rather, it was Hagener who did the admiring; Ronny's interest in ancient art was far from all-consuming.

Let us recapitulate, said Hagener to himself: the picture I've seen hanging at the cabaret, is now exhibited at the EnKu. Intendant Oberfrunck, aware of the thing, sends someone to nose around. To make sure the painting is properly stored? Is it his property? Was it Keller who sold it to him? That would be great news for Dunkels.

Oberfrunck, who is at his best making speeches against immorality, against all the "filth" of modern life, has inclinations that few people imagine. But Hagener knows. Hagener knows everything about the city's night-life, its taverns, lounges and hangouts.

He knows that Oberfrunck, in the good old days, was a regular at the Grüne Trompete and also at Paradiso, Frau Schramme's "shop", close to the Blaue Maus. But how could Dunkels be aware of that, he, a provincial from a traditional Catholic family.

Wer ohne Sünde ist, hums Curt Hagener. "He that hath not sinned ..."

A verse by Rudi Nadolski. From a number of a Scala revue, five years ago. No, it was in 1926 in fact, the same year as *Laterna Magica*, the masterpiece of Hollaender, at the Renaissance-Theater.

Dunkels. There is one who will cast the first stone with enthusiasm and without second thoughts.

16

Violetta had seemed to take Harry's infidelity with the tolerance and open-mindedness that characterized the era, those twenties that some call golden. So, how explain the embarrassing encounter she had plotted between Harry, his lover Lotte, and Vittorio Carraro, with whom she, Violetta, was conducting herself an affair? How understand her delight at Harry's confusion?

Harry and Vittorio had met a few times during vernissages, but their intimacy did not go further than that. One evening of 1927, when Harry came home, he found Vittorio in the living room with a cup of tea in his hand. And five minutes later, the doorbell rang: it was Lotte. Violetta had invited her without telling Harry. He looked at her in amazement.

"I called the Schimmel to warn you but you were not there," she whispered as Violetta went to the kitchen for some beer.

"What do you make of this story about the People's Party?" Violetta commented casually, with four bottles of Kindl under his arm. "If even they accept the Republic as an irreversible fact, it's a good sign, huh?"

"You see," answered Lotte, grateful for the change of subject, "they were forced to say that if they wanted to enter the ministry."

"But the industrialists, and it's they who have the real power," slipped Carraro, "do not compromise."

"Yes but not all bosses are anti-republicans", objected the journalist, "and anyway, now that the economy is recovering, they are quite happy."

"The recovering of the economy, if there is one," said Harry, "is good news for Krupp and Thyssen, not for the workers."

"Yes, but I was talking about those industrialists who ..." clarifies Lotte.

"Well, as for me, I'm talking about the workers," Harry proclaimed.

"But I'm Left too," Lotte argued.

"Oh, but just yesterday you were still a Social Democrat," scolded Harry, making her pay for her naïveté, for having bitten Violetta's hook.

"I still am. As for you, you're just a sectarian of the Comintern," she replied.

"My children," interrupted Violetta, amused. "You quarrel like a married couple, 'Founding love, wise love that discovers and invents,'" recited Violetta. It was a poem by Heinz Brehme, refused by his fellow members of Der Bruch because of its sentimentality and individualism.

"Do not talk about love lightly," said a sententious Carraro. "Because behind love there is sex, and the importance of the sexual question is well established by now."

"Love?" said Harry, "A glass of water, forgotten as soon as drunk."

Lotte: "I've heard that too many times, that's pure cynicism. And it's the fault of all those romantic songs that make people lose sight of the eminently progressive nature of love."

"*Bei mir bist du schön*, 'We only love once', 'With you everything is so sweet'," Harry hummed. "The new opium of the people. What society really needs, and that was the core of our criticism to Heinz, is not confused puerperal feelings, but vigorous and regular sexual relations. Moreover, in a socialist society there will be no soppy songs like those, because they will no longer be needed. And if someone takes it into his head to compose them, it will be suggested to him, fraternally but firmly, to devote his time and forces to something more useful to society. "

Carraro: "Provided that the role of sex is recognized in that society you are talking about, which does not seem to be the case in the USSR."

Harry: "Reactionary slander. If there is a country in which psychoanalysis is going to develop, no, to reach new heights, it is doubtless the Workers' State. The logic of history leads it inexorably that way."

Carraro was not his friend yet: still, the situation was embarrassing for Shadow. He could accept that Violetta had affairs, the opposite would have been considered a primitive, an antediluvian reaction. But he expected discretion. Besides, if he could have chosen a lover for her, it would never have been Carraro; the Italian had at that time the three things that Harry most cruelly lacked: success, success and success.

"I did not know you were so Machiavellian," says Morel.

Violetta smiled satisfied. Her fury when they left the Russian restaurant, ten minutes ago, seems now forgotten. They walk side by side along the Lietzenburgerstrasse.

"But your Harry, does he still paint?" asks Morel.

Harry? Paint? If she's going to answer, Violetta would have to begin with Droysen's story. And what's the use? What's the interest of enumerating the discussions with gallery owners, the complications of last minute, overcome thanks to the generous Mr. Wilton? What difference does it make to Morel?

"Harry Shadow exposes at Droysen," announced the poster on the advertising columns. The vernissage was well attended: the bunch from Der Bruch, Lotte and Vittorio, who after their unexpected encounter at Violetta's had formed a couple of sorts, but also personalities from the show-business as well as radio celebrities. Sylvia von Harden, a brief Anita Berber and even Gropius in person, although after ten minutes he took polite leave, to Harry's frustration; he missed him, busy as he was flirting with Lotte Lenya.

Next morning, he hurried down to the Romanisches. The café offered its customers the latest issues of twenty different newspapers, but there was nothing about his exhibition.

Finally, one day Harry was honoured with a criticism, and this in a major newspaper. It was ruthless, vicious. Only one reaction had the exhibition provoked, and it was devastating. He never forgot the name of that critic.

"That's today's art world for you," summed Harry up his feelings at table eighteen.

"And you are surprised?" said Heinz Brehme. "Half of the critics are bought, the other half are so worthless that nobody even bothers to bribe them."

Harry made a sombre assent.

"In the current situation," he said, "there is no longer any point in art."

Back in the apartment, Harry solemnly communicated his decision to Violetta.

"Don't be discouraged," she consoled him. "Do you think Kirchner was immediately accepted?"

"The situation is different: the press has undergone a process of concentration and monopolization, as already Marx had vaticinated. There is no space for dissent, everything is standardized. It's a thick brick wall I keep running into. "

Harry looked down and could not suppress a sob.

"My love, don't take it like that," said Violetta.

"I don't make the grade. I'm tired of fooling myself."

Looking her straight in the eye, he said:

"I will at least have the courage of lucidity. You must admit that I have always looked at reality in the face."

Those violent bouts of self-denigration served to preserve him from a deeper depression. In spite of everything, Violetta loved him. Despite his obstinacy to devote all his efforts to just the thing for which he was the least gifted. Because Morel was right, he had perceived it all too well: Harry lacked confidence, that's why he clung to known models, that's why he imitated more than he created.

But, Violetta suggested, why not enlarge his register? He had a verbal talent. What the paintbrushes refused him, the pen seemed to grant. *Die Welt am Abend*, the communist newspaper, had published his cartoons. Why don't you try to write for them? she suggested.

They would never publish it, he objected. "I don't follow any political lines. I am a revolutionary, but my thinking does not wear uniform."

No, decides Violetta, no reason to go into these old stories with Gaston.

They set out to cross the Uhlandstrasse, but have to stop for a column of cars: four black Horch which lower almost imperceptibly their speed at the intersection, and then take the Lietzenburgerstrasse. SS cars.

"I wasn't aware of your Machiavellian side," he repeats.

When provoked, she is dangerous. But Morel is sure that, after having played him that bad trick, after having embarrassed him with Lotte and humiliated him with Vittorio, she gratified Shadow with a night of torrid love.

After having snubbed me, ponders Morel, she's become gentler. And from reconciliation to affection it's just one step.

"I'm surprised," she teases him, "that you lose your time with me while Nina Bovrik must be anxious to lavish her caresses upon you."

"My story with Nina," he protests, "was like yours with Carraro: a one-night stand. Do not compare yourself with her."

"Excuse me so much," she laughs, "I had not grasped all the depth of your feelings for me."

"You should," he replies, suddenly serious.

She looks at him surprised. He, who has let the words spring from his lips without giving his brain a chance to examine them beforehand, is surprised too.

They walk in silence. They arrive at the Olivaer Platz. He chooses a street that leads to the hotel.

"No," she says. "It's not this one. We have to cross the Kurfürsten."

"I know, but my hotel has a nice bar, not very frequented. You won't refuse me a last drink?"

"But you stay a few more days, don't you?"

There is something in her tone. Could it be concern?

"Anyway, it is late for me," she decides. "But if, instead of a drink, you offer me a taxi, I'll accept graciously."

An Opel approaches with the small "*Frei*" flag on the taximeter. But a few meters before them, an old gentleman stops it. No other taxis in sight. They'll have to wait.

"Just one more thing," says Morel, "am I prepared to hear about this universal genius, about Herr Shadow: tell me why you stayed with him for so long."

She laughs mischievously.

"That's strategic information."

"Well," he says, "this is how I see it: things were going well for you, but not for him. You pitied him."

"No!" she reacts vehemently. "It was not pity. Call it my maternal instinct if you have to."

"He was something you had to protect?"

She nods and stares off into space.

"How should I say? There were all these tiny details ... His face when he sipped his first coffee in the morning, somewhere between pleasure and relief ... "

There is still desire in her voice when she speaks of him. But a somewhat faded desire, little washed-out, concludes Morel.

"I enjoyed his laugh, but when he was sad I wanted to be at his side too."

"Would you call that love?" he asks, with a hint of sarcasm.

She weighs it up for a moment. Then she replies: "What else should I call it ?"

Violetta gives him a quick kiss, not on the cheek but in the mouth, and in a jiffy, she's already climbed into the back seat of the taxi. He makes a last farewell gesture, but she looks stubbornly forward. The car accelerates westwards along the Kurfürstendamm.

The street is as lively as it used to be, the neon advertisements still bright and colourful. It seems strange, incongruous, to see all the swastikas on this avenue that was once the symbol of free, joyfully decadent Berlin.

It is only eleven, he doesn't feel like sleeping. Call Nina? And why not?

17

"Harry, try to understand," said Gertie. "I have nothing against you, you do publish an interesting, a really innovative magazine, Der Bruch, isn't it? But we're talking here about the *Morgenpost*, three hundred thousand copies sold all over Germany."

Gertie was a cultural reporter at *Neue Morgenpost*, Lotte's newspaper. Lotte, with whom Harry had moved after breaking with Violetta, and after Lotte had broken with Vittorio, lived in Hansaviertel. It was a well-to-do middle class neighbourhood, near the Spree, very different from Moabit, its northern, more working-class neighbour.

The building where Lotte had her flat was the only one in the block designed by a functionalist architect, with large windows that let in all the sunlight. Otherwise, what prevailed in the area was the "reminiscent architecture" of the end of the century: imposing neo-Gothic, neo-baroque, neoclassical residences with airs of Renaissance castle or Nordic cathedral. Wide avenues framed by linden trees and maples planted at the end of the previous century and which had already reached the age of being leafy.

Lotte was Violetta's opposite. If Violetta was an artist, Lotte was interested in social issues. Where Violetta was impulsive, Lotte was cerebral. Lotte's clothes were practical, of good quality, but above all functional. Her hair was short, not to follow the fashion but to save time. Violetta dressed in a feminine way without being traditional; Lotte wore always pants.

Violetta was Hungarian, there was something about her that came from the East: the deep, intense gaze of her black eyes, her unpredictable reactions. Lotte was firmly German, with both feet sturdily anchored on the ground, and a rock solid practical sense.

Living with her was a balm for Harry: she did not question him constantly, on the contrary, she admired him because he was all she was not. Everything he said she found wonderful and she had hung his paintings on the walls.

With Violetta we kept colliding with each other, thought Harry. With Lotte, it was the division of labour. Rational. Effective. And, all things considered, happy.

The time that Harry no longer devoted to painting, he could now use for the magazine. But it became clearer and clearer that, whether they threw a fierce attack on New Objectivity or rushed to the defence of post-expressionism, the cultural world followed its imperturbable course, as if they had not written a word, as if the review never had left the printing press and been distributed to kiosks and book stores. What they wrote was of interest only to their friends, as well as to the editors of other literary magazines, who read Der Bruch exclusively to look for blunders, to pinch ideas or just to feel less alone in that editorial cosmic immensity where they were all but asteroids.

At the weekly meetings, he contributed little to the discussions, sometimes he didn't come at all. Even the café-owner asked for his news. "The Schimmel is not the Schimmel without Herr Shadow," he said, he who had always regarded the whole band of Der Bruch as

162

parasites, because they occupied a table for hours, with just a coffee at fifty pfennigs or at most a vermouth.

One evening - Lotte and he had an appointment at Café Josty - he surprised her in the middle of a discussion with a colleague: a young woman dressed in purple, short hair but with a protruding lock on her forehead, deep carmine lips and a monocle on her left eye.

"Gertie, from the culture section," introduced her Lotte.

After which Gertie went on talking without even a glance at Harry.

"It's my worst month in memory," she complained. "This week we have not only Lovis Corinth at the *Sezession*, but, in addition ,Soviet posters at *Der Ring*. Alright, Huber takes care of that, but in exchange he gave me, can you believe it, Matisse at Flechtheim!

"At least you won't have to go to Dessau," Lotte said. "For Kandinsky, I mean."

"I would have nothing against it, I have a girlfriend in Dessau. But you know, he sends me to cover Wright instead."

"Who?"

"Lloyd Wright, the architect, it opens on Saturday at the Wintergarten. Lotte, you know English, don't you? Be an angel, do it for me ! "

"Architecture? Me?" said Lotte, staring at her in disbelief.

"It's not difficult: you read the catalogue, the photographer takes three snapshots and, that's all."

"Amazing to see how seriously our most prestigious organs cover the artistic scene," said Harry, not used to be ignored.

"I would not ask just anyone," replied Gertie. "I ask Lotte because I know she would do it properly. Oh, and wait! I did not mention the presentation of the Van der Rohe Pavilion for the Spanish exposition! Lotte, darling, is that human? Is it? "

"Why don't you ask for reinforcements? Huber will understand the situation."

"Lotte, my darling, please take the architect! If you refuse, you leave me only one alternative," Gertie said, illustrating her warning with a feigned self-strangulation.

"I wish I could, but ..."

Gertie looked at her in despair. Then she repositioned her monocle, which threatened to fall into her glass of dry Martini and, with a pleading smile, asked:

"But then, couldn't you at least stop by Richter's? It's a stone's throw from your place, you could do it on your way home, it'll only take you ten minutes, I swear! "

"Romanian Dadaists, you mean," said Harry.

Lotte looked at him, relieved: "But of course, why didn't I think of it? Gertie, your plight is over, help is on the way. In fact, you have it in front of you, wearing a checked waistcoat. "

"But ..." Gertie hesitated, looking at Harry. "Are you a journalist?"

"He runs an art magazine, and he's a painter," said Lotte fervently.

Gertie tried to disguise a smile.

"That's great," she conceded. "But we are talking about a chronicle of five hundred words on page twenty-two of the *Morgenpost*. To have a lively interest in art is fine, I mean, it's absolutely great, but... "

"Gertie, I assure you that Harry is better qualified than me, whether he has a press card or not."

Gertie considered it for a moment while chewing the olive from her cocktail. Spitting the kernel on the saucer, she told Lotte:

"It don't care who writes the chronicle, provided it is properly done. But it is you who sign, Lotte."

"I don't sign anything that I haven't written," Harry replied, "but what I write, I sign."

"He could do it as a freelancer," Lotte said. "That's usual."

"But only if Huber, as section editor, decides it."

"So talk to him."

Gertie sighed, looking sceptically at Harry. Finally she spoke, decided to settle the argument once and for all:

"Harry, please try to understand, I don't have anything against you, on the contrary, but we're talking about the *Morgenpost*, the flagship newspaper of the Ullstein press group. Three hundred thousand copies, every day. You have this experience of having published this cultural magazine which is highly commendable in every possible way, of course, but... "

"Have you ever read Der Bruch?" he asked, in an effort to control himself.

"Once, yes. I mean, I think so."

"And if I mention *Der Sturm*, do you have any recollection of having read it too?"

"I have read all the issues of *Der Sturm* right from number one," she replied, haughtily. "Further questions?"

"In that case you have surely read some of my pieces, and at the head of those articles you could have seen my name. Mine, not my girlfriend's, my sister's, or my aunt's."

Lotte confirmed: "Herwarth Walden is Harry's friend. He was at our place a few days ago, actually."

Gertie looked around as if searching for an excuse to run away. Then she concluded, in a cold and objective tone.

"Alright, prepare the article, I'll take care of Huber."

"Very well then," he said. "And while you're there, suggest him a piece on Oskar Schlemmer's exhibition at Nierendorf's. You cannot miss that. Lovis Corinth is nineteenth century. We are in 1928 in case you haven't noticed. Are you art critics or archaeologists? "

Harry did not wait for Huber's confirmation to write the review, after all he did not have much else to do. Lotte read the text and she had nothing to say about it. She had, however, an objection:

"It's much too long. It's not a literary magazine you are writing for, it's a daily newspaper," she said, extirpating three paragraphs.

"I'm not a reporter, even less a telegraphist."

"Of course, but if we just eliminate a few sentences, the article will pass, and they will pay you eleven marks."

That was an argument hard to disregard: Harry hadn't been able to pay his share of the rent last month.

In the evening, when Lotte came back from work, he was waiting impatiently.

"So," he asked, "did the article find favour in the sight of the arch-priest of Kochstrasse?"

"The boss does not have time to read everything. Gertie has approved it, that was enough," she replied.

"And my signature?"

"It will be there. And you did well to stand firm about that: having written for the *Post* is good for your résumé."

"Résumés? I couldn't care less for that," he said.

"But you should, because they hire substitutes for the summer, and if you have already published you will have a fair chance."

"And who told you I'm looking for summer jobs?"

June came, and by recommendation of Lotte and a reluctant

Gertie, Harry got a one month job at the newspaper's offices at the Kochstrasse. He humbly accepted Lotte's every advice, and covered without protest all the events Huber sent him to.

When the month was over, Harry asked Huber, in a meek tone he didn't know he was capable of:

"Do you believe I could be of any value to the *Post*? On a permanent basis I mean."

Huber laughed.

"If you knew how many applications I receive every week. Look here: a doctor in philology from Leipzig. Another one, with a degree in history from Karlsruhe. And look at this one: she's at the Bauhaus in Dessau. Working with mural painting, of all things."

Harry pressed his lips together.

"But," continued the chief, "you do have something that I appreciate more than medals and diplomas: an ability to take initiatives, and also that touch of impertinence which is always a good spice in an editorial staff. We have no vacancies just now, but as soon as there is one, well, nothing is impossible."

"So, you're a reporter now?" Dieter asked when Harry came to the table eighteen for the first time in a month.

"Am I a reporter?" Harry repeated in a nonchalant tone. "What do you mean? I'm still the same."

"No, not the same. You're Hans Schattendorf now."

Harry had signed his pieces in the *Post* with his real name, which he had never used in his previous career. Like John Heartfield and other artists, he had chosen to anglicize his name ; "Schatten" means "shadow".

"Shadow and Schattendorf may be two. As for me, I'm still one," he replied.

But he had to admit that having written for an important journal had given him a sense of achievement well beyond the two hundred marks he had earned: knowing that he was going to be read by one out of every three Berliners, that his words would have an effect.

Three months went by. And in November, Huber's letter arrived.

Culture reporter at the *Neue Morgenpost*. It was like for a footballer to sign for the Rapid of Vienna. Like for an actor to be discovered by Max Reinhardt.

Grolmanstrasse. The Kronen Gallery.

If it had been Baumgarten, if it had been Obermayer, Curt Hagener would put the question directly: who is the owner of *Still Life*? But, Erwin Keller? He hardly knows the guy.

"Business are going well?" he begins.

"I cannot complain."

"I see you rearranged your shop windows a bit."

"I change them regularly. Anything special you're thinking of?" asks Keller.

"Contemporary art, does it sell these days?"

"I have a Hommel somewhere, a medium format, or small rather. And I could have shown you a superb Ziegler if you had come yesterday. An early work, mind you. Still... "

"But what I mean is Kirchner, Kandinsky. Or Grosz."

"Not much right now. What are you looking for more precisely?"

"Grosz. Are you sure you don't have anything by him? In some corner?"

The gallerist shakes his head.

"Because I have once seen a work by him here, *Still Life with Three Characters*."

Keller bends over to pick up a piece of paper blown away by the draft when Hagener opened the front door.

Hagener: "I happen to know that Oberfrunck, from Heritage, was interested in that painting. Perhaps he still is."

He scrutinizes the merchant's face. He detects a blink of the eyelids.

"Richard Oberfrunck?" asks Keller.

He's pretending, Hagener says to himself.

"No, not Richard. I am referring to the Chief Intendant at the Prussian Heritage Department."

Keller shakes his head. But he avoids the eyes of the other.

"I thought he might have contacted you. After all, your gallery has a solid reputation in contemporary art."

Flattery works wonders, thinks Hagener.

But flattery is not always enough. It is clear that if the Intendant bought the painting from him, Keller is not going to tell it to anyone, especially not to a journalist.

He takes a taxi to Lichtenberg. If anyone can give him information about Bang, it's Frau Schramme.

"Ah, Herr Hagener, always so courteous. And always so naughty," she greets him. She is stouter than last time he saw her.

She is glad to see him again. Since the new regime's regulations forced her to move to the suburbs, she no longer meets the same gentlemen from the times when she was in the Jägerstrasse.

"I'm not complaining, but it is not the same kind of people, if you see what I mean. They were public servants, artists. I had an University professor, a researcher in Ancient History, who came

169

punctually every Tuesday, I will not mention his name, but of course, you know him well, nothing escapes you, Mr. Hagener."

And Bang, what about him?

"I think of him often," she sighs. "A good man, serious, honest." He had to leave, she understood that. He decided it already in 1932. But what could she do in Copenhagen? And then, she had the girls under her responsibility. Where would they go without her? "There are terrible places in Berlin, you know, Herr Hagener."

No, she does not have the Dane's address. Geza Nemes could have it. The painting, yes, she remembers it.

"When Bang offered to lend it to me, I accepted."

Have I got this right? asks himself Hagener. The picture had gone from the cabaret to her brothel? She confirms. *Still life* was hung at Paradiso's entrance.

"And it caught the eye, I can tell you that," she adds with a mischievous smile.

So, Hagener concludes, it must have been at Paradiso that Oberfrunck spotted it. He was hardly a regular of the Blaue Maus.

"That man, do not talk to me about him," the woman replies. "Nobody would call that person a gentleman, even if he nowadays is a director or supervisor, I don't know what. You know, I had to ban him. Mine was a honest establishment. Girls are not supposed to submit to certain things. I prefer not to go into the details. "

Oberfrunck. The scandalous painting. Paradiso.

There is no evidence, not for the time being. Still, Dunkels will be delighted to hear all that.

18

The Chevalier of Koenigsberg was being shot in Babelsberg studios.

"Herr Wassingher!" calls Braillowski. "Last minute changes in the garden scene."

Sasha had been working with Braillowski for six months now, beginning in December 1929. The working days, theoretically of eight hours, extended often to twelve. The others grumbled, and verified carefully that the overtime was duly recorded. But Sasha saw scarcely the time pass; for him this work was something more than a livelihood, more than just a job.

Civil or industrial engineering were areas in which he had much to learn and little to invent ; cinema, on the other hand, was a developing technique. New demands every day, which challenged his ingenuity. No, it was not geometric designs of roads or grain storage systems he wanted to work with. It was film engineering, a field no one had yet heard of.

Working closely with the sound engineer, Sasha handled the microphone, placing it at the right distance to record the actors' voices, suppressing at the same time unwanted noises, such as the camera's. It was he who came up with the idea of wrapping the microphone in a silk stocking - cotton was less effective - to further limit the interfering sounds, a method quickly adopted all over Babelsberg.

It was also his responsibility to dampen other unwelcome noises, sprinkling the floor with water to prevent it from cracking or covering it with a thick carpet. In short, tinkering and more tinkering, dealing with unexpected hurdles that had to be overcome at all costs, with all kind of unpleasant surprises he did everything to prevent, by carefully reading the film scenario beforehand.

It was also vital for him to move in such a way that neither the pole nor its shadow fell into the frame of the image, which was why he needed to grasp the principles of lighting, to distinguish the main sources of light from the secondary ones, all things that made it easier to work together with the chief photographer.

"For the garden scene, no problem, Herr Braillowski," he replied, "I have already marked the path step by step."

"Yes, but there is something new: Lehmann wants to do it in the opposite direction. Your notes will be of no use. How are you going to pass with the pole under that branch? It is too low. "

Lehmann, the director, was known for his obstinacy. If he found it aesthetically motivated that the two main performers walked the path not by approaching the camera but by moving away from it, the change would be put into effect regardless of the cost. The fact that it forced the boom-operator to rethink all his movement schema meant nothing to him.

"He's against sound, you know," said Braillowski.

For the director, sound was an uninvited guest into the seventh art, annoying chatter, which denatured cinematography by depriving it of its unique character. By turning poetry into ordinary prose. Worse: into verbosity.

"For him you are a parasite," concluded the director of photography.

And it was precisely because of the poor esteem in which many held the sound technicians, that he had been able to build a career in Babelsberg. "It's a passing fad," they said, "it will never be a real profession." The sound people were the lowest in rank. A field, hence, where even a stranger, a foreigner could make his way.

Despite his aesthetic pretensions, the value of Lehmann's works was doubtful: light comedies with Vienna or Budapest as background, but without the wit of Lubitsch. "The Roman circus of the twentieth-century," called Sasha's Lena those productions, located in Imperial St. Petersburg or in Golden Prague, if not in an idyllic Polynesia which no spectator had the slightest chance of visiting unless he was a Ruhr tycoon or a currency speculator.

He understood better for every day Braillowski's words during their first interview: "You don't make a film as you paint a picture." The more he realized the importance of technicians in the industry, the less he thought of directors' pretensions.

Was Eisenstein the author of *Potemkin*? The general coordinator, at most. The real work was done by the cameraman, by the lighting designer, by the prop men. Not to mention those who cleaned the studios' toilets.

Cinema was not an art but an industry. Masterpieces were achieved not by the director but often in spite of him. "Some day, the director will be replaced by someone who understands all aspects of film industry, someone with a truly comprehensive view", believed Sasha. By an engineer. A film engineer.

"Sorry, Wassingher," finished Braillowski. "You know what I think of Lehmann's whims. And to make things worse: you have one hour, not a minute more, to make the changes."

No problem, decided Sasha ; he would skip lunch, go and buy a sandwich at the canteen, which he would eat while putting together the new scheme.

The queue was long, Sasha was not the only one to replace lunch by a snack.

"*Scheisse*, how long is this going to take?" complained a voice behind him. He turned around. It was a brunette with her hair combed like a helmet around her head. Thick eyebrows highlighted her black eyes.

"Oh, excuse me. It's just that I have to be back in the studio in five minutes," she explained.

"Take my place," he offered.

"Ah, thank you, awfully kind of you ! I am Vicki."

The girl's studio was next to number four, where *Koenigsberg* was being shot. They walked briskly together, exchanging information between two mouthfuls. Vicki was an extra.

"But," she hurried to explain, "not in mass scenes. In fact, it's more like small roles I play." Vicki would appear as a waitress, a bank clerk or a housekeeper. Her face was clearly distinguishable, unlike the other extras, the anonymous ones, but her name was not listed in the cast.

Her dream was to secure a role in Lehmann's next production. A real role this time. "It would not be the first," she said just before dealing the final bite to her herring sandwich. "I have already had one. In *Divorce in Budapest,* you surely have seen it, it was premiered last autumn, at the UFA-Palast."

They reached studio four and took leave of each other with a handshake.

At eight o'clock, Lehmann being finally happy with the garden sequence, Sasha's workday was over. Leaving the studios, he heard someone call him. "Are you going to Berlin?" Vicki asked. "I take that train too." They had to wait twenty minutes at the station, a time she put to good use by cross-examining him about Lehmann's film but above all about the director's future plans.

"Has he already completed the cast of *The Czarevitch's Love Affair*?" she wanted to know.

"But, it's Herdinger who will make that film," he objected.

With a mischievous smile, Vicki explained:

"Herr Kettner has changed his mind." Kettner was a producer.

"You are better informed than me," Sasha had to admit.

"Well, if you ever had the opportunity, couldn't you ask if he still has a role to assign? I'm thinking of Ekaterina. It's a small role, cut out for me. She's a woman a little older than me but not much, and physically I'd be perfect, being a brunette. "

Vicki had managed to get hold of a summary of the script, something which was normally confidential.

"You see, Vicki, it's Braillowski I work with. Lehmann never lowers himself to speak to me."

"Ah, if I only could get an interview with Herr Braillowski ... That would be an important step for me already."

"But the casting is not his business, you know."

"But maybe Lehmann will ask for his opinion ..."

Next day, during a break, Sasha reported his chat with Vicki to the chief photographer. Braillowski smiled.

"A girlfriend?"

"No. I already have one."

"One is not the limit, for some. In any case it's surprising that she had access to the script."

Later Sasha found out that Fredi Körner, Vicki's boyfriend, knew the fiancée of the film's screenwriter. That's how Vicki got the information. And that's how she obtained her second role in German cinema, a very secondary role but still "a further step and a key move in my career," as she put it.

To thank him, she invited Sasha and Lena to Fredi's birthday party.

Fredi was a jovial boy, a musician. His real name was Bedrich Kovner. "But here no one can pronounce it, so I transmogrified it into Fredi Körner." He had arrived from Prague two years before.

Thirty people were crowded into Fredi's bedsit, drinking beer and munching biscuits flavoured with onion and cumin. Many were foreigners, mostly Czechs and Poles. One was a painter, another a reporter, the third a tango dancer and there was even a boxer, a Lithuanian Jew with very fine features which contrasted with his flattened nose. He had just become champion of the Neukölln district.

"By crushing the Gorilla from Treptow," Fredi explained. "A Nazi."

"He's not a Nazi," the reporter said.

"So why did he call Bubi a dirty Jew at the weigh-in?"

"Alright, he's an anti-Semite, but not a Nazi."

"He may not have the party card, but for me he is a full-fledged Nazi," insisted Fredi.

"Full-fledged he may be, but his set of teeth wasn't full any more when he left the ring," said another, greeted by a roar of laughter.

There were also girls at Fredi's party, girls who, like Vicki, hoped for a career in film or radio. One of them, Lissy, danced at the Scala. Being a dancer at that revue theatre was like being a foot soldier of the Sixth Infantry Regiment of Brandenburg ; the Scala productions involved hundreds of chorus-girls.

"But I do solos too," she explained to Sasha. "Four evenings a week at the *Elysée*."

"A disreputable scene," teased her Fredi.

"Not at all," Lissy protested, "and they pay better than the Scala."

"I played the piano at the *Elysée*," said Fredi, "and towards the end of the number I had to give the cue to the dancer."

"What cue?" asked Sasha.

Fredi looked at Lissy and they both burst out laughing.

"Sasha, you are so naive. You haven't been in Berlin for long, have you?" Fredi laughed.

The cue he talked about, a gesture with the arm, was intended to give the dancing girl time to make a last pirouette and remove her bra, just two seconds before the tune came to an end and the lights on the scene went out.

"But I dance there just to pay my rent," Lissy explained. "Dance is my life, but by dance I mean Mary Wigman and Isadora."

"If the Duncan knew you were dancing at the *Elysée*, she'd beat you to death."

Lissy shrugged.

"One has to make a living."

Turning towards Sasha, Fredi said:

"You know, I am also in the cinema business, like Vicki and you. More exactly at the Alhambra cinema, from six to midnight."

Fredi was the pianist who accompanied the films in that small theatre of the Frankfurter Allee.

"Which means that you," he added, pressing an accusing finger on Sasha's chest, "you are my rival. Worse, my enemy, because you are paid to put me out of work."

Vicki was from Cologne. She had attended a drama school and one day, back in 1925, she decided to move to the capital, where she thought it was easier to "break through" or to "take off", as she put it.

To begin with, she had taken an artistic name, euphonic but at the same time international, something that couldn't be said of the one on her passport: Wibeke Leimkühler.

The first name, as well as the family name, had to have two syllables, neither more nor less, she maintained. Like Greta Garbo, Vilma Banky, Dita Parlo, Pola Negri. Then it was necessary to exclude letters that didn't exist in English, as well as accents, circumflexes and *umlauts*.

After long consideration she had chosen Vicki Lander. "It sounds German but could also be Danish or Swedish," she explained. "And it's easy to pronounce for an American. *King of Broadway*, with John Barrymore and Vicki Lander. It sounds good, *nicht wahr*?"

"She's a little naive," was Lena's opinion. "And quite superficial, even is she keeps quoting Ibsen and Strindberg."

"Well, as for me, I don't even know for what team those two play," said Sasha.

"I'm not sure she is more enlightened than you," she answered.

A few days later, Vicki invited them to a cabaret where her boyfriend Fredi was playing the piano. Lena wasn't keen on coming, but she let herself be convinced. It was in the Jägerstrasse, in Friedrichstadt. Fredi was already at the keyboard when they arrived.

A black haired woman was leaning on the counter. At one point she put down her glass, climbed on stage and, after a pair of chords that Fredi adorned with a few arpeggios, she attacked the opening stanza:

"Eine Villa im Grünen mit großer Terrasse,
vorn die Ostsee, hinten die Friedrichstrasse"

Violetta Brenner, the singer, strolled across the floor, smiled seductively at a customer as she hit a vibrato, looked sternly at the next one as she would look at a naughty boy, spirited away the cup of *sekt* from a third one, gulped down a sip taking advantage of a few songless notes, then put down the glass with a casual gesture and resumed her cruising through the audience of the Blaue Maus.

"Tucholsky," explained Lena to Sasha. "The lyrics of the song are by him."

"A communist writer," Vicki added.

"I'm not sure he's in the party," said Lena.

"Of course he is!" Vicki persisted.

It was unclear whether she was a member of the KPD herself, but she always presented herself as a communist.

Vicki's artistic ambitions seemed ludicrous to Lena.

"Do you have any idea of how many girls who are looking for the same thing as you?" she asked her one day.

"Plenty," replied Vicki.

"They arrive every day from Munich, Hamburg, Thuringia, Bohemia, even from East Prussia, and what do they come for? They

179

will all give you the same answer: to make it in the movies, to become a star, a new Mady Christians, a second Truus van Alten. They all say the same, without exception, like a chorus. "

"And some will succeed," Vicki replied. "The film industry is not only directors and screenwriters; actresses are needed too."

"Of course, but: who says that the new star's name will be Vicki Lander?"

"Sure I cannot be. But I trust my talent."

If at least she was a beauty, Lena thought, but the girl was nothing out of the ordinary. Her face was pleasant, but she was far from a Garbo. Her nose could have been smaller, her eyebrows less thick.

What she did not lack was tenacity. That's how she had managed to get a foothold, or rather a toehold, in Babelsberg. But two secondary roles were not really imposing as a résumé.

"Lena: it's this simple: I'll never be happy if I give up what you call my fantasies. Those fantasies are my life."

"But: is it so important to play maid roles like you always do?"

Vicki stared off into space.

"You know what the great Erika Glässner once told me? 'When I enter the stage I am no longer me: I slip under the skin of another human being, I incarnate another destiny.' "

"Desdemona's destiny? Juliet's? Or a lady-cook's?" asked Lena mercilessly.

"That's exactly the challenge," replied Vicky with passion. "Pudovkin said: 'Proletarian cinema's mission is to give a voice to the silent.' "

"No, that's the mission of my Sasha with his padded microphone," corrected Lena. But the other didn't flinch:

"If you saw *Battleship Potemkin*, you must have noticed ..."

"What I did notice is that there are no glamorous girls in that movie. Could you name a single star of Soviet cinema?"

This time Vicki remained silent.

"In any case," she finally said, "I will be an actress or I will be nothing at all. I neither want nor can compromise."

Ready to die for her calling, thought Lena, oscillating between irony and compassion.

But when she was done with mocking Vicki, melancholy overcame her. To what ideal was she, Lena, ready to devote her life? When she was younger she thought it would be art; she wanted to work in close contact with creators, with their works. That is why she persisted, against her parents' advice, to enrol in History of Art.

And all these dreams, where had they led her now, 1934? To a secretary position at the law firm Lutz & Spennert.

"We've got to move on to pastures anew, Sasha is right there," she thought.

She is at a dead end. And he, with his Jewish mother, will never find a job here ; it's close to a miracle that she managed to procure him that post at the expo.

"We must leave," she concluded. Make a fresh start elsewhere.

19

Hans Schattendorf, formerly Harry Shadow, had not met Vittorio Carraro for two years. Carraro had had a brief affair with Violetta Brenner. After that evening when Violetta, for Harry's greater confusion, succeeded in making them both converge in her apartment of the Passauerstrasse, they had met a great number of times at Café Schimmel, but since Harry entered the *Morgenpost*, his visits to the café became sparse.

Carraro had been a kind of ambassador of Italian futurism, a fashionable trend in Germany around 1920. But it happened what it always happens sooner than later with Berliners: they lost interest in futurism. They were too busy in their frantic pursuit of that rare pearl, that Holy Grail which goes under the name "*etwas Neues*". "Something New."

Things were not going well for him, which did not make Schattendorf unduly sorry ; he had not forgotten Carraro's benevolent but patronizing air when he turned up at the Schimmel with his cane made of lacquered beech wood and with a beautiful silk tie, always different. It was said that he owned three hundred of them.

Schattendorf – Harry – was at that time the natural leader of Der Bruch, its founder and its soul. Everyone in the review acknowledged his pre-eminence. Vittorio troubled that order. One day he got them to change their printing house, the next day he brought his own guests to table eighteen: a poet he had just discovered, or an actress who drew the attention of all, turning them away from the day's deliberations.

Even Dieter had changed since Carraro's arrival: he was acting more independently, distilling more and more irony into his remarks to Harry.

Everyone loved Vittorio. He was so good-natured, so cheerful. He had a kind word for everyone. However, Harry mistrusted people who smiled all the time. A smile always hides something, a honest person does not need to be nice, he thought.

No, Schattendorf had no desire to get back in touch with Carraro. But one morning, that must have been in 1930, as he was leaving the baker shop of the Lessingstrasse to go to work, he ran into a customer who was coming in. Vittorio.

"But, you live here too?" asked the Italian. "That's what I call a coincidence ! Wait for me, I'll buy some *pretzels*, then we'll go for a beer."

"I'm in a hurry," replied Schattendorf.

"But, where are you going with all those *brotchen*?"

When he learned that he was now working for the Ullstein group, the Italian congratulated him warmly.

"I'll drop by your office one of these days, then."

It was at the Kochstrasse that Schattendorf had his office, in the imposing building of the press group to which *Neue Morgenpost* belonged, a massive construction of red brick, between fortress and Gothic cathedral. In the Ullstein citadel worked thousands of people. According to a typically Berliner joke, a lion had escaped one day from the zoo, entered the premises and started devouring editors; it

184

was only when he had ingested a hundred and twenty of them that someone realized what was happening: so countless was the staff.

Their employers, politically liberals, were concerned about the employees' well-being: social benefits, leisure activities, a good restaurant. Schattendorf's office was twelve square meters, it was equipped with a leather sofa as well as a Continental typewriter of the latest model, with noise-damping mechanism. The office was separated from the corridor by a glass partition, which let pass the light but not any glances from outside.

He had already forgotten his meeting at the baker-shop when one day the reception called him: he had a visitor, an Italian gentleman. Since the building had been attacked by the brown shirts, the guard let nobody in unless someone from the staff came to meet him.

"Say that I'm not here."

"Can you repeat that, Mr. Schattendorf?" asked the guard, who was somewhat hard of hearing.

He had no choice but to invite Carraro to a beer at the canteen. Vittorio didn't paint any more, he said. Now he had a post at the Italian embassy and was also correspondent for a Trieste newspaper.

"Great *pilsener*!" he said, admiring at the same time the paintings hanging on the wall: a portrait of the director of the newspaper by Dix and a breath-taking Max Liebermann landscape.

For Schattendorf it was a pleasure to let the other see that he was not spending most of his time in café discussions any more. That he was now an editor of a major newspaper. It was a way for him to correct the past, to obliterate his failures, to put things in the place where they should always have been.

Vittorio did not even try to play down his admiration.

"I knew you were meant for something important," he said. "But

185

what about your painting? The last time I saw you was at a vernissage, I think. At Droysen's, wasn't it? A remarkable exhibition, whatever that idiotic critic might have written."

"Sauer."

"That's right: Ludwig Sauer was his name. Still, you were right in switching career. In art, if you do not have something new to say, it's better to clean the paintbrushes, dry them carefully, and move on to new challenges."

Annoyed, Schattendorf replied:

"I did have things to say."

"Of course, of course, and your Droysen show is there to prove it," said the other. "What I mean is that if we are at all able to live without painting, then living without painting is an imperative. Art is not an activity, it's not a ... a job. No, it is a way of life."

"I do not regret anything in my career," emphasized Schattendorf. "I just realized that my true mission is not to paint, but to reconnoitre, to map and evaluate the various paths that art must pursue. I am not a rower, I am a prospector. But I talk too much, Vittorio. After all, we don't know each other that closely."

"But we have shared women, that's what you were going to say, right?" interrupted the Italian with a knowing smile.

"In short," continued the other, "I realized that if I painted, it was because of Violetta, she had been a sort of mentor for me and, by following her, I strayed away from my true path."

"Scarcely a good model, a woman," Carraro agreed.

As for him, he was a married man now.

"Nina Bovrik, an artist. You know her, I think. We have a kid."

And upon hearing those glad tidings, Schattendorf took leave of his guest; he had to prepare for the weekly editorial meeting.

186

Schattendorf's working days at the *Post* extended well beyond eight-hours. It was the case of everybody there, but he had to strive even harder. On that point he was prepared to admit that Gertie had been right: at Der Bruch his freedom was complete, he could give free rein to his rhetoric, yield to every whim. Writing for the leading morning newspaper was a different matter.

Yes, every editor had his phone, two or three for some. Yes, the canteen offered excellent meals at low prices. Yes, there were editors whose offices were decorated with oriental carpets and even in his own room there was an original watercolour. But in return, the *Morgenpost* expected total availability.

Schattendorf, who had always found it difficult to start the day, who wasn't productive before afternoon, was transformed. At work, he did not see the hours pass, and sometimes didn't return home until midnight. Passing by all the cafés full of life, he was tempted to cross the threshold, just to have a drink, only one. But his professional conscience - he owned one now - reminded him that next day he had to be at Kochstrasse at eight o'clock to finish an article to be submitted to Huber before noon.

One day, having lunch with Lotte and Gertie, they talked about a colleague who had been transferred to the Travel section. "Just imagine" said Gertie, "Locarno in May, St. Moritz in January, instead of covering boring exhibitions, interviewing pretentious artists? Imagine: Wiesbaden, Cortina, maybe even Corfu, with all expenses paid?"

Nothing could be further from Schattendorf's ambitions than wasting time in fashionable resorts. For a long time he had been happy vegetating in the suburbs of the intellectual and cultural life. If he had bid farewell to bohemian life, it was to become someone, to make a name for himself.

Huber's letter and the interview, which ended with his being hired by the *Post,* came at the right moment. To give a meaning to his life. What meaning? He couldn't explain it. "Things are moving," was all he could say. No mean feat after all those months of stagnation after his fiasco at Droysen's.

He had put everything in that exhibition. All his imagination could conceive was embodied in those works, a creativity guided by his lucidity, by all the analytic power he was capable of. He could have defended each painting, justified each brush stroke.

To what avail? None. No reactions at all. Except, of course, for Ludwig Sauer:

"A bar, rather than an art exhibition, one would guess, judging by the sandwiches and the alcoholic beverages that circulated generously. The paintings did not appear to be the focus of attention, the audience – ladies, gentlemen and other sexes – being too busy exchanging kisses and helping themselves to one more caviare sandwich. And I do not blame them: to call Herr Shadow's works bad would be an understatement. No, a compliment. "

The final sentence was engraved in Harry's memory: "Leave all hope, ye who enter this exhibition: the caviare sandwiches are finished."

He had wagered and he had lost. He could not afford another setback. That is why, as he walked by the cafés and imagined the passionate discussions that were being carried there, while he devoured with his eyes the handsome women sitting at the tables, he clenched his teeth and resumed his walk. Forward! he spurred himself. Always forward !

Vittorio continued to call him and they met from time to time. Schattendorf wondered why, for the Italian irritated him, even more now than in the old times at the Schimmel.

During the discussions at the table eighteen, one would have thought that he was more or less left-wing, like all intellectuals in those circles, for whom the political rainbow began in furious red, and extended no further right than to social democracy. But now, tête-à-tête, his standpoints were different.

"Parliamentary democracy is inefficient," declared Vittorio. "And immoral: where do these politicians derive their legitimacy from? From the fact that they had three more votes than their competitors? Usually, they have not even a majority, just a minority somewhat less insignificant than the others. I'll tell you, Hans, what the true origin of power ought to be. Listen to me. "

The discussion took place one day of 1930 at the Italian Embassy, on the Tiergartenstrasse. For a mere counsellor of the cultural attaché, Carraro had an imposing office, found Schattendorf to his surprise. It had belonged to the Deputy Consul, but as that post had been abolished, Vittorio had managed to get hold of the premises, in fierce competition with a career diplomat, who was his sworn enemy since then.

Sitting on a comfortable armchair opposite the Italian, Schattendorf was impressed by the place's splendour. An oak and crystal bookcase, a five centimetres thick carpet, and on a side wall a marble statue of the goddess Demeter with a wreath of wheat ears in one hand and a bunch of flowers in the other.

"Just a façade," said Carraro modestly. "What I really need is neither marbles nor crystals, but a secretary. Let us hope that next year the budget will deign to bestow that luxury on me."

He got up to fetch an ashtray, then sat back down at his large mahogany desk.

"People need a leader, Hans," he continued, "and once it's found him, it's not about to break that relationship. The people has no need to test it periodically in those general inventories, in those cash counting and audits called 'elections.' No, the relationship between a people and its leader tolerates no mediation. The leader does not represent the people, he is the people . "

Schattendorf could not believe his ears.

"But how do we know that it is that fellow and no other, who incarnates the people?"

The Italian looked at him with an air of superiority:

"When 'that fellow', when the true leader emerges, you know it without having recourse to phylogenetic research or to the wise monks of Tibet. You know it with your heart, with your muscles, with your guts. Everybody knows it, those who follow him and those who fight him. "

On one point and only one, Schattendorf agreed with him: the Republic was a corrupt regime. It was enough to turn the eyes to today's politics: Chancellor Müller resigned, Brüning returns, tomorrow it's Brüning who will resign and von Papen come back, then Müller again and so on. Scandals, corruption without limits. Lotte gave him every day new details of the Sklarek brothers scandal, where even Berlin's mayor appeared to be involved.

"But what we need is not a mystical leader but a real proletarian democracy," he replied.

190

"Like in Russia? Hans: Communism is nothing but a Christian sect. Compassion for the exploited. An ideology for sheep."

"But, do you have an idea of what you're talking about?"

Harry could not fathom Vittorio's metamorphosis. He had never actually talked with a fascist. Those people did not exist for him, they were only abstractions.

"Fascism, my dear Hans, does not make up philosophies, fascism rolls up its sleeves and starts building, fascism constructs the future here and now. Fascism, allow me to tell it to you who are an art critic, sees politics from an aesthetic point of view. It craves beauty, but a beauty born out of the struggle. This is why I decided to quit art. Because it's time to act, because politics is the continuation of poetry by other means. It's time to change the world, not to portray it. Communism, on the other hand ... "

"But it is precisely Communism that ...!"

With a patronizing smile, the Italian interrupted him:

"Communism? A dead theory: sterile practice, a dogma conceived by old bearded farts in dusty libraries, a materialism that is already historical."

Had he simply sold himself? Was he merely a vulgar careerist, ready to champion the ideas of whoever gave him a luxurious office?

One day Carraro went beyond the limits in his utterances. Schattendorf sent him a short letter: "I do not feel our discussions have any sense and I think we should stop seeing each other."

20

Schultze does not speak to Clausen. Clausen does not speak to Schultze. But Sasha speaks with both Clausen and Schultze.

The exhibition is to open any moment. The paintings are hung, the lighting is perfect in every detail. This is the time chosen by His Excellency the Culture Commissioner to pay them a visit.

It's the first time Dunkels honours them with his presence. He makes a quick stroll through the exhibition-rooms, his gaze sweeping the walls without stopping on any single work, like a military spotlight which sheds light solely in order to detect enemies.

"Good work, Herr Professor," he says. Clausen nods his head in acknowledgement.

"Having said that," Dunkels goes on, "we must talk about the lighting."

My God, said Sasha to himself.

"If what we see on these walls," he explains, "were works by Dürer, by Rembrandt, I would have nothing to add. It is clear that the professor is experienced in his field. However: in our days, lighting must be conceived as a part of a whole, designed according to the laws of scientific propaganda."

Schultze, standing at a distance, nods in assent. The Commissioner completes his argumentation:

"If a picture depicts reality in a distorted way, the lighting must be consistent with that anomaly, it is a matter of coherence. We are not just showing pictures here, Professor Clausen, we are promoting our principles."

Clausen tries to object:

"My concern," he says, "was to present the works in the clearest possible way, give the viewer a precise idea, that way he will be able to judge better ..."

Dunkels shakes his head with a smile of superiority.

"It is plain that you are not in the political struggle, professor. You don't seem to wholly understand that this exhibition is not about showing pictures. No, this exhibition puts forward an idea. We know very well what we think of these 'creations' and we are not going to wait for the judgement of the 'sovereign public', like liberals do. No. We know. And it is our duty to make that truth known, to fight for an art committed to the political struggle. Do not forget that when the Führer created the Ministry of Culture, he also called it 'of Propaganda' Art for the elites, Byzantine controversies, all that belongs to history. "

Sasha couldn't care less whether culture is propaganda, science or Babylonian religion. What makes he feel like vomiting is the prospect of having to rearrange once again the damned lamps.

"It will not be necessary," tells him Clausen when the Commissioner leaves with the same martial step with which he had entered. "It will be enough to hang the paintings a bit higher. Like this, you see?" he says, holding a small painting against the wall.

And indeed, that changes it, the light comes not from the front but from below, producing a bizarre effect. With that lighting, the room of Negroid painting looks scary, like the ghost train of the Luna Park.

Still, driving another fifty nails on these porous walls will not be an easy task. And even when it's done, they will still have to unroll the carpets and, unbelievably as it may seem, the last layer of paint at the building entrance will have to be applied. The rooms have all been painted in different, very vivid colours. Red, green, blue. The entrance is a shrill yellow that gives headache. That's how the Commissioner wants it.

"Professor Clausen, a parcel from Hildebrandsstrasse," Leni announces.

That is to say, from Dunkels' office. Clausen sighs and opens the package. A dozen rectangular panels, black text on white background, accompanied by a letter with a few vertical, horizontal and oblique lines below, a sort of monogram: the signature of the Commissioner of Culture.

On each panel's back, the name of the room for which it is intended. "The texts will be exposed in a clearly visible way," specifies the letter.

Well, said Sasha, they are made in cardboard, I can fix them without nails, a few drawing pins will do the job. But the cardboard is too thick for pins.

Sasha takes up one of them: "Are they fools or is it us they take for idiots?" "Avant-garde, the swindle of the century." "For this 'Art' have taxpayers paid millions of marks."

"You know what you have to do, Wassingher," says Clausen. "I have other matters to deal with."

Sasha reads another sign, intended for the pornographic room: "Those who have painted this junk will be permanently evicted from the artistic community."

195

He goes to the "factory" for a hammer. That's when he spots it: strolling quietly around the garage between the objects awaiting restitution, a black tail. And behind the tail, the white rump of Macke.

He runs after him, but the cat, disoriented by the disappearance of the pile of pictures on top of which he used to climb, hesitates for a moment, watching now right, now left, taking at last refuge behind a futuristic canvas. Sasha manages to catch it by the tail, but the cat threatens to retaliate with its claws. Sasha tries to kick him, but his foot hits the board instead, tearing up the back of the frame. Macke, perched on the carpenter bench, keeps an eye fixed on him, determined to defend his position.

If Clausen sees the beast, if he, furthermore, notices the degradation of the painting, who knows what his reaction will be? Sasha makes a threatening gesture with the hammer and this time the cat gets scared. It turns around and in less than a second it disappears out the window.

From the factory, he hears someone speaking loudly. Sasha approaches the entrance discreetly. A man in his fifties is standing there. Over his beige checked garment he wears a sort of cape and a black strip daintily knotted around his neck by way of tie.

"I demand to speak to the person in charge," he says loudly.

"You'll have to wait," answers Leni. "The professor is busy right now." The fellow stares angrily at Sasha as well as at young Willi.

After a few minutes, the professor's tall figure appears in the front door.

"What can I do for you?" he asks.

"Mr. Clausen, it's a shame, a real scandal!"

"I'm sorry," interrupts Clausen, "I did not hear your name."

"Hoyer-Lemke. Leopold Hoyer-Lemke."

The name sounds familiar to Sasha.

"Mr. Clausen, I must ask you, no, demand you, to remove my picture from this exhibition where it has nothing to do."

Without losing his calm, Clausen takes the blue notebook and leafs through it for a moment.

"Hoyer-Lemke, yes. *Schweriner Platz,* belonging to Baumgarten Gallery. An oil painting. Valued at two thousand marks. It is among the selected works."

"What does that mean?"

"It means it is one of the fifty-five selected for the exhibition."

Sasha fears that the man will have a seizure. He turns red, opens his mouth, but fails to articulate a word.

Clausen: "Fräulein Leni, bring a glass of water to this gentleman."

But the man rejects the glass.

"Who decided that my work would be brought here?" he asks. "Without asking for my permission?"

"I was just going to tell you that your painting was borrowed from the Baumgarten Gallery by order of the Culture Commission of the Capital Region."

The other glares at Clausen, then at Sasha and the secretary.

Sasha remembers the painting. It's in the green room. All in yellows, greens and blues, a street scene. A road junction with buses that cross each other, high buildings American style, and a crowd hurrying in all directions.

"I demand to see my work," says Hoyer-Lemke.

"Follow me please," says Sasha.

The man is going to do it, but he stumbles on a threshold and drops his leather briefcase, which opens, revealing its contents: a bundle of files.

"Wassingher," complains the professor, "when are you planning to even that threshold? It's ages since I asked you to do it."

"It's because I was waiting for the painters to apply the final coat," Sasha apologizes, as he helps the man pick up his belongings.

"And in the meantime, visitors will break their necks, is that the idea?"

"Mr. Clausen ..." begins the man, then he corrects himself: "Professor Clausen ..."

His tone is humbler now, more an appeal than an ultimatum.

"I've been an artist for thirty years," he goes on. "I went to the Dresden Academy, I did fifteen exhibitions. You're from Dresden too, aren't you?"

"From Breslau."

"Not a Berliner then. You see, living in Dresden, I have, like so many other young people, been attracted by the people around *Die Brücke*, a circle or artists that..."

"I know which group you mean," Clausen said.

"An artist goes through different stages, you are perfectly aware of that of course. The things I do now are not at all the same as then."

He pulls out one of the files from his briefcase. He shows them some photographs and the style is indeed different. A portrait of a woman, a mountain landscape, both very realistic.

"Truly accomplished works ," says Clausen. "But as for your painting here, the final selection has already been approved by the Commissioner. It is not in my domain to ..."

"But wait, I am a member of the party," exclaims Hoyer-Lemke, opening the folds of his cape. On one of the lapels of his jacket, a golden pin with the swastika. "What you are exposing here is the work of communists. I took part in the war, I have two decorations."

"I understand," says Clausen to calm him down. "Mr. Hoyer-Lemke, I suggest that you contact the Culture Committee. It's at the Hildebrandsstrasse, near Potsdamer Platz. Ask for Dr. Dunkels. "

"But, couldn't you ... Because it is a mistake ... It would be so simple to replace it with another work, you have so many here, no one will notice. "

Sasha feels sorry for him. Clausen seems to pity the man too, but Sasha knows that he will do nothing, that for no reason will he go against the regulations.

Leni offers Hoyer-Lemke a chair, but he asks for the bathroom instead. He puts his briefcase on the floor and Leni shows him the way.

"I did not select that work by chance," explains Clausen to Sasha, "there is no misunderstanding here, it is a perfect example of Expressionism. The urban theme, the jarring colours, the crude brush strokes, the distorted lines. See how these buses seem to clash with one another, it's unreal. Look at the buildings, that's not Dresden, that's Chicago. "

Clausen studies the picture as if he wanted to add still more elements of analysis to better justify his election. He leans over it to study the stylized figure of a passer-by. He consults his notebook.

Sasha: "It's a good thing that I did not have time to hang up the panels. If he had seen them, the poor gentleman would have a heart attack."

He shows one of the panels to the professor: "Vision problems or criminal will to distort reality? In the first case: the hospital, in the second: justice must be done."

Leni cannot avoid a little laugh. The professor looks at her disapprovingly.

Someone's knocking at the door. Leni opens.

"It's the Feininger!" she announces.

The gouache that's been damaged during the flood. Clausen removes the protective paper and examines the work. A blue human figure seen from behind. A yellow bridge. To the left, an orange house, to the right another construction, light blue. In the background, a factory's chimney.

"But," exclaims Clausen, "what have they done?"

He proceeds to the office and comes back with a ring binder.

"I wrote it quite clearly: two damaged areas, one in the lower left part, the other twenty-two centimetres higher up. They have repaired the first one but they have done nothing at all about the other. "

"I'd say they mended it, at least partly," says Sasha.

Clausen fetches a magnifying glass.

"No. The stain is still there," he concludes.

In the meantime, Hoyer-Lemke has come back. He is wiping his forehead with a large checked handkerchief.

The professor instructs Sasha to hand over the gouache to Willi, who will pack it up again and send it back to the restorers. Sasha takes two steps towards the "factory", but Clausen stops him. He checks his notebook and muses for a moment.

"Get me item number 124," he says. "Fourth row, by the wall. Gallery Obermayer."

Object 124 consists of several bits of yellowed newspapers glued to a canvas, a photograph - a smiling man with some kind of gear in his hand – a number of blue, green and black brush strokes, and some words written in large print: "We are all Dada."

"What do you think of this creation, Mr. Hoyer-Lemke, you who are a connoisseur of the artistic scene?" asks Clausen. "In which school or movement might it belong?"

Hoyer-Lemke looks at the picture, then at Clausen. He stammers something, half excuse half complaint.

"I hope you'll have nothing against this piece," Clausen said, "because it will replace your *Schweriner Platz* in our exhibition."

The man looks at the professor, then turns his gaze towards Sasha. Finally he throws his arms around Clausen, his eyes in tears.

"It would have been a great injustice, Professor," he says as he picks up his briefcase. "And for me a disgrace, the end of my career, I will never forget your gesture."

"You did the right thing, professor," says Sasha, when the artist has left.

"Member of the party or not, that will change nothing for him, it changes nothing for Emil Nolde either," answers Clausen. "If someone wants to hurt Herr Lemke, he'll just have to dig up a painting like this one. Having produced it will always be a stain on his record, whether it's publicly exhibited or not. "

Clausen looks critically at the Dadaist collage. Then he concludes:

"At least we will have spared him public humiliation."

"But won't the Commissioner react?" wonders Sasha.

"The Commissioner would not see the difference even if we replaced all Expressionists with Macedonian icons."

21

Cultural Editor at the *Morgenpost*. 1929. That changed his life thoroughly. As if a writer had been appointed editor of the *Weltbühne*. Better, in fact, as the *Bühne* printed fifteen thousand copies, the *Post* twenty times more.

Now that he had access to more exhaustive information, Schattendorf could develop a more precise overall view of the artistic field. And more radical. His reviews became more caustic.

He denounced especially reactionary painting. The German Art Defence Association, for example, an organization that advocated the so-called *völkisch* traditional style and denigrated everything that had been produced in the last half-century, especially Expressionism, but also Impressionism and Cubism, styles which were by definition "anti-German", either because these creators were not ethnic Germans, or because they belonged to the political Left.

They were rabid reactionaries. Nationalists, racists, anti-Semites. For them, modern art was a Jewish and Bolshevik conspiracy. They swore only by beautiful landscapes or by portraits of happy girls or old peasants. But their fight was not only ideological: it was about marks and pfennigs too.

In the good old days, painters like them sold fairly well, museums bought them a canvas from time to time, they managed to live by their art. But since the war, the market had changed, now it was the expressionists or the neo-objectivists who were popular. And it was not only the museums that bought that art, but also private collectors.

"A bunch of Jews," said the magazine of the Association, "exploiters of the German people who use the money they steal from us to corrupt our taste, our Germanic soul." That is why they demanded, without success, that the official institutions stop buying modern art and organizing exhibitions such as the Dresden International Art Fair, where both Liebermann, Kokoschka and Klee had been exposed.

Schattendorf began to be feared. People complained, but the chief tolerated it. For Huber, he was like a pinch of pepper in a cultural section otherwise too placid.

With Lotte, the relationship had become less harmonious. The deterioration that threatens any relationship? Professional jealousy? She had lived harmoniously with Harry Shadow, but Hans Schattendorf was a different matter: whereas she was no more than a competent reporter, he had become a well-known signature.

She became more critical towards him. The gap between them widened day by day and it became clear that if he continued to live with her it was out of gratitude. But he didn't really feel in debt to her ; she had taught him the ABC of the trade but the rest was his own merit.

One day he had to attend an inauguration at the Kaisersaal. It was something awful, *völkisch* painting of the worst kind.

A colleague introduced him to a young woman. Tall, elegant, a great mane of golden hair falling on her shoulders. She was not an artist, yet everybody treated her with respect. When he heard her surname, he understood why.

Adolf Furtenberg was an industrialist who had embarked on the press world and bought newspaper after review, publishing house after distribution company. The main organ of his group was a major daily newspaper: the *National-Zeitung*. Furtenberg held also a leading position in the German National Party, conservative and patriotic, hostile to parliamentary democracy.

Under normal circumstances, Schattendorf would have inflicted the exhibit a merciless critique. He would have trampled it, demolished it, pulverized it, he would have knocked down each leafy chestnut, profaned all the little alpine churches with richly adorned bell-towers, pissed in each murmuring brook. And what he would have done with the nymphs of the wood, with all naiads and loreleys, it is better not to describe.

But this circumstance was not normal.

Irene Furtenberg was dazzling, and Schattendorf succumbed without resistance to the charm of her sky-blue eyes. A true Valkyrie, the descent her very Germanic father, whose name was prominent among the exhibition's sponsors, had every right to expect. Schattendorf refrained from covering the event, and asked a colleague, less severe than himself, to do it instead.

She was the youngest of six daughters, and her father had always treated her with condescension. He had not succeeded in engendering a male heir despite his half dozen attempts. Being the last such attempt, the final blow, Irene embodied for him that series of failures.

Her beauty attracted men, but not men that pleased her father. That was why Irene was so delighted to learn that the charming young man she had met at the Kaisersaal was a reputable journalist and that he was not bound to any political party.

"He is a Jew," retorted his father.

205

"Schattendorf is a German name," replied Irene angrily.

"According to my sources, he has lived in the Scheunenviertel."

"That's a lie, his flat is in the West End."

"But he did live a few yards from the synagogue."

Irene was shocked. And Schattendorf reacted badly:

"My dear, I do not like to be investigated as if I were a criminal."

"I understand, Hans, it's surely a mistake."

"No. It is strictly true that I lived in that part of the East. I had a bad spell at the time, and lacking money is not a shame."

"He may not be Jewish," conceded the patriarch, "but I'm sure there's something fishy about him."

But his information service did not find anything serious. And one thing was certain: Irene had long since reached the age of marriage. Who knew what other character she would be capable to bring him if he vetoed this one? Still, he imposed a condition: it was unthinkable to have a son-in-law who worked for a competitor. He must leave the *Morgenpost*.

"But Herr Furtenberg," objected Schattendorf, appalled, "I hold an important position there."

Although Furtenberg boasted of paying zero attention to the culture section, he had heard that Schattendorf was widely read in certain circles. He loved the idea of snatching such a name from the *Post*.

"*Mein Herr*, what I'm offering you is not an 'important position'." he said.

The *National-Zeitung* had also a culture section. Its chief editor was soon to retire, explained his fiancée's father.

Chief editor at a major national newspaper! A dream for any journalist. And the *NZ* was one of the most read newspapers. Not only in Berlin; it was sent every morning by air to Hamburg, Munich and Cologne.

"Herr Furtenberg, I am truly grateful, but I need to talk to my superiors before taking a ..."

"Schattendorf," said Irene's father, staring at him, "let's not waste time: I want an answer within twenty-four hours. And if it's the salary that worries you, let me get that crystal clear: it's not a matter of discussion. You take it or you leave it. "

A matter of discussion? One thousand eggs? That was twice his salary at the *Post*!

Dumbfounded, Schattendorf left Furtenbergs' luxurious residence.

When Huber offered him to work for the *Morgenpost*, he did not have to consider it for more than one second. But an organ like the *National-Zeitung* ... If being hired by the *Post* had changed his life, Furtenberg's proposal could shatter it, turn it upside down.

He walked twice around the block, ruminating the question and desperately looking for an answer. He walked and walked until he realized he was lost. He had to search for a street-sign to find his way back to the Furtenbergs. He found the sign, and a minute later he found also the answer to his dilemma. Relieved, he knocked at the door again.

"I refuse," he told Irene.

"But Hans, why?" she moaned.

"If you knew me better, I would not need to explain. First, the *Zeitung*'s line is absolutely and drastically incompatible with my ideas. Second: ..."

"But Hans, Dad is just a little stubborn, you have to pretend to play along with him and then ..."

"He's a reactionary old man," said Schattendorf. "Just because he's got money, he believes that everything is due to him."

"My dear, you're overdoing it. He's a traditionalist, old-fashioned if you like, but ..."

"Traditionalist? He's a Nazi!"

"Ah, no, that shows that you do not know him. He finds all those people despicable, of a stunning vulgarity. You see, only yesterday he told me that he would not hire Hitler even as a valet. 'That clown who thinks he will rule Germany', that's what he said."

"Secondly," he continued, "I don't accept to be bribed. A thousand, eh? Well, tell him that my talent is not for hire and that my pen will not be auctioned off."

She burst into tears. "If you really loved me ... What he is offering you, the only thing he offers us, is a happy future. It's not to him you say no, it's to me. To us."

He left the Furtenberg house. He strode along the nine hundred meters which separated it from his apartment. But once he got home, he did not open the entrance door. Instead, he took the Welserstrasse.

He walked for a good twenty minutes. First he kept bumping into people: a crowd was just leaving the Ufa-Palast am Zoo and pouring onto the avenue. Schattendorf's gaze was captured by the film posters, he read the big capital letters but couldn't make head or tails of their meaning, not even of the film's title. Just the name of one of the actresses: Erna Morena.

Erna Morena, Erna Morena, he kept repeating for himself. But he got tired of dodging people, so he turned onto a quiet side street.

What an idea! Should he work for Furtenberg, for that pig? He would rather hang himself.

"Hang myself", he repeated three time, four times. Then Erna Morena came to his lips again. And suddenly, the calm street was no more and before him stood the pompous silhouette of the *Haus Vaterland,* at Potsdamer Platz. He had been only once at that huge entertainment palace, with some friends from Vienna. They had sat at the Italian tavern listening to syrupy songs which someone pointed out were not Italian but Spanish.

Spanish! Erna Morena! Why would that Bavarian girl choose such a name for herself? Why not Lola Sevilla? He had a good laugh, and a passing by looked suspiciously at him.

After some glasses of red wine, he and his Viennese friends had moved over to the French café, but there was no free table there, and no music, so they"complete with song and" went on to the Rheinterrasse, which was decorated with Rhine landscapes and stunned the public with simulated storms, complete with rain and lightings. His friends were impressed.

Did it mean anything that his steps took him to just this place? He tried to remember who those friends were but could only remember the name of one of them. He hadn't seen any of them again.

Ten minutes later he was at the Wittenbergplatz, going through the revolving door of Café Schimmel.

"It's been a long time," Heinz greeted him. "Welcome home again!"

"And Dieter? And Geza?" asked Schattendorf.

"At the Maus," replied Paul. "You know, Harry, the interview with Max Beckmann will appear in our next issue."

It was Schattendorf who had convinced the painter to answer Der Bruch's questions.

"If you're interested," he said, "I can arrange a meeting with Döblin too. He's in Prague, but will be back next week."

But it was already time to leave the café for the usual peregrination to the Blaue Maus, Bang's cabaret. The place was full and the noise level higher than he remembered. Schattendorf bought cocktails for everybody, then some Franconian wine, and to top it off he ordered a bottle of *Veuve Clicquot* and blew up the cork, causing an explosion of bubbles that sprinkled the blouses and tunics of the girls around.

But Geza, lost in his thoughts, didn't notice. "Something, we have to find something," he kept on repeating.

"I might convince Herwarth to come, if you want," Schattendorf offered.

"No thanks."

Harry had already brought Walden once, but the well known art expert confined himself to studying the people around him with an air of superiority and to utter a couple of caustic remarks.

"You know, Harry, Marlene was here for a drink yesterday," said Dieter.

"Dietrich? Are you serious?"

They all burst out laughing; that was another proof of Geza's creativity. The Berber shows up here every now and then, he reasoned, Lotte Lenya and Kurt Weill have also made quick visits, but how many people can testify of that? If I told that, in addition to the Berber and to Walden, Rosa Valetti came too, who would be able to prove me wrong?

He began to spread rumours: that Emil Jannings was often seen at the Maus, that the Dietrich used to come after her act at the *Komödie*.

One night, Willy Fritsch, the actor, actually showed up, in flesh and blood. "I thought I ought to see at least once in my life the place where I am such a regular customer," he explained.

"Good old Geza," laughed Schattendorf. "But, you know, I can bring you Tucholsky. For real." He knew well the writer, who sometimes contributed articles to the *Post*.

"But," Geza replied, "what are you waiting for? Bring him, tomorrow if you can."

When he had pilgrimed to the Schimmel three hours earlier, his intention was to confer with his friends. About Irene, about her father, about Furtenberg's outrageous proposition. But during the whole evening he spent with them, he did not even mention those subjects. He even managed to forget about them, his attention attracted by little Vicki, Fredi Körner's girlfriend, for whom he had always had a weakness.

"It's been a great evening, a wonderful evening," he said to himself, over and over again during his way home. He stumbled over the first step of the staircase that led to his apartment, but he continued repeating: "A great evening. Those are my friends, that is my world. How could I ever forget it?"

He slept deeply, without dreams, nine hours straight . He woke up serenely, without a hangover and – as he noticed in the bathroom's mirror - with an inexplicable smile on his lips.

He opened the room's window and let the sun enter. He brew himself a coffee. He sat down at the table.

He took a notepad and wrote:

211

"First: I refuse to live without her."

He took a first sip of the black, very hot, sugar-free coffee.

"Second: the old fart is a reactionary as few remain, a tyrannosaur."

He blew on the liquid, to cool it down.

"A tyrannosaur. But: he is not interested in things cultural and, once I am the section chief, I will do as I please."

"Tertio: if he doesn't let me, I'll resign. He can fire me but he cannot force us to divorce."

Furtenberg bought them a flat. With this gift, and with the wedding party for a hundred guests he arranged, the Patriarch considered to have fulfilled his duty to her daughter.

And there he was, Hans Schattendorf, former editor of an obscure bi-monthly review, today, in February 1932, chief of the cultural section of a newspaper that sold half a million copies daily. There he was, set up with her ravishing Irene in a large apartment on the Kastanienallee, in the heart of Charlottenburg.

But it's 1934 now. Bang's cabaret no longer exists, thinks the Chief of Cultural Action, sitting at his office in Spandau. He saw with his own eyes that the blue and white panel of the Blaue Maus had been replaced by a red one: "For rent." All the establishments of that kind have been forcibly closed, with very few exceptions.

If anyone can give him information about the picture, decides Schattendorf, that person is Geza Nemes, the Dane's handyman. Geza was never an intellectual. He was a regular of the Schimmel, but without being part of the review. Neither a communist nor a social democrat, what reason could he have to leave the country?

He's got his business card somewhere. He searches his drawers but he sees only notepads and forms. The bottom-drawer perhaps? It is full of objects without any given place: used pens that he does not make up his mind to toss in the trash, keys that open God knows which doors. And finally, there, among postcards stamped in the island of Rügen, in Capri, in Nice, a business card was hiding ("Geza Nemes, impresario") with a solitary palm and sea waves in the background. A pattern in good old Geza's taste, thinks Schattendorf. He slips it in his pocket.

It's over two years since last time he saw him. It was at the Maus, of course. He does not recall seeing the painting there that time, it was probably at Schramme's already. Before that, it was in an inner room, near the toilet.

Metzerstrasse 43, says the card. In the building's hall, a table with the names of the tenants. Nemes, second floor. He goes up, knocks at the door, no answer. He snatches a sheet from a notebook and writes down: "Call me to Spandau 3567. Hans." Then he adds, between brackets: "Harry."

He walks down again. The Metzerstrasse is a quiet street, although just a ten minute walk from Alexanderplatz. No bus lines, little traffic. A low middle class neighbourhood. People are dressed properly, but with no elegance. At the corner of the street, the local office of the NSDAP, the Nazi party, with three brown-shirts at the door, cigarettes in mouth. A lady passes by with two straps in her hand and a dog at each end. On the opposite side walk, an employee from a bakery carries a large tray covered with a white napkin.

Schattendorf stops at the crossroads to wait for a horse-drawn carriage to pass. On the other side of the street, a man with reddish hair and a striped suit.

"Geza!" he shouts. A broad smile crosses the face of the other.

213

There is a bar right across the street. Schattendorf invites him to a beer.

"Do you remember that picture that won the Argus Prize a few years ago, Geza? It was hanging near the toilet."

Geza laughs.

"Yes, I remember it. By the way: do you know why the prize was called Argus?"

"Not a clue. But Geza, what I would like to know is how the painting ended up ..."

"Yes but, wait, this story is really funny. Do you know the name of the Dane?"

"Well, he was called Bang as far as I know," replies the other impatiently.

"Yes but, August Bang? Hans-Peter Bang? Rudolf Bang?"

"Oh, you mean his name was Argus?"

"Argus Absalon Bang. Is it not hilarious? And I am the only one to know, the only one who has seen his passport. It was the day we signed the lease contract for the premises of the club."

"I see. That explains the prize's name then. However..."

Geza inspects the other's face with the disappointed smile of a man who has just told the best joke of his repertoire without reaping the laughs it deserves.

"The picture, yes," he says finally. "You see, Bang saw things coming, and his decision to return to Denmark did not come overnight. He prepared his departure with the same care as he had set up the cabaret."

"But tell me, Geza ..."

"Those were the times, eh, Harry? The Maus was not the best cabaret in Berlin, but surely the funniest. Those were, frankly, my

214

best years. Bang had hired me for a month, little did he imagine I would stay with him for all that time."

Geza's present is surely less bright. And he does not have many people to recall the past with.

"Great times, indeed," Schattendorf agrees. "But what interests me, you see, is why in the world the painting suddenly reappears, and signed by Grosz this time."

Geza shrugs.

"What I know is that Bang sold everything he could sell, including that painting, before he left. It was at Schramme's before that, maybe you didn't know that?"

"I did. Listen Geza: it's very important for me to know all the details. Are you positive you don't remember anything more? To whom Bang sold it, for instance?"

Geza regrets, but he has no idea.

Schattendorf felt lucky to have unearthed Geza, but that hasn't helped him a bit.

"Harry," says Geza, "you're in a good position now, right? Working in the cultural spheres. If you see anything I could do ... At the moment I work at a music store, *Elektroland,* you know, but I would like to go back to journalism. "

Schattendorf promises to contact him as soon as he knows anything. The other listens with a melancholy air, as if he didn't trust much that promise. And he is right, thinks Schattendorf: today it is not easy to find a job for a foreigner like him. He could do some research, of course, and he will. But not just now, there is no time for that.

22

Morel watches Violetta's taxi drive away. Eleven o'clock, too early to go back to the hotel. The Kurfürstendamm is as lively as before, the neon lights always as bright. At the top of a building's façade, on a black strip, by turning on and off successively, thousands of lamps draw letters and numbers and let them scroll from right to left. Elektra-Dresden 102.5 Auto-Union 96.4 Pound Sterling 13.84 Franc 3.54.

He would have gone to the Jockey Bar or to Rio-Rita but, do they still exist? The Eldorado is now one of the NSDAP's headquarters, he saw it with his own eyes.

He goes down the Leibnizstrasse and as he reaches the Kurfürsten, he runs into a telephone booth. Call Nina Bovrik maybe? If it's the Italian who answers, he could just hang up.

Westend 2916. Nina. She seems pleased to hear him. She was just leaving for the Red Top to meet some friends. "Why don't you come too, Gaston?"

His taxi drops him off at Kantstrasse, in front of the entrance. A black brick façade with no windows. Two lanterns and, on a panel, "Red Top. Bar-meals-music."

All the tables are taken, as in the good old days. But the atmosphere is not the same, people are dressed more formally. At one of the tables, a black uniform.

Nina greets Morel, not with one of her little sparkling kisses on the mouth, but on his cheek this time. She introduces him to his friends. Curt Hagener, a journalist in his fifties, dressed in a strict yet elegant style: a striped shirt, a large black and violet tie, and cuff links with a small blue stone each. Next to him sits a fragile-looking woman and a man of about forty, with ash-coloured hair.

Two boys in brown shirt make their entrance. The doorman warns them that there is no free table left, but the SA don't leave ; instead they look around, searching a place where to sit. The SS in black gives them a short dissuasive sign. With a quick Heil, they evaporate.

The Nina he knew a few years earlier was an intellectual flapper: boyish haircut, short black dress and her arms covered with bracelets from the wrists to the elbows. Now the hair is longer, as is the pale pink dress. Around her wrist, a bracelet, only one, but of gold.

Her most seductive smiles are aimed at Hagener, which annoys Morel. As soon as an opportunity arises, he asks her about her sentimental situation.

"But, I'm always with Vittorio," she answers. As if it were self-evident. As if he did not know they had been separated for a year. As if she did not know that he knows.

In any case, Morel does not rule out the possibility of a more intimate contact with her, perhaps because of the looks she is giving the journalist, not wholly suitable for a married woman.

"Curt is at the *Lokal-Anzeiger,*" says Nina. "The culture section."

"At the *Tribüne* now," Hagener corrects her. "Since one month."

"Oh, congratulations," exclaims she. "An important step in your career, isn't it?"

The *Tribüne* is an extraofficial party organ.

The guy makes a gesture of modesty.

"When is your next exhibition?" he asks.

She makes a face.

"I have trouble finding the right gallery. I got the canvasses, but ..."

Morel has seen two of Nina's paintings at some dealer's by the Savignyplatz. Her style, slim figures, subtle traits, something between Oskar Schlemmer and Chagall, have become less extreme. The subjects are no longer erotic; romantic at best.

"Try Schoelcher," suggests Hagener. "They have a few empty weeks."

"Oh, thank you," Nina chirps. "Would you mind if I mentioned your name?"

"Not at all," replies he. "They owe me a favour."

"You are a darling," modules Nina.

"Do you know anything about the *Entartete Kunst* exhibition?" asks Morel.

The other examines him attentively before replying:

"It opens soon, in Kreuzberg."

"What a place for an exhibition," Nina frowns. "I prefer Schoelcher... "

"And at the same time, another one," Hagener continues, "of contemporary German art. Non-degenerate art, I mean."

There is a touch of irony in his remark.

"One of my works is there," says the second man, who had been silent up to now. He is tall above average and looks somewhat maladroit. He does not seem comfortable in this environment.

"Degenerate or decent?" asks Morel.

Nina looks at him disapprovingly:

"Eberhard is an esteemed artist. And nobody gave him a free ride, he had to fight to get the position he has now."

"Sorry, I did not hear your name," says Morel.

"Novak," answers the man.

"In what style do you work? Excuse my curiosity, I'm a dealer."

Nina answers for him:

"Eberhard has a great quality of draughtsmanship and he's a talented colourist too. His paintings have ... a sense of life, or rather... " she searches in vain for the exact word, "... they have a soul."

Novak listens to her without comment, his gaze fixed on the white tablecloth.

"My style," she continues, "has been experimental for a long time, but I admit willingly that a more classical art like that of Eberhard moves me deeply."

"I'm not really classic," he says.

"That's not the right word, it's true," she says.

"I feel a kinship with the impressionists, for example."

"Of course," confirms Nina. "That is palpable in your textures, and in your colour."

He is, Morel figures, one of those artists in the regime's liking, something Nina would probably want to be too. Nina, a native of Kiev, a passionate revolutionary, a symbolist later, then a surrealist, and always uncompromising nihilistic on the erotic front. Nina, official artist of the Reich? He cannot avoid a smile.

Novak, who seems embarrassed to speak about himself, comments in a low voice:

"Style does not matter, but art has to talk to people. For me, painting is another way of ... of taking part in people's lives, in their hardships."

"But there is also joy in your works," protests Nina mildly.

"And that happens to be the name of my piece for the exhibit: *The Joy is Back*."

"I got a good training at the Academy," he concludes. "But it was life that taught me how to paint."

Morel tries to identify his accent. Bavarian? Swiss?

"I have a painting too," he comments. "At the EnKu."

All look at him.

"A Grosz. I'm looking forward for the expo to close, so I can get it back."

"You bought a Grosz?" Nina asks, surprised.

"I have always admired him," says Hagener. "A man of integrity, even if politically he is impossible."

"A Communist?" wonders Novak.

"Anarchist, if anything," replies Hagener.

"And a well known womaniser," adds Nina.

"A real artist will always chase girls," says Morel.

"I didn't know you had an artistic vein too, Gaston," she drops with a mischievous smile.

Everybody laughs, especially the frail looking woman, silent until then.

"Maybe you have seen it? My painting I mean?" asks Morel to Hagener.

"No, that exhibition hasn't had a pre-opening. But a Grosz, well, that's hardly a surprise; it is exactly the type of art they want to put in the pillory. Given that it passes the final selection. "

"Selection?"

"They have assembled hundreds of works in that gasometer, but they cannot expose more than one hundred. A matter of space."

Excellent news. If the Grosz is not selected, Morel will get it back sooner. Maybe tomorrow, during next week at the latest. As soon as he receives confirmation, he will telegraph to Navarro. If the affair drags on, the guy might get carried away by some rare licentious engraving of the eighteenth century, or by an ancient Roman winged phallus, and decide that his investment quota for the year is full.

Hagener: "May I ask if it's the same painting that belonged to Gallery Kronen?"

Morel jumps: "Yes, do you know anything about it?"

"Not really."

Morel: "I hope I'll get it back as soon as possible, I have a buyer waiting impatiently and, who knows with which care the works are kept in that gasometer."

"Your client must be someone with erotic interests of a very precise kind," says Hagener.

But Morel confines himself to a smile. "While not being a father confessor, I still have to observe some discretion."

This Morel, and not Keller, must be Oberfrunck's go-between, figures Hagener. A Nazi dignitary cannot go to a gallery and buy such a picture openly. And if he did buy it, he has every reason to be worried about his investment now.

His reflections are interrupted by a saxophone's euphoric notes, accompanied by the piano, all this to announce a newcomer in black suit with red lapel and golden bow tie of disproportionate proportions: the funny man of the Red Top.

He looks at the audience with a big smile. Then he launches a rapid series of jokes. The first one about the Mahatma Gandhi, then another one about President Roosevelt, a third on Joseph I, Tsar of all the Soviets. Finally, he tells about something he saw in Berlin's

222

neighbourhood, a kind of facilities, surrounded by fences and surveillance towers.

"Barbed wire everywhere," he says, "and armed guards, with ferocious dogs. It made me mad. 'Surround yourself with all the barbed wire you want'," I yelled. 'The minute I decide to break in, nothing will stop me!' "

Bursts of laughter. Morel observes that the SS looks around the audience before he reacts. Finally he claps his hands too. The comic moves quickly on to his next joke, this one about a man named Israel and his wife Sarah.

Hagener leans towards him and Nina: "The one on the camps he stole from Karl Valentin, I heard him tell it in Munich."

The waiter blows up the cork of another bottle of *Henkell*. Morel feels how the sparkling wine cheers him up. The place's atmosphere is not as animated as it used to be, but it is far from lugubrious.

For Hagener it is time to go. Nina starts to get up too.

"The night is still young," whispers Morel in her ear. "Why not continue our conversation at the bar of my hotel?"

"Where are you staying?" she asks.

"At the Lilienhof as usual."

"Ah, I never understood why you don't go to the Kempinski instead, just around the corner."

"I see that your social status has risen a couple of steps," he says, a bit annoyed.

She looks at him regretfully.

"Do not get angry. Never be angry at me, Gaston."

That is another reason why he has always liked her: for this cute face of mischievous girl, ready to do anything to be forgiven.

Anything?

"What about that drink then?" he tries.

"Not at your hotel."

The server brings them a *white lady* and a *gimlet.*

"What do you do with the kid? Put him in bed and then go to the bar?"

"I do not go out much. This evening I had to meet Curt, it's important for my career. And we have a nanny."

Vittorio Carraro is a diplomat, they can afford that and more.

"So you are a faithful wife now. Has it gone that far?"

She smiles wistfully.

"I have fond memories of you Gaston."

It is not my night, he resigns himself, and asks:

"What about that Hagener? He does not look like a Nazi."

"He's got his party card, otherwise he would not be at the *Tribüne*, but in his private life he's very free, I can tell you."

"By own experience?"

"No, I'm not his type," Nina laughs.

"He prefers blondes?"

"Blonds."

"Oh? I hadn't realized."

"Let us say that he spent his evenings more often at the Cozy-Corner than at the Café Braun."

The Cozy-Corner, unlike the Café Braun, was a nightclub frequented exclusively by boys. Both have been closed.

"And Violetta?" asks Morel.

Nina shrugs her shoulders.

"Violetta and reality are not on speaking terms. Times have changed, they have always changed, Gaston, the times keep changing.

There has been a Dada era, then expressionism, realism, tomorrow it will be neo-introspection or retro-modernism. "

"I see, and now it's 1934. Early Novak era?"

She ignores the question.

"Violetta bangs her head against the wall again and again. For me, once is enough. You see Gaston, creative work is the most important, you have to adapt. If you want to paint with gold, like Klimt, but you do not have a penny, then you make do with a tube of oil. If you want to paint large frescoes à la Michelangelo, but you are not buddy with any pope, what do you do? You change plans. "

"Yesterday she asked me a weird question. She wanted to know if she was still alive or already dead."

"You too?" exclaims Nina. "She asked me exactly the same question, and in a terribly serious tone. I was so stunned that I did not know how to react. What did you answer?"

Next morning he leaves the hotel and heads for Grolmanstrasse. In a few meters he reaches the Kurfürsten, which at this hour looks different. The Kurfürstendamm, in the West, has long been one of the city's two night-life hubs. The eastern one, Friedrichstadt, around the Unter den Linden, lost ground as the "march to the west" intensified, the East being handicapped by its shabby neighbourhoods.

True, to the east of the Tiergarten are the royal palace, the great museums, the university. But the West has all that is modern, it is here the well-to-do chose to move, and with them the big department stores.

One of those is Wertheim, a majestic stone building with a Hanseatic touch, where everything can be bought, from Portuguese sardines to French silk stockings, or a radio-gramophone of the most recent model. But how much longer? Its owners are Jewish.

People came to the Kurfürsten after sunset too, not to shop but for fun. There were the Gloriapalast, the Universum, the Ufa-Palast and other cinemas, restaurants like Kempinski, theatres, cabarets. And, of course, girls and boys *"de joie."*

It was the kingdom of sophistication, of the brand new fashion, of the latests craze. If Berlin was a transatlantic, the Kurfürstendamm was its high prow. A scene like such could arouse nothing but abhorrence in boors like Hitler, who felt lost in that frenzy of cars, trams, and neon.

These people are obsessed with their swastikas. They hang them, stick them and nail them everywhere, so that no one can forget that this is the New Germany. They want everything to be "new", but their novelties are very different from those that once galvanised the Kurfürsten: talking pictures, racing cars, jazz-music, Charleston's irresistible rhythm.

He goes on walking and takes the Grolmanstrasse. Keller is already at the gallery, but the door is still closed. He knocks.

The art dealer is moving a canvas to the back room. A street scene, an elevated train that runs over a suburban street.

"But," says Morel, "I have already seen this picture. At the Moritzburg Museum. How come you have it?"

"You must be wrong, this one comes from a private collector, another Jew who feels it's time to weigh the anchor."

"So? Still, I'm sure I have seen it."

"Kirchner may well have painted the same scene twice, that's not unusual. Go to Moritzburg and you will see that it is still there, unless it has been cleansed away."

226

"I buy it from you, provided I won't have problems getting it out of the country."

"What problems? I'll give you the certificate of authenticity, as usual."

Keller uses always the same expert, a former professor of the academy, but who, being a Jew, could decide to "weigh the anchor" too, any day.

"But it's a real vein you've found, Keller. Are there any more nuggets in that creek? The Feininger I see over there for instance?"

"It has already a buyer, but there could be others, yes."

"Always of the same origin?"

"No, no, the veins, as you put it, are many. Don't think I'm happy about it. It's not good for business when people are forced to leave."

"Erwin, I confirm my interest in whatever you can find me. Russians especially."

Keller nods.

"There could be a Malevich. And a Kandinsky too, a small watercolour."

"Set them aside. I'll pay you in advance. Always with certificate, right?"

"Gaston: I sell nothing without a certificate."

Only yesterday, such works could not be purchased. They were not in the market. And they will be there just for a short time. He has to seize the opportunity. But his capital is not unlimited, that's why the sale of *Still Life* is so decisive. The bargains that crop up may be mouth-watering, but he needs the financial means.

Morel examines another piece, a Macke. Ladies and gentlemen in a bar. *The guinguette at the park,* informs the bronze plate at the frame's bottom.

Strange that a private collector should affix such plates. Instinctively, he returns the canvas. There are letters and numbers written with a big black pencil: "Ex-47 Mac." "166." And a label: "Moritzburg Art Museum."

Keller looks at him but says nothing.

Morel: "The Malevitch you mentioned, and the others: do they come from the same museum?"

Keller shrugs shoulders.

"They are of different origins. Museums have to get rid of embarrassing works. And the state needs money."

"Let us understand each other, Keller: until now I have bought you works of your property. But things with the stamp of a state museum .... How can I be sure that they will allow me to leave the country with them? "

"I repeat that I will provide all the documents: certificate of authenticity ...."

"I'm not questioning the authenticity. It's the ownership."

"You buy the painting from Galerie Kronen, not from any museum."

Morel ponders the answer.

"The situation is not clear, Erwin. I'm not going to buy works for thousands of marks, running the risk of having them confiscated at the border."

"All they will ask you," says the gallery owner, "is a proof that you have acquired them legally, that is, you'll have to produce an invoice in your name. They will not require you to account for all changes of ownership. Have they done that with the other paintings you have bought? "

They have not, admits Morel.

"It would be a different thing if it were a Dürer we are talking about. But none of these things are more than thirty years old. Besides, there are tens of thousands of works from that period. Do you figure the customs officials are aware of which Macke and which Kirchner belong to which museums? Do you think they care? The only thing they are interested in is the amount you paid when you bought it, because it is on that amount that the export tax will be determined. You will have to pay that, of course, but you know that already. "

"Erwin, I need to know from whom you buy these things."

Keller smiles:

"Of course. Would you like his address and phone number as well?"

"I need to know the origin of what I buy."

Keller gets up and goes to the kitchen. He turns on the gas, holds a small aluminium saucepan under the tap, then puts it on the gas stove. He fills a brown cloth filter with the contents of a blue and golden box with "*Jacobs Kaffee* " on it. He waits, immobile and silent. When the water starts simmering, he slowly pours the contents of the pan into the cloth filter. He takes two cups with their saucers and brings them to the small table.

"Sugar?"

"In this case, yes," replies Morel.

Morel stirs his coffee without taking his eyes from the other.

Finally, the gallery owner speaks:

"It's about the exhibition, *Entartete Kunst*. I mean, the works that have not been selected."

The same selection Hagener was talking about last night.

"The organizers have requisitioned a few hundred, but only fifty will be exposed."

The others, thinks Morel, could well be destroyed. Except if they are sold to galleries like Kronen.

Keller takes a sip from his cup.

"I know someone who has access to the works," he says.

"That Macke should not be here then, it should have been incinerated. If anybody finds out ..."

"Incinerated? When did you turn into a horror writer, Gaston?"

There's no time to lose, decides Morel. He has to buy, and then leave the country.

"But what about my Grosz? Has it been selected?"

"It doesn't matter if it isn't. The Grosz is mine. What they may destroy, if they ever do, are pictures belonging to them, those which are state property."

"You wouldn't happen to be a Jew, Erwin?" asks Morel.

"Even if I was, property rights are still in force. Jews may be discriminated, but what they own, is still theirs."

For now, thinks Morel.

No time to lose, he repeats to himself.

23

The Auditorium of the State Art Library is crowded. Heads of Cultural Action of North Berlin, Friedrichshain-Kreuzberg, Charlottenburg. Alois Schardt is there, as are Ruprecht Wendtland, the old Expressionist Adalberth Thiermann, Konrad Berg, the young painter discovered by Vittorio, and the people from Ferdinand Möller Gallery.

The boys from *Nation und Kultur* brought a whole bunch of students. On a small table at the entrance of the room, they stacked a few dozen copies of *Culture in our time.*

"Concentrate," Schattendorf urges himself. But he cannot stop brooding about the Kreuzberg exhibition. About the painting. About Grosz.

Bang had assured him, when he asked him the question a year ago, that Schramme had gotten rid of it. "She threw it in the trash." One of her brothel's customers had complained of the lack of respect towards the marshal.

Well, someone must have been rummaging through her rubbish bins, because the painting is now in the gasometer. In a matter of hours, if they really have the nerve to expose it, the picture will be seen by thousands of Berliners. First they will laugh, seeing the Head

231

of Cultural Action of Spandau with his dick in the air. But it will not stop at that. Other questions will be asked.

Schattendorf can no longer afford to wait. Peter Litzke is the right person for the job. He is a determined and courageous lad.

But here arrives Nolde: he greets him and shakes his hand.

"I do not know what you will talk about today, but I find it always stimulating to listen to you," says the elderly painter.

"It is a great honour. May I sign it for you?"

He takes a pen out of his pocket.

"Thank you for taking the trouble to come," he says. "I know you are not very keen on the capital's atmosphere."

"I'm no longer keen on anything. But over there, in my village, at least I manage to survive," replies Nolde.

"But these are exciting times, my dear and respected Emil. Isn't it a privilege to be part of all this?"

"I am above all a worker, an artisan, but things appear to be finally on the right track, yes."

When Schattendorf, having exchanged some gossip with Schardt, steps up to the microphone, he feels anxiety, as always in these occasions. Although he has done it so many times, he still feels the adrenaline rush. And the apprehension chases away the damn painting and the gasometer from his mind.

But it is not really fear, it is not even stage fright. It is the concentration of energy, and also the foretaste of the exhilaration to come. To feel the eyes of the audience fixed on him, of that audience that is waiting to be seduced, ready to submit to him.

Once the echo of the last cough disappears, he looks up and starts speaking.

"Respected Heads of Cultural Action, Commissioners and Directors of Promotion and Propaganda. Comrades."

He prepares his speeches in detail. In front of him on the desk, he has a diagram with the main points, but it is essential to leave room for improvisation, it is only thus that he can reach maximum intensity.

"You are a born propagandist, Hans," flattered him once a colleague. "You have a bright future and not just in the art field. Minister of Education, why not? Don't laugh, I'm serious."

And that much is true that politics is never absent from his reflection. But art must go along with politics. Art can even guide it, but the word "guide" must be used with caution. And not at all with tonight's audience. As a politician, he must not lose sight of his goals, but he has to choose the right occasion. Expressionism is a big word for some; the potion should be administered at a safe dose.

"The task of the artist in the twentieth century," says the invitation card to the lecture. This is not the first time that he approaches the subject, and if he still needs speech notes, it is not to avoid embarrassing silences, but rather not to expand too much; he has only fifty minutes at his disposal.

A limit that he usually exceeds without scruples. The person in charge of the auditorium will look at him reproachfully, a look which Schattendorf will scrupulously ignore ; he will pursue his argument to its conclusion.

The idea of the artist as sovereign creator, he argues, raising for the first time his voice, the idea of the genius which, alone in his studio, produces masterpieces like a magician astonishes his public by pulling one, two, three rabbits out of a hat, that idea belongs to the past. It is time to face twentieth century's realities, which, paradoxically,

233

demands us to go back to the roots of German art: to the Middle Ages.

The mention of the Middle Ages has a strong impact, regardless of the audience. That's the idea he emphasizes, that's the climax of his speech. From there on, the ideas unfold effortlessly, the lecture delivers itself.

"The sculptures of Strasbourg Cathedral," he asks rhetorically, "those summits of medieval art, are they signed? Did their author engrave his name on the pedestal? When he did not work for the bishop, did he exhibit in galleries? Was he an expensive artist? Did his name sell? "

The medieval artist was not an individual, he was but a drop in the ocean of the people, of the nation. It was from this unpretentiousness that he drew his greatness.

And it is just at the moment when he mentions the sculptures, that the door opens and a group of people enters the auditorium. They are half a dozen, in uniform. In their middle, a man tall below average, brown hair, black striped suit. He proceeds, surrounded by his suite, towards some seats which are promptly evacuated by their occupants. The man limps.

Schattendorf is touched. Of all the party's cadres it is him that he admires the most. A true intellectual, an intellectual and an activist. And it is his presence that encourages him to emphasize more than he had intended his concept of art as companion, as an associate of the political action. He feels that this thought reflects the doctor's own ideas, and he dares to take a step further: art not only follows political action, it can, moreover, guide it.

Because, where do the ends of action come from? Not from rational speculation at any rate. No, those goals are linked to the nation's identity, to atavistic forces, forces to which the people only have access through forms and colours, not through reasoning. That is why those images must be constantly created, recreated. It is the task of each generation to re-formulate the ancestral certainties in images that are new. "And that is in fact what 'avant-garde' means", could he had added.

Schattendorf feels the doctor's eyes looking intently at him. He feels his sharp, penetrating gaze.

"Art is political, but I want to go further and advocate the idea that politics is an art, not the sixth, but the first one. And we all know that the Führer sees himself above all as an artist."

Once the lecture finished, Goebbels approaches the podium.

"Very interesting ideas," he says. "I take note."

He looks him straight in the eyes and adds:

"Our movement cannot do without people like you. Men who are both loyal and creative, that's what we need, urgently."

He shakes hands with Schattendorf and leaves the place.

The Council of Fine Arts. With the minister's backing, no one, not even Rosenberg, can stop him. And Dunkels can go back to the hole he crawled up from.

But before, he must get rid of the painting. He looks for a phone to call Peter and tell him to take Gerhard with him.

But back to 1932: due to his union with Irene Furtenberg, Hans Schattendorf had become Head of Culture of the *National-Zeitung,* the *NZ.* It is true that no one in the cultural circles ever read the *NZ,* too conservative. The *Morgenpost* had more prestige. But at the *Post* he was one editor among others, here he was the boss.

The *NZ* exalted patriotic values which he thought moth-eaten. But the newspaper also attacked the Republic, a Republic he had always despised, yesterday as bourgeois, today as corrupt.

Without subscribing to the newspaper's opinions - but had he ever subscribed to any opinion? - he felt more at ease than expected at the *NZ*. A reactionary newspaper? Maybe, but in the editorial board there were also young journalists, academics with innovative ideas. Seen from close range, the monster was not that repulsive.

He announced his new job to his friends of Der Bruch in a playful tone. As if it was one of his practical jokes, like that time when he had managed to sneak in the congress of the venerable Catholic Party asking inappropriate questions about the relationship between Mary and Joseph, and starting thereby a gruesome brawl. As if it was still one of those character traits, free, rebellious, for which he was admired. Pure Dadaism, in other words.

But they did not see it that way.

"Well, I can stop overnight if I feel like it," he argued. "And you can bet your life that I will if they ever try to impose anything on me."

"And say goodbye to the thousand eggs of salary?"

"Ah, so you think I sold myself? Here, take these two hundred. And I'll give half of my wages to Der Bruch."

"Der Bruch does not accept subsidies from Furtenberg."

His first reaction was astonishment; these people were his best friends after all. But then he got furious. And finally, bitter. He, a traitor? But it was they who betrayed his friendship, who accused him of the most appalling things without the shadow of a justification.

And then, who was Heinz, who was Paul to demand loyalty to God knows what ideology? As if Der Bruch had ever had a political affiliation. "My thinking wears no uniform," had always been Harry Shadow's motto, but also the review's.

It was easy to criticize the *NZ*, and Schattendorf himself did it wholehearted. But he knew what he talked about. Had Heinz even bothered to take into consideration the standpoints he so sharply denounced? He just stuck a label on them. The idea of putting them to the test without preconceived ideas, of examining them with the critical spirit he always boasted over, did not come to his mind.

If there was a newspaper which revolted Schattendorf these days, it was the Social-Democrat *Vorwärts*, because of its hypocrisy. At least the *NZ* called things by name. The organs of the Left misrepresented, pretended, faked.

He was nevertheless shocked when Der Bruch, at a meeting to which he had not been summoned, excluded him from the editorial board. Police manners. A political trial worthy of Stalin's soviets.

After the surprise, after the indignation, came resentment. And desolation. Never had he felt so alone. Not after leaving Violetta, nor when his relationship with Lotte came to an end.

He took refuge in work. Hard work became his drug. And that drug was hardly in shortage, now that he was head of a culture section.

One of the old-timers among the editors had a name that Schattendorf had never forgotten. He treated Ludwig Sauer with courtesy, without ever mentioning the exhibition at Droysen gallery, which the old critic had probably forgotten after having butchered it.

"Leave all hope, ye who enter: the caviare sandwiches are finished."

The time for revenge would come sooner or later, told himself the Chief of Culture. And it did come, in the person of Ruprecht Wendtland.

Schattendorf had understood that what irritated Sauer the most in contemporary art, even more than its avant-gardism, was the fact that many of those creators dared to exhibit and even to sell without having a degree. They painted without having paid the license, so to speak.

Wendtland was an autodidact. Perhaps he felt that, being a close relative of H. Neubrandt, a prestigious architect and sculptor, he could do without an art education. His new exhibition was shortly opening. In the weekly distribution of tasks, Schattendorf managed to send Sauer to cover it. "An innovative artist, technically not very skilful, but with the fresh touch of the self-taught," that's how he presented Wendtland for Sauer, who had never heard the painter's name.

On Monday, his review was devastating. Improvisation, lack of discernment for the combination of colours, inadequate disposition of the subjects, "ill-digested mixture of variegated influences."

Devastating, but after the subtle modifications that Schattendorf introduced, reinforcing an epithet, adding an adverb, it became ferocious.

"What is this Wendtland thing?" asked Furtenberg, who called him early in the morning. Furtenberg knew nothing about art, but there had been complaints.

"That's the problem, you see," Schattendorf explained. "Some people have had their day, they have lost their tact, their flair. I've already mentioned it to you."

"Don't throw this back to me ! You've accepted the chief position, with all that it implies. Am I wrong?"

Without waiting for an answer, he went on:

"This blunder has occurred under your authority and responsibility, I accept no excuses."

"You know, Herr Furtenberg, Sauer is a tricky case. He's been an editor since ..."

"Did I ask for details? That is your job, these incidents must not happen again. And you'll call immediately Neubrandt to apologize."

Among the informations that Schattendorf had given Sauer about Wendtland, there was one missing: Neubrandt, the painter's uncle, was also Madame Furtenberg's cousin.

Schattendorf watched the old editor clean his desk, pick up one by one his mementos, his photos, his medals. Justice had been done. Sauer's cruelty had been punished by his own pen.

He held out his hand, but the man stared at him with hatred and left without a word. To go to the Family Announcements and Obituaries section.

Today, he realized it had been a mistake; revenge is the pleasure of the weak, and he had got himself an enemy gratuitously. When he's got his position at the Council, he will find some way of compensating Sauer. An honorary position or a medal.

No, Schattendorf was not proud of that episode, but still, it did earn him the sympathies of Ruprecht Wendtland, sympathies that were so important for him in his new political career.

For some time, Vittorio Carraro had been a politically dubious figure for Schattendorf. Not a renegade, he did not use such words as lightly as Heinz or Paul, but someone who was better avoided.

But now that he had been himself accused and brought to justice, tried and condemned, proscribed and stigmatized, he wondered whether he had been fair to the Italian. He called him. He was surprised at the warmth of Vittorio's reaction. As if they never had quarrelled, as if Schattendorf never had blamed him for having sold his soul to the Duce in exchange for a luxurious office with a view to the Tiergarten.

"Nonsense!" said the Italian. "Didn't we fight all the time, you and I, like guys do, loyally? Of course we are friends, we have always been! So, how is Lotte? And Violetta, do you still see her?"

Vittorio's cordiality comforted him, a cordiality which the people of Der Bruch never had been generous with, and which today they refused him.

"Lotte, that's the past," replied Schattendorf. "Vittorio, you're talking with a man who has contracted those sacred bonds which go under the name of matrimonial."

"No more bohemian life, huh, Hans? Well, all must end one day. But when something dies, another thing begins."

After which, he moved on to politics:

"Things are changing, Hans, things are finally going in the right direction. You're part of the movement, I take it? "

"No... "

"But, what in earth are you waiting for? Everyone who aspires to play a role in the new Germany must take sides, without further delay. History does not wait, Hans. Each day counts!"

Schattendorf found it shocking. As if working for a newspaper that was sympathetic to the new Chancellor forced him to join his party.

"Hans: National Socialism is essentially the political version of the expressionist movement. In the same way that Kirchner and Nolde express the very deepest in the Germanic soul, the Führer interprets the most authentic sentiments of the German people."

"You're quite mad, you know. And your prose is a tad pompous, if you don't mind my saying so," laughed Schattendorf, uncomfortably.

But he had to admit that the world was changing at terrific speed. Nineteenth century ideas were dusty, he had to agree with Vittorio on that point. The twentieth century demanded new solutions. But, was it the National Socialists who propose those solutions?

He had always been proud of his freedom of opinion. He was cured from his left-wing illusions, but the traditionalist right did not attract him either: his father-in-law's German National Party was a nostalgic, a reactionary force.

A few days later the Italian telephoned him.

"Hans," he said, "I have a job for you."

"You may have forgotten it," Schattendorf replied, "but I already have one."

"When I say 'a job' I mean a mission. Enough of writing art reviews, Hans! The time for action has come. "

Becoming Head of Cultural Action of a large district of Berlin. That's what he wanted to discuss with him.

"But... " Schattendorf objected.

"You see, I know the new minister of education for the Prussian State. They are desperately looking for capable people in the field of culture. Well, I gave him the name of a journalist who knows that field perfectly, someone with a clear political position, a person who is both energetic and brave. And this person is a member of the party, I presume, the minister asked. Of course, I replied."

"But...."

"So, Hans, what you're going to do now is go to Dresdenerstrasse 14. No, forget it, stay where you are, I'll send my secretary to fetch the registration form and hand it over to you. What you do is, go to the Civil Registry and get a certificate of aryanity. And don't forget your family record book. "

"I will do nothing of the sort," replied a furious Schattendorf. "My thinking will never wear a uniform, I don't let myself be enrolled."

It was a mistake to get in touch with him again, he thought. He resolved to cut off all contacts with him. He was going to tell him so, but the Italian had already hung up. So much the worse, he decided, and ordered the reception not to pass any calls from Carraro.

All the same, he had to admit that he had never seen a communion between the different strata of the population comparable to those early days of the new regime. This fraternal climate, this rebirth of forgotten social ties. January 30, 1933 had released energies with a potential that seemed impossible to estimate.

If one day I adhere to the NSDAP, Schattendorf said to himself - and I do not see how I could take such a decision - it will obey to a certain logic; my thinking has always been radical and the National Socialists are today the only party that can be called revolutionary. They are, in fact, what the German left would have been if it had not been anaesthetized and submitted to the Kremlin.

Fifteen days later, Schattendorf had got his party card, number 2.640.243.

"Well, Hans, was I right or was I wrong?" Carraro asked.

"You were wrong. Dead wrong. You don't understand the reasons for my decision."

It was not because he subscribed totally to Hitler's ideas, far from it. Not because he found the swastika appealing; in fact he considered all those symbols ridiculous. No, it was because the Party was a breath of fresh air in the oppressive, stuffy atmosphere of an impotent parliamentarism. And above all, it was a need for action, the desire to get down to work once and for all. To change the world, to put an end to the sterile reflection. As Head of Cultural Action in a large district of the capital, he would have a free hand to implement a transformation, to finally clean the stables. To do away with all octogenarians, professors, teachers, deans, rectors. To transfuse new blood to the German culture. To revive it, to regenerate it.

24

Peter Litzke and Gerhard will come to the office at three o'clock.
Schattendorf can go home in between.

He gives Irene an absent-minded kiss, she reproaches him for not
having come to lunch.

"Excuse me, darling, I was terribly busy."

"But Hans, couldn't you have told me in advance?"

"Irene, try to understand. If I miss a lunch, if the soup gets cold,
that's trifles. It's my career that's at stake."

"But... what's going on?"

He does not keep her up to date on all his affairs. No point in
telling her about the picture.

"It's complicated, but it has to do with the *Entartete Kunst*
exhibition, the one organized by Dunkels."

She sighs. "That man is really unpleasant. But Hans, I do not find
it a good idea to associate with those students either. They are
troublemakers," she adds with a gesture of dislike. "What you need is
to cultivate the friendship of serious people, people of substance, like
Wendtland."

He caresses her hair.

"Thank you for your patience, I will never be thankful enough for
having met you."

And it is true that Irene - elegant, refined - is perfect to have at his side in formal receptions. Violetta or Lotte would have been impossible.

The apartment of the Kastanienallee is not very spacious, but it is well located and with a large living room which she has furnished herself. Wing chairs covered in yellow velvet, porcelain vases, a baroque oak table, solid, massive, a large sideboard, everything on a thick Persian rug, a wedding gift from an uncle of Irene, ambassador to Tehran.

The Bauhaus gang would have sent all this to the stake; the salon exudes the bourgeois composure that he himself has always loathed. Much has changed in his views, but on this point Schattendorf remained faithful to Harry: he does not feel comfortable here. He is not at home, even if his name appears on the deed of property. But the fact is that this traditional atmosphere is the one he needs. Irene's taste is the taste of the people whose confidence it's essential for him to win.

At three o'clock he's back in Spandau. Peter is already waiting, together with Gerhard, another member of the group, and a third one which Schattendorf has not met before. He looks at him suspiciously and asks him politely to leave them alone for a moment.

"Who is it?" he asks Peter.

Gerhard explains: Carl is a student in economics. "He has been a Communist, he has lots of enthusiasm but no political education. He has had big problems at the university, communists are not welcome there. But I defended him."

"You did well," agrees Schattendorf. "Many of them are sincere people who have chosen the wrong path, as Minister Goebbels says. But about this Carl ..."

"That's exactly what I told him," interrupts Gerhard. "There is a lot of truth in Communism, but it is a cold doctrine. But an excellent raw material because, you take Communism, you infuse it with a soul and, what do you get? First-rate national socialism. "

"Well put. You're a born propagandist, but what I wanted to talk about was the *Entartete Kunst* exhibition. It is, as you know, Dunkels' attempt to get at me, at us."

"Yes," Gerhard alleges, "but who will see it? If it was at the Palais maybe, but in Kreuzberg?"

"In any case, that exhibition will take place and we can do nothing about it. But there is one thing we can do: to prevent a work in particular from being shown there. If it were, it would cause us serious problems. Peter knows what I mean. "

Gerhard wants to ask another question, but Peter interrupts.

"Tell us what to do," he asks simply.

"Peter, you know someone at that gasometer."

"The Pole, yes. I know how to handle him."

"But it's no longer a question of just having a look at the picture, you understand? Now we are going to get things done."

Kastanienallee. Vittorio comes in. He kisses Irene's hand.

"How is the dazzling Madame Schattendorf-Furtenberg today?" asks the Italian.

"Always so courteous, Vittorio," she replies coldly. "Shall I bring you anything to drink?"

"Not for me, thank you," says Carraro, "I have to be in Friedenau in half an hour. I'm tired of all these formalities, only to assign us what is just a vacant lot. As if it was a palace we are asking for. No, we need just the building land, the rest will be paid by us, Rome has already allocated the funds. Hans, you'll have to take care of this, once you are in the Council! "

"It's the Italian Cultural Institute," explains Schattendorf to Irene.

"Ah yes, it's a pity," she comments, and walks away to the kitchen. She does not like Carraro, she finds him pretentious, insincere.

"Did you get any more information?" asks Vittorio.

Schattendorf shrugs.

"And she?" asks the Italian, "what does she say?"

"Irene doesn't know."

"I don't mean Irene."

"Ah."

"What does she think?"

"I have not seen Violetta for a week."

"She might know something. After all, she was involved too."

"Listen Vittorio," replies Schattendorf annoyed, "we have all the information we need. Now we have to get rid of the damn thing, that's all."

"I do not understand why you did not do it long ago."

"You think I did not try? I went to see Bang immediately after starting at the *National-Zeitung*. It's in the trash, he told me."

"Well," says Vittorio, "then the Dane took you for a ride. And watch out Hans: do not let Violetta fool you too."

"What are you saying?" reacts Schattendorf.

"I'm telling you to be careful. Not to leave any loose ends."

"No loose ends here."

"Violetta can cause you more harm than that bleeding picture. You know what we should do? Take her out of the country. I can find her a job in Vienna, I know the director of the *Albertina*."

"I meet her once a month, and always discreetly," says Schattendorf.

"Once a month? Or once a week? You're not serious, Hans. Irene will find out one day or another and you cannot afford to break with her. Without Irene, without her father, you lose half of your backing."

Send her to Vienna, what an idea, thinks Schattendorf. Her place is here in Berlin. Only, she must redirect her creativity in a positive sense, she must join this great current which has set in motion never to stop. "The negativity is over," he has told her so many times, "it's time to build now, with joy and enthusiasm."

"You want me to betray myself" was her reaction.

"On the contrary, I want you to be faithful to what really matters. Have I betrayed myself? Am I an apostate?"

"You're Harry. I am Violetta."

She's Violetta, no doubt about that. She is so amazingly Violetta. He misses her, her boldness, her freedom. The Muse of Moabit. She was not yet called like that when he first met her, an evening in 1924 or 1925. Anita Berber was with her and attracted the attention of all. But his visual field was filled, saturated, by Violetta.

She was still a model at that time.

"A model: an actress at rest," he improvised, his creativity suddenly aroused at the sight of her. "A model: abruptly stopped movement. A murder? Frozen movement, but not really dead. Dead, yes, but still alive. Petrified, turned to stone, but stone ready to become flesh again."

He barely understood himself what came out of his mouth, once his inspiration was awakened, unbridled. "Not easy to be a living statue," he insisted. "Antinomy requiring superhuman concentration, a focusing in the pure Being."

She looked at him amazed. In admiration? Astonished in any case. And that was what he wanted. It always worked. It worked with her. Even though she later realized that his monologue was based on a poem by Dieter, published the week before in Der Bruch.

Everybody has seen Violetta, but few can recognize her. She is in *Suffering Nude* by Thiermann, in *Venus in Hat* by Fuchs, in *Margot* by Minkowski, although she is blonde there.

She has talent the broad. But she lacked a guide, like all the others, martyrs of art, truncated destinies. She will return, as others will. And that is precisely his mission, only he can carry it out.

"Violetta's place is here, Vittorio," he insists. "If it's important to recruit Nolde and Thiermann, it is also necessary to bring her to our side."

"But ... She has not changed, she ... she's not one of us ..."

"Every truly creative artist will inevitably be with us, with our movement."

"Let me handle this, Hans. She'll stay in Vienna for six months. Once your position is consolidated, we bring her back. But now I have to go."

Carraro wants to say goodbye to Irene, but she is out, says the maid. In the landing he bumps into Peter Litzke.

"I was there," Peter tells Schattendorf, "but I did not see the Pole. The boss, the professor, was there though, and he wouldn't leave, he was immersed in his files and folders. Eventually he spotted me. I had to go."

"Zero result then," says Schattendorf.

"I would not go that far," Peter corrects him with a mischievous smile.

"Get to the point!"

He begins to regret having used the students.

"The fact is that Carl ..." begins Peter.

"Again this Carl? I told you to go, not bring a whole escort with you. And especially someone as inexperienced as that boy. That's why Clausen spotted you."

"Wait, Hans, it turns out that Carl recognized another guy, someone who lives in Friedrichshain, like him."

"Stop it," Schattendorf asks, "this is going too fast for me. Carl has a friend who works at the exhibition, at the EnKu, is that right?"

Peter laughs.

"Hardly a friend. The bloke broke once Carl's teeth in a street fight. Carl was a communist before, remember?"

The previous night he had had trouble falling asleep, but now he is sure to sleep like two logs. Peter went to see the guy that Carl knows. He agreed to get the painting for them, for a fee. The problem is solved.

That is the point of having a network. Vittorio overestimates the importance of Irene's father for him, and underrates that of *Nation und Kultur*. They are not many, but they are dedicated and resourceful.

What with the exhilaration of having solved the problem in such an effective way, he felt, for the first time in weeks, the urge to make love to his wife. But Irene is already asleep. His gaze stops on the mirror in front of the bed. The reflection of a picture hanging above the bedside: a Rhine landscape, a forest. He would gladly throw it into

251

the fireplace of the living-room; those pines, larches and firs would burn like hell.

He lifts the sheet, hoping to see his wife's half naked body. But tonight Irene sleeps in a nightgown. He caresses her with a light hand. She moves, but instead of waking up, she turns around and starts snoring gently.

He falls asleep too.

When Dunkels showed him the photograph, Curt Hagener recognized the painting right away, even though it was badly lit, small-sized and in black and white. And it did not take him too long to remember where he had seen it.

The intendant Oberfrunck is interested in it. Hardly a surprise, as the piece is plain pornography. Has he bought it through the French dealer? Nina Bovrik cannot confirm it, but she does know that Morel has a customer, an important person who collects erotic art but whose name he never mentions.

He was about to pass on this valuable information to Dunkels, when the idea came to him to look for Geza Nemes, who used to work for Bang, the Dane. Why not go to *Elektroland*? At the same time, he could see if the recording of Berg's *lieder* had arrived. At *Musikhaus* they did not have it yet.

"Take your patented automatic gramophone right now and pay in twelve monthly instalments," urges a signboard. And for those who already own a music player, the store offers the latest song hits: *Heartaches*, with Ted Wheems and his orchestra, and *Veronika der Lenz ist da*, by the Comedian Harmonists.

Nemes was busy demonstrating to a customer how simple it is to operate a phono-suitcase, irreplaceable for a picnic.

"No, I do not see what picture you're talking about," is the answer he gives to Hagener.

"It won a prize, doesn't it ring a bell? The Argus Prize."

Nemes bursts out laughing.

"Well, yes, actually I can tell you something about it," he says playfully. "Do you know why the prize was called like that? It was created by Bang himself, that you know, but ..."

Hagener interrupts him:

"Geza, what I'm trying to find out, and I'm pretty sure you know it, it is to whom the Dane sold the picture."

"Sorry Hagener, I can't help you."

As if Geza Nemes had not been aware of everything that took place at the Maus, as if it was not he who decided even the colour of the toilet paper - coral red, an exclusivity in the universe of Berlin's public toilets.

But Hagener notices that Nemes did not say, "I do not know." He said, "I cannot help you."

"Listen, Geza, are you making a good living here?"

"Last month I sold twelve gramophones, but this month has started so-so."

"Haven't you thought of going back to journalism? You have lots of experience, don't you?"

"You can say that twice. I worked at *Pankower Tageblatt*, among others, but above all, I was in charge of press relations for Max Reinhardt's group. And I can prove it."

"So you must have many contacts."

"Today, contacts are of no use. They would be, if I were a German citizen."

"You see Geza, I know a newspaper where both a Polish and a Czech are working."

"And the authorities say nothing?"

"They don't have time to take care of everything. Mind you, it's not the *Vossische Zeitung* I'm talking of. It's a small local newspaper."

Geza looks confused. He thinks. Then he asks: "Do you believe you could help me to get a job there?"

"I do. The editor is an old buddy. And by the way, do you know Gregorius?"

"The professor? I know him from Café Schimmel."

"Well, it's precisely in that paper that he writes his astrology column. Geza, let me ask you something in my turn: are you absolutely sure that you don't remember anything about that painting? Not even if you make an effort?"

The other looks at him without replying.

"Can we meet in an hour? At the Red Top?" he asks finally.

When the Hungarian enters the bar, little frequented in the afternoon, Hagener is already standing at the counter. At Geza's request, they take a table at the back.

"Are you sure you can help me, Hagener? Are you serious about it?" asks he anxiously.

"I'm not in the habit of lying."

Then, Geza makes up his mind:

"Do you remember that Bang had a few paintings at the cabaret? The Dane didn't know much about art, but he knew what he liked. He had a number of etchings and even an oil by Grosz. So, when he realized the big changes which would soon take place in the country, no good for his business, you understand, well, he decided to sell off everything. A dealer came, and he offered a nine hundred marks for

254

the Grosz, which Bang thought was too little. But on the other hand – would you believe it? – he was very interested in the painting you mention. He thought it was a Grosz too ... "

"And so it was," says Hagener. "Erwin Keller would never have bought it if there had not been a certificate of authenticity."

Geza smiles.

"There was a certificate, alright. I know all kind of people in Berlin and I could help Bang to obtain the necessary papers. But in addition to that, Grosz himself authenticated it! "

Hagener looks at him, nonplussed.

"Grosz came often to the Maus, he had got chummy with Bang. The last night before closing down for good, we threw a party. Everybody was drunk, including Schramme and her girls. Grosz, plastered as the others, signed a paper to Bang certifying paternity. With all due papers and even a document signed by the author, no problem to sell it. By the way, it is with the money he got for that fake that Bang paid me a lump sum that kept me alive for a few months until I got the job at *Elektroland*. "

"A fake? But, if it was not Grosz, who had painted it?"

Geza stared incredulously at him.

"But, don't you know that?"

25

"Listen, Wassingher," Herr Braillowski had said that day of May 1933 when he had to sack Sasha. "You are of German origin, right? So apply for the citizenship and I will be able to rehire you."

Easy solution, simple. Of an irrefutable logic, considered undoubtedly the chief photographer.

There followed three months of unemployment, only interrupted by a few assignments in sectors of lesser strategic importance; neither the Chancellor nor Göring seemed to regard the post of dishwasher at the Bar Lichtburg in Bergstrasse or the distribution of *Morgenpost* in the letter boxes as key to the Reich's destiny.

At the end of those months, Lena got him finally a job. While at the Art Academy, she had make friends with Hannelore Günther, who had afterwards obtained, unlike Lena, a post in accord with her skills, thanks to her father, a professor in Breslau. The professor, who was in charge of a Berlin exhibition, was temporarily lodged in his daughter's flat and it was there that Lena met him.

"Herr Professor: I do not want to bother you, but if you ever needed someone with an artistic background, then ..."

"Fräulein, the exhibition will last barely two months, it would not make sense for you to leave your job for so little."

But Lena was intimate with someone who would be thankful for any work however temporary.

"If he's hard-working, if he knows about electricity and carpentry, there may be a possibility for your fiancé," said the professor.

But even for that insignificant job, German nationality was important, not to mention the certificate of aryanity.

At the same time, being a short-term job and Clausen having testified to the urgent need for something as rare as an electrician and carpenter with experience in the field of art (of film, in Sasha's case), the local delegation of the Ministry closed its eyes.

Sasha Wassingher had entered Germany as a Soviet citizen in 1928, at a time when no one cared whether his parents were Aryan or not. Wassingher is a German surname, the ancestors of his father had left the Rhineland for Russia a century and a half earlier.

But since the Nazis took over, things have changed. The fact that a family name sounds German is not enough for them. The current authorities require a certificate of aryanity. Sasha must prove the German origin of his four grandparents.

And if Sasha's father's name is clearly Germanic, his mother's name is Rebecca Perelboim.

But no one can expect him to produce the birth certificate of his mother; it would be necessary to contact the authorities of Tonkoschurovka, province of Saratov. And the bad relations between Germany and the USSR make these formalities unfeasible.

As a Volga German and a refugee of communism, he can count on a certain benevolence from the civil servants. But not on them giving him a racial certificate.

He and Lena were at Tom's, a cousin of hers, a few days ago. Tom works for an aeronautical company. The Nazis will calm down, he assures. If they expel all Jews, all scientists, film-makers, professors

258

and industrialists with Semitic components in their genetics, the economy will suffer. The Nazis are not stupid.

"And anyway, you're not Jewish," he said to Sasha with a slap on his back. "I'll explain to you how they reason, these people: if your two parents are Jewish, you are too. If your father is Jewish and your mother half Jewish, bad luck: you're still Jewish. But let us consider the following case: Jewish mother but wholly Aryan father: congratulations, you are not Jewish! "

"And how do you know that?" wondered a sceptical Lena.

"Because that situation arises often in our company. If the authorities asked us for your personal data, we would answer: Alexander Wassingher is a German, born outside the Reich but of German blood nonetheless. He is *Volksdeutsch*, and so is his mother."

"But let's say that someone who wants Sasha's post shows up and says, 'Her mother's name is Rebecca.'"

"Who in Berlin can know the name of that lady? But if so, I'd say: You are lying. Case is closed. "

"But if he cannot prove that her name is Jewish, you cannot prove either that her maiden name is German."

"In fact, no one can prove anything, since those archives are thousands of miles from Berlin, but I would give him the benefit of the doubt. After all, his appearance is more Teutonic than mine."

"But Tom... "

"Yes, I know what you are thinking: let's suppose someone makes an expedition to Tonkoschurovka and comes back with a briefcase full of documents proving that Sasha's mother is not Aryan. As he cannot prove, because it is not true, that any of his two paternal grandparents is Jewish too, the case is settled: Sasha has, at worst, two grandparents of Hebraic race and is therefore a *mischling*, a fifty-fifty,

259

a half-breed, which is very different from being completely Jewish. You see, I know a senior Air Force official whose father is Jewish, his name is Milch, Erhard Milch, Göring's man of confidence, nothing less. "

"A half-breed?" said Lena in disbelief.

"But with skills that are valuable for the Reich, and a war veteran moreover."

"It is true that in order to determine who is Jew and who is not, they will need regiments of ethnologists, of lawyers, and finally, we are all half-breeds in some degree," Lena admitted.

"That's what I mean," Tom concludes triumphantly. "It was easy for Hitler to launch a crusade against the Jews, but what is a Jew exactly? In the end, what counts is Hitler's opinion. If he decides you are an Aryan, then you are."

"The Nazis will not last long, thinks Tom" says Lena as they head home. "He takes his desires for the reality. And in the meantime, you'll survive washing dishes, a job for *mischlings*. Why don't you write to your Kansas parents instead? In the U.S. nobody cares whether your mother's name is Perelboim, Redmann or Schultz. "

An uncle of his had emigrated, like many other Volga Germans, twenty years earlier. Sasha had exchanged letters with him. Also Lena had reasons to emigrate. She did not want to finish her days as a secretary. Perhaps her skills would be better appreciated elsewhere.

If there was no Hitler, if it was still Brüning or Von Papen who controlled the destinies of the country, Sasha would never dream of leaving. And the worst is that he does not know why he has to. If somebody told him: you have to go because you are a Soviet citizen and our country is at war with yours, then he would understand. If they told him: you have to leave because we do not need good technicians, because none of your abilities are of any use to us, then he would leave without complaining.

But, "you have to leave because you have red hair," "because you entered Germany on a Friday and not on a Monday," "because your passport has an odd number."

"You have to go because you're not Protestant, because you're neither Catholic, nor Muslim, nor Buddhist, because you are, of all things a man can be, Jewish."

He hardly knows what it means to be a Jew. He never set foot in a synagogue. It is true that he does not feel German either, although he speaks the language well, having learned it in his childhood. But still less feels he Jewish. He feels Russian more than anything else, but a special Russian, a different Russian and, at present, an ex-Russian. Berliner of Russian origin, that's how he defines himself.

Politics have never interested Sasha, but politics are very interested in him. He has to face it: people like him have no future in Germany. In the U.S.? Maybe.

Had the apartment been theirs, Lena would change everything. The dark green wallpaper, with medallions and flowers. The furniture, old-fashioned and in sombre brown tones. A clock on the wall and, on a pedestal, a blackened bronze bust representing a Greek ephebe. A night scene in a forest, lit by a lamp fixed on the frame of the painting, Lena replaced immediately by a reproduction of Renoir.

If the apartment was hers and Sasha's, she would only keep the beautiful Turkish bed-top, with a geometric design in various shades of red. Everything else: out!

The toilets are in the corridor, but in the room there is a sink, next to which they placed a bowl on a metal tripod. They have also a screen that protects from the light and allows Lena to sleep an extra half hour while Sasha is washing and having breakfast.

"Lena," says Sasha, "what do you know about Eberhard Novak?"

"Who?"

"A painter. He exposes in the gasometer, in the EDeKA."

He produces the catalogue and shows her the black and white reproduction of *The Joy is Back*. Lena looks at it and shakes her head.

"No, never heard of him. He must be one of those new talents discovered by the Nazis."

"Well, talent he has, that's for sure. This photograph doesn't do justice to the painting. It's an impressive picture, rich colours and a warm range of tones."

Lena looks at him with affectionate irony:

"That could be professor Clausen talking. I give him a technician and he sends me back what? A full-fledged art critic."

"Do not laugh until you have seen the picture in real life," he says. "The expo opens the day after tomorrow."

"I'd rather see your expo."

"Frankly, after having seen the EDeKA, I'm ashamed of ours. Either you know how to paint or you don't. Novak knows. And then, you see, Lena, I could swear I have seen this picture before."

"But you never visit exhibitions. In one of my books maybe? But I don't have books about that kind of stuff."

She gets up, goes to the book-shelf, looks at the books' spines, pulls out one of them, examines it and then puts it back in its place. Eventually she finds it: a book published by *IA-Verlag*, a publishing house close to the Communist Party. "Proletarian Art of the World."

Reproductions of Brodsky, Gerasimov, Kasatkin, and other representatives of the socialist style.

She lays the volume on the table, leafs it for a moment, checks the table of contents, then turns the pages, quickly but without skipping any illustration. But she fails to find the one she's looking for.

Lena has been once a party sympathizer, but she never cared for the brand of realism that this volume illustrates. "It goes back to the past, to the nineteenth century. The comrades will have to forgive me but that stuff is not my cup of tea."

"I had already seen that kind of things in Saratov," says Sasha. "I cannot judge if they are true masterpieces according to all the artistic criteria, but ordinary people like them and they are well made. They are ... honest."

"You mean Lissitsky and Malevich are dishonest?"

"I don't say that, but I do not understand what they do. I would need an explanation, and that is exactly what..."

"What explanations? You still don't get it, Sasha."

"... and that's exactly what Hitler says: 'Works of art that are not capable of being understood in themselves, but need some pretentious instruction book to justify their existence, are not true works of art'."

"Hitler? Did he say that?"

"I read it in the EnKu catalogue."

"So? Who cares what he says? It has nothing to do with explanations, it's about educating your taste. Do you think that the first time perspective was used in a painting, back in the Renaissance, everybody liked it? But today our taste has evolved and it is on the contrary medieval paintings without perspective which seem odd to us."

"As you like. All I say is that the kind of art you call modern does not appeal to me, it appeals to nobody."

"It appeals to me. "

"Oh, but you have a degree in Art History. Art must address itself to the people, as cinema does. If you ask Maier, the neighbour next door, if he prefers to go see a painting of Kirchner at the Crown Prince Museum or *The Vampire of Düsseldorf* at the Zoo-Palast, you can be sure he will not hesitate. "

"And what is that supposed to prove?"

And before he can reply, she adds:

"And please stop talking about Maier." The neighbour regularly complains because Lena leaves her wet umbrella in the landing or Sasha throw a cigarette butt at the building's entrance.

She begins to clear the table, first the cups with their saucers, then the glasses. She's on her way to do the same with the coffee pot, but she stops short. She thinks for a moment, then she turns towards the library. Sasha caresses her, but she ignores him. She scrutinizes the spines of the books she has already examined.

"Ah, here it is," she mutters.

She takes out an in-folio volume, large and heavy. On the cover, some athletic workers leaving their factory. The title is in Cyrillic.

"I knew I had it," she says, leafing through the volume and studying the reproductions, most of them monochromatic but some in colour.

Sasha leans over the table to read the book's spine. *Here is the art of our people* is the title in translation.

He goes out to the hall and closes the door behind him. But just when he's opening the door of the communal lavatory, he hears Lena exclaiming:

"It's this one!"

He comes back. She shows him an illustration. Sasha utters a cry of rapture.

The reproduction that Lena shows him is in black and white, but it is *The Joy is Back*, no doubt about it. Except for a few details; the architecture of the building is not identical and the women have scarves on their heads. Not to mention another detail: the portrait on the platform does not represent the Führer but another gentleman, with moustaches too, but bushier. The Little Father of the Peoples. Comrade Stalin.

"But," he mutters, "the author is not Novak."

"Viktor Germann," states the Cyrillic text at the bottom of the image.

"It must be Hermann," Sasha explains. "The h does not exist in Russian and it is replaced by a g when transliterating foreign names."

And he translates the title of the work as *Celebration at the kolkhoz*. Prize of the Culture Section of the Peasant Front, Dnipropetrovsk District.

"No wonder it reminds you of your childhood," says Lena.

He picks up Peter and in a few minutes they are at the place agreed with Schultze, Carl's "friend", not far from the gasometer. It's a quarter to seven in the morning.

"After we get rid of the painting, we go straight to my office," announces Schattendorf. "We'll make an inventory of the damage done by Dunkels."

They will contact the museums of the region to gather information about the works they have lent to the EnKu. How many of them have been returned?

A fellow approaches, tall and well built, though with a burgeoning belly. He walks briskly, waddling his hips slightly. Under his arm, a package that doesn't look heavy.

"Comrade," says Peter, who shakes hands with him, "allow me to offer you a compensation, after all this exceeds your usual duties."

He hands him two notes of fifty marks.

Schultze has a slight tremor. Then he shakes his head.

"In no way comrade. My principles forbid it. No way."

"Accept fifty at least," insists Peter.

He hesitates. Showing his disinterested dedication to the cause can be useful. On the other hand, a stubborn refusal could offend these highly placed people. He mutters a few grateful words, folds the note in half and slips it into his pocket.

A victory, congratulates Schattendorf himself, watching the scene from the car. A quick and effective intervention. Abscess removed successfully, without blood, without traces.

Peter inquires about the fate of the unselected works. Schultze cannot answer but, given the nature of the objects, he would not be surprised if many of them were eliminated.

"Some of those things are truly depraved. A real shame, I can tell you that", he adds.

He has wrapped the painting without taking apart the canvas from the frame. A parcel of one meter by sixty centimetres. Peter tries to unpack it, but it's tied up with a thick rope. Schultze pulls a penknife out of his pocket and cuts it. Peter seizes the parcel and takes it to the car.

Schattendorf removes the wrapping paper.

A naked woman, her big buttocks just in front of the nose of a man, a customer. On the other end, another character looks lecherously at her. Behind the heavy red velvet curtains we see a trio, two women and a man, naked all three and in the process of performing a number of sexual acts.

Schattendorf forgets all precaution. He gets out of the car and goes up to Schultze.

"What have you brought me?" he exclaims. "I asked you to bring a Grosz, the only Grosz you have!"

"I'm sorry" Schultze stammers. "The comrade here told me it was a scene with prostitutes."

"One. One whore. And two men. She sucks off one of them, the other is standing behind her ."

Schultze's face lights up:

"Oh, I see ! She does not actually suck, she has a cigarette in her mouth, but ..."

"That's it," says Schattendorf impatiently. "Go get it immediately, there's no time to lose."

"But ..."

"It's not seven o'clock yet. What time do the others arrive?"

"Well, professor Clausen does not arrive until eight, but ..."

"Go then, right now! What are you waiting for?"

"But, comrade, ... Excuse me, may I ask your name?"

"Oberfrunck," belches Schattendorf. "Chief Intendant at the Heritage Department."

"Comrade Oberfrunck: that painting has already been selected. "

"Are you talking about the final selection?"

"Yes," confirms Schultze. "It is not possible to change it, it is beyond my power," he concludes in an apologetic tone, handing the fifty mark note back to Peter.

"But," replies Schattendorf, "there must still be a way of ...."

"Comrade Oberfrunck, I assure you, on my honour, that the painting will be punctually returned to its owner once the exhibition is closed. Not all the objects will, but regarding the one you are concerned about, I will personally take care of it. "

Peter goes up to the car. They take the Westkorso. At this time there is still little traffic. Twenty minutes later, they are in Spandau.

"We are going to counter-attack, to open a new front," Schattendorf says, breaking a long silence. "This very afternoon I'll file a complaint with the Ministry. As for that picture, we did what we could."

If he reports the actions of Dunkels, without further delay, his position will be weakened to such a degree that no foul tricks he attempts with *Still Life* will be of help to him. If he has requisitioned two hundred works, a third or more must come from private galleries. He will not dare to attack those. One hundred and thirty left. He will not destroy them all, it is more likely that he wants to show his power by damaging a dozen, but already that will suffice to convict him. Not even Rosenberg's support will be enough to protect him. The destruction of state property is a criminal offence.

He makes a few calls, while Peter takes notes. The student goes through the catalogue of Spandau's Expressionist exhibition, organized by Cultural Action. Schattendorf is certain that it was that catalogue – his catalogue – which served as a basis for Dunkels to pick the works for the EnKu; his knowledge of modern art would not allow him to make a selection himself.

After two hours, Peter takes leave.

As long as they were working, as long as they were focused on a specific task, Schattendorf had not had time to ruminate. Now that Peter has left and he's alone in his office, the idea of what is bound to happen, of what will inevitably happen, haunts him again.

He had considered the problem solved. He had sold the bear's skin, but the beast was alive and ready to pounce on him. The battle is not yet lost, but it is better to face it: if the picture is exhibited, if investigations are carried out, his career in the Movement is over.

He reclines on a comfortable armchair, pours himself a brandy and lights a cigar. He has done what could be done. There is nothing more he can do. Nothing.

Acknowledging his helplessness has a sedative effect. A somnolence invades him.

270

A bonfire in the middle of the Unter den Linden. A group of people vociferate, others perform an oriental dance. A woman who resembles Violetta is there. All of a sudden she exclaims: "It is he, it is he!" He wants to flee, but the crowd prevents him. Violetta, for it is indeed she, shrieks with laughter. She wears a feather diadem on her head.

Suddenly, a shrill sound. "A fire engine," he thinks. The sound, which martyrs his ears, chases away the dancers as well, along with the people around the stake.

He jumps awake. The phone is ringing.

He takes a look at his watch: eleven o'clock. He lifts the handset. The line is of a frightful quality. Through the cracking and scraping noises he manages to recognize Gerhard's voice.

"Speak louder!" he asks.

On the other side, more throat clearings.

"I hear nothing! Speak slowlier!"

Finally he succeeds in identifying a word: "gasometer."

"Can't you find another phone?" he asks.

"... the employee ...... gasometer" is all that Schattendorf grasps. Gerhard hangs up.

Did he go to see Schultze? He is about to call Peter, but he stops himself; Gerhard will call again, better not to block the line.

"Hans? Are you using the phone?"

It's Irene.

"No, but I expect a call."

"Ah, tell me when you're done, I promised to call mom. It turns out that the pills the doctor gave her, the new doctor you know, well, the fact is that the migraines have worsened instead of disappearing,

271

can you believe it? What good are all medical advances if they are not able to cure a simple headache? "

Five minutes pass. Schultze may have reflected and decided to take down the picture after all, to take the sum he offered him.

Finally, a call. It's Peter.

"Where is Gerhard?" asks Schattendorf.

"He was going to make a visit to the gasometer."

"To do what?"

"That's what I asked him too. He says that we lose nothing in trying."

He hangs up and a second later, a new ringing sound. Now it's Gerhard.

"I had a hard time finding another cabin," he says. "Listen, we have an appointment, at noon, at the *Reissler* beer hall, it's near the gasometer."

"Has Schultze changed his mind?"

"No, not Schultze, it's another one, I do not know his name."

Clausen? No, that's not possible, says Schattendorf to himself.

Suddenly, an idea comes to his mind.

"He has a foreign accent?"

The expo opens on Saturday, but the professor asked Sasha to stay a few more days. It could be necessary to reposition a lamp or to fix a panel. Thereafter, he will not be needed any more. The personnel will be reduced to some attendants to welcome visitors, hand them the explanatory brochure and make sure that no one touches the paintings.

And speaking about exhibitions, who's the painter behind *The Joy is Back?* Viktor Hermann's *Celebration at the kolkhoz,* dates from five years ago, so Novak must have plagiarized it. Unless he painted it before Hermann. Who copied who?

But here comes Schultze. He busies himself with some crates at the reception. He stacks them on top of each other and carries them to the garage.

He comes up to Sasha. He behaves as if they were good colleagues, as if he had not threatened to denounce him as recently as the day before.

Sasha, who knows him well by now, guesses that Schultze has something to tell him but that he hesitates. Finally, he spills the beans:

"It's hard to believe," he says, "but there are people who are interested in this junk. Specifically in the one from room three, you know. A certain Oberfrunck, a big shot at the culture department. "

"The picture with the whore?"

"You don't believe it either, do you? And I'm talking of someone who works at the German Heritage Department. Well dressed, dark suit, tie, elegant hat. You see, Mister Sasha, high officials come to ask for our help. Maybe we are not so insignificant then."

In the evening, Sasha tells Lena the story.

"Who can it be?" he wonders. "Have you ever heard that name, Oberfrunck?"

"I haven't. Sasha, look here, a letter from the United States."

His uncle from Kansas says they can accommodate them, but only for a few days: they are seven in the family and they live in four small rooms. On the job side, everybody in their town works in the same tire factory, and the firm is going soon out of business. Sasha should better try elsewhere. But: in the same envelope there is an invitation letter, which is mandatory to obtain a visa.

"Though we'll have to get married," says Sasha. "Otherwise the embassy will not give you the visa."

They've already discussed the subject and Lena does not like the idea. Her parents will be against it.

"Let's forget about Kansas," he says. "It's an unnecessary expense. Better to go straight to Los Angeles, where I can surely find a job: crisis or no crisis, the film industry is always booming."

The bus ticket from New York to Kansas costs fifteen dollars, he learned it from a former colleague who's been in America. Which means that, up to Los Angeles it should cost around twenty-five.

A thousand marks seem to Lena a minimum to start a new life on the other side of the ocean. "My parents will surely lend us something," she believes, "once they got used to the idea of me leaving."

Sasha makes some number crunching: at this moment his savings amount to one hundred marks. To save a thousand will take them a year, assuming he finds a job after the exhibition, a daring assumption to say the least.

But Leni, the secretary, looks cheerful; she's found a position at the Tax Office when her work here is over.

"It will take me an hour by the S-Bahn, but it is a good job," she says.

Willi comes to Sasha with some fuses he has been out to buy.

"And what will you do, after the expo?" wonders Sasha.

"On Monday I start at Hentze's," replies Willi.

A bearing maker, in Wedding.

"And how did you like it, to work here?"

The other looks around him.

"Not bad, though I know nothing about art."

"Well, let me tell you a secret: neither do I."

Both laugh heartily.

Today it has rained, but now the sun has a fair chance of breaking through the clouds. Sasha goes out for a puff. He takes some steps, approaches the vacant lot which serves as a parking place for the people working at both exhibitions, but also for the employees of the *Schuhpalast*, – a shoe factory – and the Sankt Johann hospital. He sees Clausen's Opel there. A good wash would do it no harm.

It is at that moment that a young man comes up to him. He cannot be much older than twenty. Without presenting himself, but with a friendly smile, he asks him if it would be possible to exchange a few words.

"But I have to go back to work," replies Sasha.

"It's just your work I want to talk about. Could you come to *Reissler's* at lunch time?"

"What is it about?"

"Your work, as I said. It is important. At the bar *Reissler*, if you know where it is."

"Is your name Oberfrunck, by any chance?"

The other looks at him, mystified.

Sasha thinks for a moment. He sees Leni coming in his direction, to have a smoke.

"Okay, at noon," he decides.

But as soon as the young man's gone, Sasha regrets it.

He wants to talk with him about his work, he says. Is he a policeman, or someone from Immigration? He would like to discuss it with Clausen, but the professor is not there. Sasha proceeds to the garage. He has to pack two paintings to be returned in the afternoon. But, where has the boy left the roll of wrapping paper?

Clausen is back. Sasha's going to approach him, but then he changes his mind. After all, the young man does not really look like a policeman. And then, the *Reissler* is full of people at lunchtime. Where is the risk?

Two hours later, he goes up the Dieffenbachstrasse. The bar-restaurant is a large room with the walls covered in green wooden panels and decorated with deer heads. All tables are taken by people who are busy filling up with proteins and calories for the second half of their working day.

He looks for the young man, but it is hard to detect him among the dozens of heads. Sasha takes a few steps towards the exit, and then someone touches his shoulder. It's him. And he's brought another fellow with him.

The new one sports a well-groomed moustache and wears a grey raincoat. It's weird, but Sasha is sure to have seen that character before.

"Eckart," he presents himself, with a nod but without offering to shake hands.

"Mr. Wassingher," he says, after having placed an order to the waiter, "I need to recover a painting. I'm referring to a work by George Grosz. It is urgent."

Another one interested in the Grosz. First Oberfrunck, now this Eckart. And the more he looks at him, the more certain he is of having met the fellow before.

"Given the exceptional character of the procedure, I am ready to reward your efforts in a pecuniary way. Three hundred marks."

Sasha has already asked himself the question, but it was strictly theoretical: would he dare to steal pictures like Schultze does? To wait for Clausen to leave, then hurry to get out before the night watchman arrives? It should not be too difficult.

He did more than just considering the idea, he even figured the best way to carry it out. After his work, he always goes through the parking lot to reach the Fichtestrasse. But he has seen an opening in the wire fencing that runs between the gasometer and a tennis court next to it. The court, where he has never seen anyone play, has its exit gate on the Urbanstrasse. He has taken that shortcut once, just to try a new way to the U-Bahn station.

He has considered the possibility, yes, but it was pure speculation, he would never have dared to put it into practice.

"Excuse me," he asks, "the quantity you mentioned, was it three hundred marks?"

At that price it is not even worth considering. He does not remember how much the object is evaluated in Clausen's blue notebook, but it must be ten times more.

"With all respect," he says, "and without wanting to take advantage of the situation ...."

"There is no situation to be taken advantage of," warns the other sternly.

That voice. Those high tones, now that he's upset.

And so he gets it! The guy is the monologist from the Blaue Maus! Sasha was there many times, with Vicki Lander, whose boyfriend, Fredi, played the piano in the cabaret. His hair is shorter and he's dressed more formally, but it's him, no doubt about it!

277

"I would be taking a great risk," Sasha alleges. "This work has already been selected and its photograph is on the catalogue of the exhibition."

"Are you German, sir?" asks Gerhard.

"Yes. I mean, I am of German ancestry, but I do not have the citizenship yet."

"Well," exclaims Schattendorf, "I find it outrageous that a foreigner is working illegally on an official project. Let us make this clear, sir: if three hundred marks are not enough for you, I will add another remuneration: not to denounce you. Now, go get me that picture. "

Sasha's savings have always been small. An opportunity like this will not present itself again. This guy is well dressed, his hat looks expensive. He can pay more than three hundred. On top of that, he is in a hurry; the exhibition opens tomorrow.

Thousand marks would pay their fare to New York, and with the rest of their savings they could survive a couple of months in Los Angeles, time enough to land a job.

"I beg your pardon, Herr Eckart, but I am not exaggerating when I speak of major risks. I understand that one of my colleagues has already declined your proposition."

Gerhard, to Schattendorf, in a low voice: "Just ask him to make disappear the bloody thing, to hide it somewhere for a few days or to tear it into pieces. For us it would be enough, wouldn't it?"

Schattendorf is red with rage. But he controls himself and increases his offer.

"Mr. Eckart," replies Sasha. "Five hundred marks is very generous indeed, but still not quite enough. I am sorry but I need a thousand marks."

"Are you kidding me? Well, if that's a joke, it's a bad one. You'll be deported tomorrow and that's definitely not a joke. Good day."

That's when Sasha plays what he believes is his master card:

"Mr. Eckart, you do not remember me, but we have already met. At the Blaue Maus, in Friedrichstadt."

Schattendorf's face becomes pale.

"I have not the slightest idea of what you're talking about," he stammers.

"Violetta Brenner used to sing there. There was another man, Dieter I think, doing monologues, and if I'm not mistaken, there was also someone called Harry Shadow. "

"Enough! I don't frequent the same places as you!" barks Schattendorf.

Gerhard knows nothing about the Maus, about Violetta, about Schattendorf's past.

He would willingly send the guy, not in deportation but straight to hell. But after all, a thousand marks is a reasonable price to get rid of *Still Life*.

"Alright," he mumbles. "But what proof do I have of your identity, that you are really working at the exhibition?"

"Doctor, I have no papers, it's a temporary job ..."

"Well, I'll settle for your identity papers then. Because you have that at least?"

"I have a passport. But I cannot leave it to you."

Schattendorf bursts out laughing.

"Listen: I'll advance you three hundred, the rest on delivery. This passport ," he says, hitting with his finger the booklet with the letters CCCP on its red cover, "is my only guarantee that you will not evaporate with my money. "

They set up an appointment for seven o'clock that same evening.

27

"He who has never sinned ... ," hums Curt Hagener.

He imagines the conversation he will have at Schlosskeller, in half an hour:

"Listen to me, Dunkels," he will begin, "the painting is not by Grosz and its name is not *Still Life with Three Characters.* Its author is Harry Shadow."

"That rings a bell," will Dunkels say.

"He published a literary magazine, he was one of those gravitating in *Der Sturm* galaxy, it's those times I'm talking about."

"But, the painting is not by Grosz? So what? What I asked you to look for is only one thing: why Oberfrunck is interested in it. Does it belong to him? Or does he want to buy it?"

"Forget Oberfrunck," Hagener will reply, "he has nothing to do with this. And as for the painting, yes, Grosz' signature is on the canvas, there is even a certificate of authenticity. And still, the picture is not his, because the one who won the Blaue Maus prize is Shadow, Harry Shadow. "

"Prize? What Mouse?"

"The Blaue Maus, a cabaret."

There, Hagener will make a dramatic pause and revel in the irritated look of the other. Dunkels does not like riddles. He only feels at ease with clear, crisp propositions.

He has never been an habitué of the Berlin night. He despises and hates that world. Prostitutes, hermaphrodites, perverts, in his view.

"I'll give you another key: he often appeared in that cabaret, as did madame Brenner, the Muse of Moabit."

There, at long last, a glimmer of intelligence will shine in those Doberman eyes.

"Yes, Brenner, and she was the lover of ..."

"Of Shadow. She still is."

"No, no. Of Schattendorf. But that's an old story."

He is not really stupid, Dunkels. He is able to solve an equation quickly and faultlessly, as long as it has only one unknown element, as long as the solution can be found by applying precise rules. In the equation that Hagener will propose him, at the Schlosskeller, thirty minutes from now, there will be too many factors: Grosz, Keller, Shadow, Brenner, Wendtland, Schattendorf.

But at last he will get the picture.

Schatten equals Shadow. Here it is, at last: a formula as clear as a bell. It means that it will not be Oberfrunck's head that will fall, but Schattendorf's, a rival much more dangerous for Dunkels, a prey ten times larger. It will fall like an overripe fruit in October.

It is not just the fact of being the author of that obscene caricature, of that insult to the Marshal and to morality. It is, furthermore, what that picture reveals of his past. Of course, not everyone in the regime can boast an immaculate background. Here and there, sins of youth can be found, doubtful political sympathies, questionable ways.

Goebbels himself was an expressionist in his early days, and he's said to have flirted with the Left. And as for the past of Curt Hagener himself ...

But few have switched sides like Schattendorf.

Wer ohne Sünde ist ...

In fact, Rudi Nadolski, who in his glory days had sung that immortal line at the Scala, performed at the Maus on one occasion. But he was so drunk that he sang off-key and was jeered by the public. Perfectly chilled Polish vodka was the culprit. It ruined his career, in the end. A man who had tread the same boards as Kurt Gerron and Paul Graetz...

He who has never sinned ...

Dunkels, there is a man who has never been even close to sinning. When he drinks, he goes no further than a beer. Tobacco, he knows not. He penetrates his wife once a week, always on Friday (Good Friday being an exception).

And a person like that should be a member of the Council of Fine Arts? Schattendorf has at least a bit of cheekiness and a hint of talent.

"I'm sorry Dunkels, I have no idea of whatever relationship Oberfrunck may have to this painting. A mystery."

It is that account, and no other, that the Commissioner will be served when Hagener meets him at the Schlosskeller, half an hour from now.

Grosz was Bang's favourite painter, he appreciated his caustic, if often macabre, humour. No surprise then, that, to celebrate the second anniversary of the Maus, he instituted the Argus Prize, "to the most daring, the most incisive satire." The prize would have interested neither Violetta or Harry if its amount hadn't been so generous and

283

their cash-box so ominously empty. The rent bill ("To be paid before Nov. 30, 1926, as per the current legislation") had been lying for a week on the dining-room's dresser, patiently waiting to be settled. The sight of that bill cleared out Harry's last doubts: yes, they would make a bid for the Argus Prize.

"Big blobs of colour. Solid yellows, greens, reds. A punchy thing," he suggested.

"But it should be more realistic than that. Think caricatures. Think Grosz."

Violetta knew Bang's artistic taste.

"Naked women you mean?"

"Why not, but it has to be something with a meaning. Symbolic, you know."

Harry racked his brains, flipped through an art book, went on cogitating. All of a sudden, he cried out:

"Here is what we will do: we will illustrate a fundamental contradiction: on one side the bourgeois, whose only activity is to exchange goods in order to make a profit in each transaction, and on the other side the artist, the real producer."

"No, it must be naughtier than that. Bang likes daring subjects."

"Wait, wait: both of those characters are watching a woman. Naked. A whore? Yes, but even a symbol for twentieth-century's society. The bourgeois, a parasite, waiting lasciviously to be satisfied, while the artist ponders over how best to render that reality, that woman-society which is raw flesh, how to reinterpret it in sensitive forms, an aesthetic statement that contrasts sharply with ... "

"Fine, fine," she said, laughing, "you are on the right track."

She made a sketch in her drawing block, he placed a canvas of 75x50 inches on the easel. He handled the paintbrush, she stood model.

"I am the one to bare my ass," she said, "but it's you who prostitute yourself."

Next day, the painting was finished, with the bourgeois on one side, the artist on the other, the red velvet, the blue feathers and all the rest.

"Colossal," judged Violetta. "But the bourgeois, is it absolutely necessary to make him bald and pot-bellied?"

"If he was thin and handsome, who would understand that he is a bourgeois?"

"But if we're going to win those two hundred eggs, and we have to, we need something more original."

They ruminated. Harry suggested:

"I'll give him Marshal Hindenburg's head. Bang told me about his experience in military service. He hates officers."

He did so, and Violetta was satisfied with the final result.

"But I would add two little things. If you don't mind."

She mixed a little rose with a bit of beige and improved the buttocks by making them rounder. She also drew, with a fine silver tip, in the manner of Grosz, two small sketches or alternative versions of the main motif, one on the right side, the other one further down to the left.

And while she was at it, she also retouched the face of the artist. A thin moustache, a little less hair on the sides of the skull and a little more on the top.

"But ..." stuttered Harry. "Stop it ! I don't want to..."

When she was ready, in the same way as the bourgeois had been promoted to Field Marshal, the artist had seen his anonymous face changed into the easily recognizable features of the painting's author himself.

"If I accept to appear in the show, me and my naked bottom," she argued, "I can't see why you should let me alone there."

Their contribution, titled *True Love,* did win the first prize. And the rent of the apartment at Passauerstrasse was paid with no more than a fortnight's delay.

28

17.15. Clausen has left, but the boy is still there, preparing two returns.

"What time are you leaving?" asks Sasha. "There is not much left to do."

"I'll just finish this, then I'm off."

"I'll help you."

A quarter of an hour later, everything is ready. Willi puts on his cap and leaves the room. Sasha goes to the back room.

If there is a scandal tomorrow, the first suspect will be Schultze. And Clausen can always replace Grosz' painting, as he did with Hoyer-Lemke's. Come to think of it, it would not be a bad idea to replace it himself: with no empty space on the wall, it will take longer for Clausen to realize that something was missing.

He goes to fetch some wrapping paper. He cuts three yards, it should be enough to pack the canvas, which, rolled up, will make a cylinder of 50 inches. He proceeds to room three, picks up the picture and the frame, rolls up the canvas, wraps it in the paper and winds two turns of rope around the bundle. He is pondering what to do with the empty frame when somebody pulls the entrance door open.

It's Clausen.

"Ah, here you are. I need you," says the professor. "You will not believe it, but Dunkels asks for a new, up-to-date inventory. He absolutely needs to know exactly which items are left."

It is 17.35. By 18 or 18.30 the list can be ready. It has to be; if he misses his appointment with Shadow, he has no way of getting in touch with him.

There were two hundred and eight objects in the beginning. Minus the fifty-five that have been selected, there should be one hundred and fifty-three left. In the warehouse they have forty, it means that more than one hundred and ten must have been returned. But that is not enough for Dunkels; he wants to know which ones were returned and when. Apparently a requirement from the Ministry, with which someone has filed a complaint. No wonder, thinks Sasha, considering Schultze's thievings.

In order to set up such a list, they'll have to check all delivery notes. Sasha begins to worry: he is not sure that it will be ready by half past six, not sure either that the professor will leave immediately after. One thing is certain though: Sasha cannot go before him, leaving him alone in the premises. Somehow he has to make it to room three unseen, unpack the bundle and put the canvas and the frame on the floor. He will pretend the frame fell down and was broken. Only, Clausen does not leave him alone for a second.

At last, the list is ready. It is 18.20.

"If I leave by 18.50, that should be enough," reckons Sasha. "Shadow will give me a quarter of an hour."

The list of the returns includes eighty-nine objects. Twenty-four are missing, in other words; they are no longer in the gasometer and they do not appear on any delivery note.

"A scandal," sums Clausen up. "For which I decline all responsibility."

It's quarter to seven. Clausen folds up the list and slips it in her briefcase.

"I will hand it over personally," he announces. "You can go, thank you for your help."

I'm saved, thinks Sasha.

But Clausen, who had already put on his coat and opened the door, stops at the threshold.

"I forgot, I have to check that Felixmüller's name is written correctly. We've already mixed him up with somebody else once."

Sasha feels something cold, something icy, radiating from his stomach to the chest. He cannot let Clausen go to room three.

"I will do it for you, professor," he stutters.

But Clausen is already on his way. In two strides, Sasha reaches the electrical panel and cuts off the power in the room where the unframed Grosz is.

He hears Clausen swear.

"Mr. Wassingher, there is no light in the back room!"

"I'll check it right now, professor."

"Solve this, even if it takes you all night," warns Clausen. "Should that happen tomorrow, it would be a serious matter."

The professor is in room two, comparing a label's text with the data in his notebook. Then he moves to another painting, on the wall opposite. At long last, he closes his notebook. But he doesn't go back to the front office.

Something in Room Two's ceiling has caught his attention. He takes a step back to better observe it. Even though the room is in the dark, if he happened to turn his look in Room Three's direction, there is no way he will miss the bundle that Sasha left there.

"Professor, come on please, I have to show you something," says

Sasha in a voice he wants normal but that comes out more like a shriek.

He has to invent something, anything. But no idea comes to his mind, his head is as empty as the canvasless frame leaning on the wall in room three. He must find a subterfuge to keep the professor where he is, to prevent him from returning to room two, to contemplate even the possibility of crossing the threshold of room three.

That's when he hear it. The meowing.

Macke has just entered through the door Clausen left ajar.

"Get out !" shouts Sasha, at the top of his lungs. Clausen joins him, worried.

The cat makes a leap to the "factory" and disappears under a cabinet. Clausen tries to force him out and the cat throws a paw at him. It's just a scratch, but the professor hurries to the sink and puts his hand under the tap.

"People say cats are clean," he says, "but who knows what germs there are in those claws. Wassingher, get this animal out, but be careful. I'm going to the pharmacy. I'll see you tomorrow at seven o'clock. "

As soon as he hears Clausen's car start, he jumps to the door to make sure the coast is clear. Seven minutes to five. The guard has already left, the night watchman will arrive any minute. Sasha rushes to the garage, grabs a painting with two female nudes, hangs it in the place left empty by the Grosz and leaves the premises.

At the parking lot there is a police car. He is happy to have thought of an alternative route. He hurries to the tennis court.

Schultze will be accused of having stolen twenty-four paintings, it'll do him no harm to take upon him the twenty-fifth too. He has been in and out many times today, he hasn't lacked opportunities.

Sasha passes through the hole in the fence. Three minutes later, he is at the Urbanstrasse, the agreed meeting place.

It didn't start well. Schattendorf and Gerhard arrived at Urbanstrasse five minutes in advance. At 7 pm, a police car parks thirty meters from them. Two minutes later, they see another black sedan, with three agents in it, pass towards the gasometer.

"The complaint you filed is showing results," says Gerhard.

"But too quickly, I should have waited a few hours," thought Schattendorf.

19.05. They see Sacha walking in their direction, a bundle in his hand. He hesitates for a moment, then passes by without looking at them.

"He saw the schupos. You should have chosen another meeting place," said Gerhard. "Here it is too close to the gasometer".

"I know," replied Schattendorf annoyed. "But it's he who chose it, he did not want to walk around with the painting under his arm, he said. And we're five hundred meters from the exhibition here, that's not so close."

He starts the car. They pass by the policemen, who look at them. But their car does not move.

Schattendorf continues to the second crossing street, then turns left and takes the street parallel to the one of the meeting place, but in the opposite direction. He turns left again and stops just before Dieffenbachstrasse. After a while, they see Sasha, who's still walking, but now slowlier. His hands are empty.
Schattendorf stops the car without turning off the engine. Gerhard gets out and goes to meet Sacha.

291

"Where is the painting?" he asks him.

"I put it in the garden in front of a building. It's because of all the policemen here, I don't want to be found with that thing under my arm."

"Go get it then, but hurry up!"

After three minutes he is back with the roll. Gerhard brings it to the car. Schattendorf rips up the paper and takes a quick glance at the canvas.

He hands an envelope to Gerhard, who gives it to Sacha in turn.

"And my passport please," asks Sacha.

"So give it to him," growls Schattendorf to Gerhard, looking over his shoulder. The black police car is still at the same place, but the lights are on now.

"But ... it's you who has it ...," answers Gerhard.

"What do you mean? I gave it to you when we started!"

He searches his right pocket. Nothing. He wants to search the other pocket but his right hand is not free:

"Hold this for me!" he hands the roll to Sacha. He places it on the ground to count the money, but the pavement is wet; he places the roll against a tree on the sidewalk, then opens the envelope and takes out the bundle of hundred-dollar bills. They are ten.

"Do you want your passport or not?" barks Schattendorf, who has finally found it. But at that moment, the police car, which has turned around, comes in their direction, its siren on.

Schattendorf throws the passport to Sacha and starts the engine.

"And the roll?" exclaims Sacha.

"Give it to me! Hurry up!" Gerhard shouts.

Sasha goes to fetch it. Gerhard pulls his hand out of the window, Sacha gives him the roll, but at that moment Schattendorf accelerates abruptly. The roll, which Gerhard had managed to grab at one end, falls from his hands, landing on the pavement.

Sacha picks up his passport and the roll. Gerhard shouts something to him which he doesn't hear. There he stands, at the corner of Dieffenbachstrasse and Graefestrasse, with a thousand marks and a stolen painting. He tries to hide in a building's entrance.

The policemen signal to Schattendorf to stop. He does, makes his Heil Hitler and shows his card of the ministry.

"We are in a hurry, we are investigating irregularities in the gasometer," he says, and, without waiting for an answer, starts again.

Schattendorf continues two hundred meters, then turns right. He stops to drop Gerhard, who goes to look for Sacha.

Once he is back home, Schattendorf makes some calls. He gets the confirmation that the police is investigating irregularities at the gasometer.

The minister himself has taken matters into his own hands. Goebbels went so far as to demand that the exhibition be cancelled, but Dunkels, through Rosenberg, obtained support at the highest levels. Result: the exhibition will open the next day as planned, but for two weeks, not two months.

In any case, Dunkels is knock-out. Condemned for his lousy organization, for his total lack of control. Rosenberg himself will have to withdraw him his support. If the character still had a hope of saving his skin, he can now say goodbye to it: *Still Life* is no more.

"What if Grosz denies his authorship, what if a restorer scratches the canvas and discovers Harry Shadow's signature?" he wondered as late as this morning. No more reason to worry ; the painting is no longer there. From now on nothing stands in the way of his appointment to the Council.

"Congratulations!" greets Carraro him next morning. "You burned it, I hope?"

"The nefarious painting will no longer cause any harm," declares Schattendorf, satisfied.

"But where is it?"

Schattendorf tells him about the meeting at Urbanstrasse. How Gerhard went after Sasha and the painting, but the Russian was nowhere to be found.

"But that doesn't mind. What is important is that the damned thing is no longer in the gasometer."

"But it is not destroyed? You have left yet another loose end, Hans."

"First of all," he replies irritably, "Gerhard is going to meet the Russian at the gasometer tomorrow. Secondly, our primary goal was to prevent the picture from being shown. And it won't be."

"But what do you know about that guy? He may try to barter the painting. Or blackmail you."

Schattendorf bursts out laughing.

"If you'd seen him, you'd understand he's not the kind of guy to threaten me. He's an illegal alien, who can be expelled from the country at any moment. He's delighted to have pocketed my thousand marks. I bet he has thrown the canvas to the Spree, out of fear of being found with it."

"I don't like that. Your Gerhard is a moron. I'm going to question your Russian myself. And if he still has the canvas, I'll get it back, you may count on me."

"You do that. Still, I'm not the one who has reason to worry. "

"Yes, Dunkels position is not good. But Hans: do not rest on your laurels, do not turn off the engine before you've reached the finish line."

It is crucial to make his presence felt, he says, especially these last days before the decision.

"I'm going to publish an article in *Der Angriff*," says Schattendorf. "When?"

"Tomorrow or after tomorrow."

"It should have been yesterday !" roars Carraro. "I'll take care of it, the editorial secretary is a friend."

"But I know the boss."

"Do not send your article to Wolff, he's not the one who takes the decisions there, the secretary does. Send it to me to the embassy, I'll do the rest."

The article is a statement of principles. "Politics of art or art of politics." But it is also, and now without any ambiguity, a vindication of Expressionism as the most authentic German art. "The political revolution has been done, now it is time to revolutionize art."

The enemy is not only the sterile academicism, but also the "New Objectivity." Otto Dix. George Grosz. That cold realism which, under the pretext of clinical examination, produces a dehumanized, cynical vision. American, in the worst sense of the word. This charge on Grosz and Dix, considered communists or anarchists, is strategically crucial, as his enemies accuse himself, absurdly enough, of cultural Bolshevism.

And now that the damned canvas is out of the picture, he can express himself clearly. The fact is, being a simple councillor is no longer the goal. Hönig, the President of the Council, is a lukewarm character, a compromise solution which all sides can live with. He will not last long. His successor will be elected among the councillors, that is to say, among the members of the body he will soon be a part of.

He revels in the minister's words after his lecture at the library: "We desperately need people like you."

Next day, at the gasometer.

Schultze, explains Clausen, hasn't shown up. The police is questioning him about the missing works.

"Things are moving," says Clausen, satisfied. "And one question: when was the last time you saw the Grosz?"

"Well, yesterday afternoon it was still there," he replies, serenely.

"Which means, at seven o'clock it was still in the premises," concludes Clausen.

"Yes, I left at five to seven. But Schultze may have removed it earlier than that. I was in room three around ... around three o'clock in the afternoon. I don't think I was there after that."

Clausen looks at him puzzled.

"But ... the lights work now. How could you fix that without setting foot in room three?"

Sasha thinks feverishly.

"It was just a fuse, it was enough to change it on the electrical panel," he stammers.

Clausen considers the answer. He looks at Sasha, then at the panel, finally at the exhibition rooms.

"No blowing fuses tomorrow Herr Wassingher. See to it that it doesn't happen," he says ominously.

A car stops in front of the door. Two plain-clothes policemen come out. Behind them, Schultze. The first policeman goes straight to Sasha.

"Your documents."

He studies the passport at length. "Your visa!" he barks. Sasha pulls out a paper from his pocket.

What an idiot I have been, he thinks. Lena was right: I should have got rid of the damn thing right away, I should have burnt it at once. Instead, he hid it in the attic of their building. Why? Because he couldn't make up his mind to throw it away. After all, it was a well known signature. But now, if the *schupos* search their house, he will be in serious trouble.

"What are you doing in Germany?" asks the second policeman, taller than his colleague. "Why don't you go back home?"

"I do not agree with the regime over there."

"But this building belongs to the German state. As a foreigner, you have no right to work here."

"It is temporary."

"Not even for an hour. It's forbidden and you cannot ignore it. What about your certificate of aryanity?"

"I've never been asked for that."

"So you work here without a permit and you are not even an Aryan?"

He looks at his colleague and says:

"How are such things possible, can you understand that?"

The other shakes his head.

"It is just because," Sasha stammers, "to obtain this certificate I would have to ask for papers from the USSR."

"And Russians cannot write, it's well known."

His colleague laughs loudly. The other raises the tone.

"You come with us," he says.

"Where?" whispered Sasha.

"To the police station. Unless you prefer the restaurant *Piroschka*, of course."

Clausen: "Officer, Herr Wassingher is indispensable for the exhibition. And we are opening in just a few hours."

"That's not our problem. And by the way, how could you hire him? Don't you respect German law either, *mein Herr*?"

Clausen goes to his desk, opens a drawer, searches a few seconds, finally he pulls out a yellow paper.

It is the staff list, on which Sasha's name appears, with date of birth and passport number. At the foot of the page, the letterhead of the Culture Commission of the Capital Region, and Dunkels totally unreadable signature. Lower down, another stamp, this one from the local delegation of the Ministry of Labour.

The tall one reads the paper and shows it to the other.

"No," decides this one, "this is not a work permit."

And, taking Sasha firmly by the arm, he pushes him towards the car.

It is at that point that Schultze, hitherto silent, intercedes:

"Comrades policemen, this exhibition is a decisive milestone in our campaign for German culture. I occupy a post here, sent by the party to supervise the political line. I have already explained it at the police station."

He takes the NSDAP member card out of his jacket.

"Wassingher is responsible for the technical part, and without him the exhibition cannot open."

The policemen watch him closely. Then they look at Clausen.

"Furthermore, comrades, Wassingher is a person whose loyalty nobody questions. I vouch for him. If he's lacking some document, I am sure he will be able to obtain it soon. All I'm asking from you is a little political understanding. This is a special situation."

The first policeman looks at his colleague. Then, fixing his eyes on Sasha, he says sternly:

"Make sure you get that certificate. You will present to the police station every morning and you are not allowed to leave the Brandenburg area. If you do not produce all necessary documents in seven days, you will be expelled, no matter if you are a key person in thirty different art exhibitions. "

"Well, gentlemen," says Clausen when the police has left, "everyone knows what to do, we open at four o'clock."

Sasha remains alone with Schultze.

"Did they take you to the police station?" he wonders. "Why?"

"Someone has denounced me, but he did not know who he was dealing with. As for you, I got you a reprieve, but you have to move your ass to get those papers. They meant business, the *schupos*."

"Thank you, Schultze."

"For what? We are colleagues, aren't we? Brothers."

In seven days, they said. But he'll be in Holland before that. From there he will find a boat for America. Shadow's thousand marks will pay the tickets for him and for Lena. They shouldn't cost more than seven or eight hundred and with the rest, they will be able to survive in Los Angeles a few months, the time to find a job.

Sasha knows from another Russian that in Rotterdam it is easy to found a cargo ship for America. Or to the Netherlands Antilles, and from there, Florida is not far away, he has looked it up on a map. It is closer to Los Angeles from Miami than from New York.

But, come to think of it, why not take a cargo ship right to California via Suez, even if the trip is longer?

Anyhow, the most important thing is to leave Germany as soon as possible. Once in Holland, they will consider the different possibilities.

These thousand marks are the largest amount of money he has ever possessed. With that sum, everything seems possible.

He tests the lighting one last time. First the main room, then number two, finally the third one. A little weak. One of the bulbs has blown. He goes for the ladder.

Schultze is trying to tighten the screw that keeps together the two parts of a pair of pincers. "More junk," he rummages. "I'm sure it's Polish pincers."

"Czech," corrects Sasha, who passes by, the ladder on his shoulder.

"Of course," says Schultze. "If our electrician is Russian, why would the tools be German?"

"Just a joke," he adds with a smile. "And, by the way, my dear colleague, am I mistaken or have you established a profitable business relationship with the honourable Oberfrunck? Because the painting that interested him is precisely the one that has disappeared. A surprising coincidence, huh? "

"It is. But I know nothing about that, sorry."

Schultze explodes with a laugh.

"You know, Wassingher, some people find that I look silly. But I am not. You won't pretend that it's Willi who took the painting, huh? Who's left then? Leni? I know for certain that it wasn't me."

He looks amused at Sasha.

"How much did he give you, Oberfrunck? I'm asking you, not out of curiosity, but because half of it belongs to me. It was me who gave you the tip. And I'm generous, I could take everything."

"I have to say I've no idea of what you're talking about, Schultze."

"They offered me a hundred marks, but that was for an unselected painting. Taking down an object that has been carefully chosen after the most scientific criteria by the professor and by Commissioner Dunkels, that's a very different matter. Such a service cannot have the same price. Five hundred marks is a minimum. "

"Schultze, if you need money I'll see if I can lend you some, but ..."

"Do not tell me you did it for less. In that case, it's you who is the idiot. For me, that job is worth five hundred, not a mark less. I want my two hundred and fifty."

Clausen comes into the factory and gives them a wary look. When he's gone, Sasha mumbles:

"I do not have that money on me."

"But Herr Wassingher, where is the problem?" he says with a big smile. "Where is the hurry? This afternoon suits me perfectly. I have full confidence in you, as I just told the *schupos.*"

29

Strange place for an exhibition, this industrial building. A circular structure, eighty yards in diameter. The exterior is brick, an ochre colour brightened by the cornices, which are red. The openings: a number of small arched windows.

Morel has been only once or twice in Kreuzberg. The working class districts of Berlin are characterized by rows of five- or six-storey buildings one behind the other, blocks separated by courtyards that the sun rarely reaches. The façades can be pleasant; it is there, in the part overlooking the street, where the better-off tenants live. But behind that Potemkin façade, squalor and overcrowding reign.

The capital has multiplied its population in the last decades. To accommodate it, it was necessary to build, massively and in the shortest delays. The answer have been the *mietskasernen*, the aptly named «rental barracks." The largest possible number of apartments, but also spaces for craftsmen, for small industries.

It was one of those spaces that Violetta used to rent at the Invalidenstrasse. The yard was a playground for children, but a shopkeeper used part of it as a warehouse. In the third yard, a market was hold every Saturday.

When the spring approached and the days got warmer, Violetta organized a party for the inhabitants of the "barracks." A neighbour would bring his portable gramophone and, at nightfall, the dinner turned into dance. But that was back in the times, not that far away, when it was possible for her to have a workshop and even let the neighbours in.

"*Entartete Kunst*, Cultural Bolshevism against our Nation," announces a red sign with white letters posted on the round wall of the gasometer. But the doors are still closed; the inauguration ceremony has not finished yet. The exhibition was announced in the newspapers, but Morel has hardly seen any posters in the streets.

It is only at half-past three that a young man with a bundle of pamphlets in his hand begins to walk along the queue, handing a copy to each visitor.

Morel takes a look at the brochure, just four pages printed in black and white. There is an introduction with the usual phrases about *Kulturbolschewismus* and the Jewish World-view. But, on page three, something makes his heart skip a beat. He had got used to the idea of *Still Life* being exposed, but seeing a photography of his painting on the pamphlet affects him all the same.

And then, to his joyful surprise, he notices that the dates on the posters have been altered: month and date have been crossed out and re-lettered by hand. The expo closes earlier than expected, already in two weeks !

That changes everything ! He was already planning to leave Berlin without the painting and to return for it in two months' time. Now he will be able to leave with Grosz in his luggage. Great news!

At twenty minutes to four, two guards throw open each his half of the heavy entrance door. The crowd begins to enter orderly. A number of guards, several policemen, as well as some SA watch the visitors with a regard alternately stern and facetious.

In the main space, twenty works are exposed. The first thing that catches his attention is the horrible lighting, not far from that of a ghost train. On the wall, large panels: "An art that preaches class struggle!", "In this 'art' the Weimar Republic has squandered millions of marks", "'Ideal' racial types'" (portraits of African and Polynesian), "Thus insult these Semitic painters the German woman" (a nude by Chagall).

It is not out of curiosity that Morel came. No, for him this exhibition is a true Art Fair of the Avant-Garde. It's as if he had been able to attend the *Salon des Refusés* in 1863 Paris, and acquire, at dumping prices, works by Manet and Pissarro that everybody considered ridiculous.

Can Keller's man, the character in the van, get that Franz Marc for him, the one with the blue horse, once the exhibit is closed? He tries to estimate the price he could get for it. He takes notes. None of these paintings is uninteresting, but some of them are true masterpieces.

In modern art exhibitions there are always those who come to make fun of the works, but few dare to do so openly. Here they feel entitled to laugh. Here they are at home. Nobody looks down on them, they meet no frowns. At last an exhibition organized by people who see things like them, experts who do not patronize them, who, on the contrary, deem them right: yes, modern art is a scam, yes, their five years old child's drawings are better than that. Much better !

These Nazis are anything but stupid, thinks Morel. They proclaim aloud what many people feel but don't dare to say. They call a cat a cat, a scribble a scribble.

He arrives at the last room, the back room, painted in red: "Art or pornography?" At the entrance, a warning: "Watch out, offensive scenes." Which only increases the interest of the public. Who knows, *Still Life* might prove the star of the show.

It has to be here, his Grosz, the only one among all these jewels that belongs to him already. This hall, number three, is the smallest. A Kirchner, a woman with open legs. A Dix, a scene in a brothel, adroitly executed, but quite tasteless. It might appeal to Navarro though. These women, some of them mature, all ugly, waiting for a customer desperate enough to choose them, could tickle his lascivious side. Two thousand? Three thousand? We're talking of an Otto Dix, after all !

But, what about *Still Life*? He goes over the room again. There must be a fourth room. No sir, a guardian answers him. There are three sections, no more.

Have they changed their minds? Did they find it too risky? But it's not worse than other things exposed here. He calls the guard, shows him the photography on the brochure. The man barely looks at it and then says irritably: "Mein Herr, if it is on the catalogue, it is in the exhibition. Have a closer look. "

Is it in room two, devoted to degenerate prototypes and inferior races? A Nolde with copper skinned Polynesians, thick lips, rings through their flat noses and a cheerful smile. Below the table, a comment: "This artist has travelled all the way to the antipodes in search of lovely faces like these." But among these twenty poorly hung and appallingly lit canvases, *Still Life* is not.

The main room shows Bolshevik or Israelite paintings. Grosz could be there, rubbing shoulders with his friend John Heartfield. Heartfield is represented by two collages, one ridiculing Field Marshal Hindenburg ("This so-called artist who has repudiated his German name dares to affront our Great Soldier"), the other with officers and

306

skeletons ("This genius of glue, who knows how to insult but not how to paint, makes fun of our Army ").

A Chagall with candelabra, Torahs and animals hovering above the clouds illustrates the Jewish Vision of the World. ("Have you ever seen flying lambs? The Jews see them all the time, or they pretend they do"). But no Grosz here either. Yet there was every reason to believe that the picture would be selected. It is on the catalogue, for God's sake!

He leaves. He walks the two hundred yards that separate the gasometer from the Grimmstrasse, a broad avenue with a wooded central promenade, and goes into the first bar he finds. He asks to borrow the phone, but another client is using it, a young fellow in his Sunday best. He is speaking with a girl, judging by his syrupy smile, and is so identified with his role of seducer that he even gesticulates in front of the telephone.

Morel comes out on the street and discovers a bakery with the legend *Fernsprecher* on the shop window. He pays in advance the required five pfennig and the employee pulls the black telephone out from under the counter. Morel dials the gallery's number. No answer. He tries Keller's apartment. "Hold on please, I believe he's in," answers a woman's voice.

Twenty minutes later, he goes through the door of the café where the art dealer is waiting for him.

"No idea," it's the only answer he gets from Keller. "My contacts assured me that the painting was in the final selection, but with these people you never know. But for you it's good news, isn't it? You'll get it back sooner than expected."

"Good news, eh? And what if it was stolen? By your famous contact, for example, on behalf of some other gallery owner. What if

307

Still Life is in this same moment in his van, on its way to another gallery?"

"They wouldn't dare: I have a receipt from the Culture Commission. But let's not waste time on guesswork," says Keller, and walks up to the counter to make a call. He makes an appointment with his contact, then they go both out and hail a taxi. The driver does not take the Tiergartenstrasse, closed to traffic for repaving work. He takes a detour to the south, bypassing the Landwehrkanal. They get off one block after the Alexanderplatz and walk into a bar. A young man is waiting for them: the guy of the van.

"Many people at the exhibition?" wonders Schultze, Keller's contact.

"Yes."

"It is good, it is important that it is a success. It's a decisive milestone in the campaign for German culture."

Morel is sure of having read exactly that sentence in the brochure.

"But, Herr Keller," says Schultze, "that painting is not my responsibility. We've never talked about it before."

"No one is blaming you," says Morel, "we only want to know why it is not exposed, despite having been selected."

Schultze pulls an ashtray towards him and, by knocking his cigarette lightly against the edge, drops the ashes that are growing alarmingly at the end of it. He allows himself a little smile.

"I happen to know that some important people are interested in the object you mention. Please do not ask me for names."

"Mr. Schultze," insists Keller, "you can count on our discretion, no one would be served by a scandal."

Schultze makes a gesture of helplessness.

308

Morel: "That information would be generously rewarded, that goes without saying."

At this, Schultze reacts vehemently:

"But, do you think you can buy everything, absolutely everything? Don't you French people know the concept of honour?"

He has got half up from his chair. He sits down again and takes a long sip of his beer.

"The person concerned is Oberfrunck," he utters. "Chief Intendant at the Heritage Department."

"And why in hell is he interested in that painting?" asks Morel.

Schultze motions as if asking for patience and understanding.

"I repeat that we are talking about classified information here, but ..."

"Yes?"

"I have my suspicions about the person who perpetrated the removal itself."

He makes another pause and looks intently, first at Keller then at Morel.

"Anything you can do to help us will be welcome," Morel says as he pulls out his wallet. "Will fifty marks be enough to cover your expenses?"

Schultze takes the note, folds it meticulously and puts it in his jacket's upper pocket. He gets up, clicks his heels and leaves the bar.

Keller: "Listen, surely he will give us a name and an address, but the thief may have already given the painting to the other guy, to that Oberfrunck."

He tells him about Hagener's visit. He had asked just about an Oberfrunck, a high official at Heritage.

"But let's go see Hagener then!" exclaims Morel.

The gallerist does not know where to find him. But Morel knows someone who might know. He calls Nina Bovrik. No answer. He asks for the telephone directory and looks up *Deutsche Tribüne*'s number. But Hagener is not there. It is Saturday after all.

"In the meantime," says Keller, "there is a way to put pressure on the authorities and, if the worst happens, receive compensation."

He proposes to make a sales contract, antedating it a few days. That will make Morel the rightful owner. He may then go to the Ministry of Culture to demand the painting to be returned or, failing that, the thousand marks he has paid for it.

"Thousand? Haven't we settled on five hundred?" wonders Morel.

"Five hundred for you, five hundred for me."

A poor consolation. But it is true that, being a foreign businessman, the authorities won't treat him as they could treat Keller.

"Violetta, I appeal to that maternal instinct you spoke so tenderly about, last time we met. I'm in desperate need for comfort." They are at the bar of the Ackersstrasse.

"Do you have a picture of your painting?" she asks.

He had thought of picking some more copies of the exhibition flyer, but with all the excitement, he forgot it. But he does have the copy the guard gave him while he was queueing up. He searches the pocket of his jacket, then the back pocket of his trousers. Finally he finds it.

"Look at this reproduction. The quality is miserable, but it is still recognizable."

But when he opens the leaflet he realizes that it is not the right one, but a brochure he got at the Baumgarten gallery.

"Well, it's not my day," he moans.

"Go and pick another one. I could very well recognize the picture," she suggests.

But that is not possible; he has to go back to the hotel in case Schultze calls him. And finally, how would that help him if she did recognize it?

"It's a brothel scene," he explains.

"Ah yes, that description is really useful," she mocks him. "George must have painted dozens of scenes like that."

"But I'm talking of an oil, not a watercolour or a drawing. A naked chick, a guy in front, the other behind her."

"Gaston! It's a lady you're talking to."

"Come to think of it, Keller must have a photography too, I could call him."

But he does not call Keller. He does not call anyone.

None of his father's commandments, none of those excellent precepts that govern his commercial activities, prescribes the words he presently articulates:

"Come to the hotel with me. I expect a call from Schultze there."

None of them do. Because what he suddenly feels the urge for, as the scent of *Jasmin du Siam*, Violetta's perfume, excites his nostrils, is not to call Keller, not to exchange a few polite phrases with his wife, not to make up an appointment to pick up a photo of *Still Life*. No, none of that. What he does crave, intensely, acutely, furiously, is a good fuck, one of those afternoon fucks that restore strength and build confidence.

Violetta looks at him amused.

"Follow you to your hotel, eh? You never give up, do you?"

But to his surprise, she agrees.

Once at the Lilienhof, he informs the receptionist that he is waiting for an important call. Then they take a seat in the lobby, in front of the crackling fireplace, with a cup of coffee and a brandy.

"I'm sure you have done other good deals here. Your visit to Berlin won't be fruitless," she tries to comfort him.

"Violetta, that depends on you. If you want it, if you decide it, I will not have come to Berlin in vain, even if I go back to Paris empty-handed."

"I see, I see. And for that gift you are expecting, you will not even have to pay an export tax ..."

He lays the palm of his hand on the back of hers, which is resting on the little table. She returns his caress, then she withdraws her hand to grab the cup's ear. She drinks a sip of mocha. She pours another drop of cream from the little white porcelain jar, mechanically, with her mind some place else.

"If it's like Keller says, that they are pillaging the exhibition, I do not see why you're surprised," she observes.

"But my painting was in the final selection. It had already been hung, according to Schultze. "

"Remind me, what's the title of your painting?"

It rings no bell to her.

"If it makes you feel better, I can sell you, not an oil but a drawing by Grosz, it's something ... well, colossal I would say. Those fine lines, delicate, almost feminine, don't you think? Yet they convey an impression of vigorous, almost brutal intensity."

Then, with a mischievous air, she adds: "In fact I do know another oil, with the same subject as yours, a love triangle too. But it is not by Grosz."

"By whom then?"

She bursts out laughing and shakes her head. "Forget it. I couldn't get it for you anyway."

Her laugh – somewhat teasing, not really cheerful - arouses his suspicion:

"That Shadow, do you still see him?" he wonders.

"Are you jealous, by any chance?"

"Should I be?"

"No reason."

A concise answer, categorical and yet ambiguous, concludes Morel. But, does it matter? At this very moment she is here with him, not with the other.

"Listen," he suggests, for there are occasions when even the most cautious player puts all his eggs in the same basket, "instead of waiting here, why don't I tell them to put Schultze's call through to my room? "

30

Dr. Dunkels' office is located at Hildebrandsstrasse, not far from Potsdamer Platz or, in fact, from Margarethenstrasse, where mighty Dr. Rosenberg himself has his headquarters. Schultze has already been at Dunkels' place several times. He greets cordially the janitor, who answers with an *Alles gut*?" after the mandatory *Heil.*

The doctor has always treated him properly, even though Dunkels is a Commissioner of Culture and he a simple member of the party. But with long-standing merits: he had his party membership book as early as in 1927. Schultze was in the party already in the heroic days, risking his neck against the Communists, fighting for the honour of the Movement, to conquer yard by yard the streets of Friedrichshain.

He takes a seat in the small waiting room of the office in which, besides the doctor, three employees work, one of them very pretty, by the way. She's blonde, made up but in a tasteful manner, a nice girl. Short legs, it is true, but a cute face. He tries to meet her gaze, but she has only eyes for her typewriter.

On a table, he sees a copy of today's number of *Der Angriff.* Schultze flips through it. Reading the press is part of the ideological education of a good party member, but he hasn't always the time.

Marshal Göring inaugurates the new Daimler factory. The plant's director, the engineer Speicher, explains to him the new organization principles.

Western powers must recognize once and for all our country's independence, said Minister von Neurath. Germany respects its neighbours' sovereignty, but it demands the same respect for its own. Nobody loves peace more than us, but there are limits to our patience.

The US call for global monetary stability. Detentions in Vienna after the attacks. On page two, a long article on agricultural policy; it does not seem important. Page three: The peasant, foundation of the nation. "The débacle of liberalism", an interview with an Italian intellectual. At the very bottom, an article: "Politics of art or the art of politics." There is a small photograph of its author, not much more than an inch, but the face looks familiar to Schultze. That nose, that moustache ...

But it's Dr. Oberfrunck!

At that moment, the Commissioner's door opens. Schultze walks in, closes the door behind him, takes a chair and moves it closer to the desk.

"Who told you to sit down?" explodes Dunkels.

Schultze, dumbfounded, puts the chair back in its place.

"Do you realize the damage you have caused me?" roars the doctor. "I picked you for your post because I thought you were a good National Socialist, but you are a common thief in fact."

"With all due respect, doctor, I was under the impression that the EnKu's works were going to be ..."

"Destroyed? Have I ever said that?"

Yes, remembers Schultze. The word the Commissioner employed was "eliminated." But he remains silent, his eyes fixed on the beige carpet under the desk.

"And even if I had suggested anything of the sort, I never implied it was up to you to carry it out, let alone laying your hands on those paintings for your own benefit. How would you call the act of appropriating what belong to others? Our rich German language has a verb for that, a verb at once precise and expressive. "

Schultze keeps staring at the carpet.

"But if it was just a matter of petty thievery. No, you did something worse, you caused me incalculable damage. I recruited you to help me, not to help my enemies."

"Dr. Dunkels, please, how can I make up for that? It was never my intention to..."

"I want a complete list of the people who bought those paintings from you. Names and addresses. "

That gives Schultze an idea.

"Herr Doktor, there is in fact a person who has approached me. He is an official, in the culture sector."

"There are thousands of officials in that sector."

"But this person has published an article in today's *Der Angriff*, you may have read it. Wait, I'll go fetch it, it is in the waiting room."

"You're not going anywhere," barks Dunkels. He turns around, takes his own copy of the newspaper and hands it to him.

Schultze browses it, finds the article and shows it to the Commissioner. "Politics of art or the art of politics."

Dunkels' index finger, which was tapping rhythmically on the table, freezes. The Commissioner raises his gaze from the newspaper and fixes it on Schultze.

"Are you sure?" he asks.

317

Dunkels organized the Degenerate Art Expo because it was a logical step in the cultural crusade. They did it in Karlsruhe in April 33, they did it in Nuremberg too. Shouldn't they do it in Berlin then? Rosenberg approved the idea without a moment's doubt.

Strategy and tactics. In the short term, advance his positions in Berlin. But his aim was more ambitious than that: to enter the Chamber, the organ where everything in the world of art is decided.

The expo should have taken place at the Crown Prince's Palace, the Kronprinzenpalais. Intrigues prevented it, leaving him the gasometer as the only alternative. But the task had been completed; the EDeKA was already a success and the other expo would be it too, in its own way.

Unfortunately, the irregularities, the imbecility of that little crook Schultze, have jeopardized his position. Minister Goebbels interfered with the case and even tried to prohibit the exhibition.

But now Dunkels discovers that the one behind the stealing of one of the paintings is nobody less than the Leader of Spandau's Cultural Action. Schultze's thefts have been commissioned by unscrupulous gallery owners, that is scarcely a surprise. But, by a government official?

And he commits that act the same day he publishes his piece on *Der Angriff.* "That cold, bloodless realism." "Which merely criticizes reality from its ivory tower, without proposing any solutions. One of the most conspicuous examples of that cynicism, is an artist like George Grosz." And, the icing on the cake: "A sex drive that is not healthy, that is sheer depravity."

And the same character that signs this proclamation, this manifesto, the person which presents himself as a "national minded intellectual", obtains through criminal means the most obscene, the most depraved picture of the whole exhibition, a work of the most "Bolshevik", the most "cynical" artist. To hang it in his boudoir?

This same afternoon, when everyone has read the article, he will reveal everything. By publishing this infamous piece of writing, Schattendorf has put his neck on the guillotine; tomorrow, the steel blade will detach head from body.

Schultze is still there, a dog waiting to be disciplined.

"Do you know how to contact that Wassingher?" asks Dunkels.

Schultze nods.

"And, he's working without a permit, is that right?"

"And besides, his mother is Jewish."

"Perfect! Here's what you're going to tell him: he'll testify about his dealings with Schattendorf, otherwise I'll personally see to it that he's deported overnight."

Schultze assents emphatically.

"But if he does his duty, he can count on my support for a residence permit. Tell him so. Now!"

31

Lena had already made a scene when he told her where the thousand marks came from. But when she found out that, instead of destroying the canvas, Sasha had hidden it in the attic, she was furious.

"Any neighbour could stumble on it!"

"It's at the very end of the corridor," he tried to placate her, "I put it behind a pillar, it's just a canvas rolled up and wrapped in old newspapers. And anyway, nobody goes up to the attic."

"I will. And tear it in thousand pieces."

And yet, he had told her about Schultze. That he had been forced to give him a part, that they had only seven hundred and fifty left. That he had identified the legitimate owner of the painting, a gallerist who would surely pay a handsome sum for it.

"Seven hundred fifty are enough," she alleged.

"For a ticket, but we'll need two. I'm not leaving Germany without you."

While Lena is getting washed behind the screen, he goes out on the street and heads straight to the telephone booth at the corner. He dials the number of the Kronen Gallery.

Morel has known Violetta for five years now and once, only one time, has he been on the verge of success. It was in the big apartment she had at Passauerstrasse. In the living room there was a very comfortable avant-garde armchair, a present of a friend (a friend?) who worked in Dessau, at the Bauhaus. There were also tropical plants, whose life on these latitudes would normally be impossible, but which in the Brennerian micro-climate thrived and flourished.

He was allowed to enter her room that time. He even managed to pull off her velvet trousers, her white muslin blouse. Everything was developing flawlessly, the preliminaries were duly completed one after the other. But at that point the phone rang. Everything froze. She said she had to leave right away. Because of that guy again? It was as if that Harry kept casting his shadow on her.

In any case, next day everything had changed. She had recovered her tone partly flirtatious partly mocking, but more mocking than flirtatious. This tone is a kind of fortress he cannot conquer. He is not used to that mix of feminine seduction and masculine distance, he lacks the key to open that door.

Five years has he waited. But his key finally turned out to be the right one, and the lock - robust, tamper resistant – gave way at last.

Morel watches her sleep. He does not hasten to wake her up. This is the first time he sees her like this, without tactics, without a mask.

That's why she has always resisted him, he thinks; out of modesty, yes, but not the kind of modesty that abhors nudity. What she refused him was not sex; it was to see her like this, without defence, without armour.

He has someone in his life. She works for a fashion house and is, like him, always busy. Lack of time is a real fact, but the true problem is elsewhere. If he is sincere, he must admit that the first thing for him is his work. The second thing? None. The third? Still nothing. A fourth place, at that position in Morel's life can a woman aspire.

322

He's free. "His heart is available," would a sentimental novel put it. But it is not true: his heart is jealously guarded. And among those sentimentalities against which he has always shielded himself, against which he has erected ramparts with their crenellations and their arrow-loops, the first one is love.

What does he feel for Violetta? She has finally given him what he desired, but he's still in want of something. What is that something, what is its name, which category does it belong to?

She wakes up by herself. First an eye, then the other, surprised, almost frightened. But just a fraction of a second, she needs no more to realize where she is and with whom. And yet, her breathing - quiet and steady- seemed to indicate deep sleep.

She wakes up, she recognizes, she smiles. No good morning, no words whatsoever. A kiss on his mouth is her first gesture.

She gets up and goes to the bathroom. He stretches out on the bed, on the crumpled sheets, on the cretonne bedspread, in an effort to reach the phone. He doesn't succeed. He sits up, seizes the device and places it on the bed.

No message for me? None, Mr. Morel. But... oh, excuse me, I'm very sorry, as a matter of fact someone did ask for you. Didn't I ask you to wake me up in that case? Please excuse us, my colleague must have forgot to tell me. Enough; what is the message?

"It's from sir ..."

"Keller," tries Morel to help him.

"No, here it's written ... Keller, yes, that's it. Mr Keller wants you to call him. It is urgent."

It's a good thing that the hotel is so charming because, in terms of efficiency ...

323

"Keller here," says from the other side of the line a voice that for once is excited.

No, no news from Schultze, but somebody else called. Asking for the owner of *Still Life.*

Morel stands up. Violetta comes out of the bathroom and looks amused at him. There he is, stark naked, discussing excitedly with a black Bakelite appliance he holds in his hands.

"General von Moltke," he stammers.

"The count you mean? He's been dead for fifty years now," she jokes.

"His statue, I mean. Do you know where it is?"

"Listen, young man," argues Keller after having burst into a wholehearted laughter, "this painting was worth less than a thousand marks a few months ago. Today it is difficult to draw more than five hundred for it. And you ask the double?"

"In the inventory of the exhibition it is valued higher than that," replies Sasha.

It is at the Tiergarten that Keller made the appointment. Morel had trouble locating the exact spot, at the foot of the monument built to honour a Prussian military hero.

"Excuse me," he asks to the young man, "do you have any connection with the exhibition, with the EnKu?"

"No, no, I came to talk about the painting, nothing else," answers Sasha. "The compensation takes into account the risks. The painting is being sought by the police."

"I doubt it," says Keller. "The *schupos* have other things to do."

"Come to the gasometer then, and you'll see all the police cars. Besides, I can tell you that there are people willing to pay that money."

"Art dealers? I doubt it."

"Not necessarily dealers," says Sasha.

That Oberfrunck again, thinks Morel.

"I know nothing about that," he says. "But what I do know is how to evaluate a painting, all the factors that affect its price. Speaking of this specific one, I'm ready to pay you the sum of three hundred marks."

Now it's Sasha's turn to laugh, a forced laugh because he feels less and less at ease.

Keller intervenes:

"We can go up to four hundred."

Eight hundred.

"Five hundred," retorts Morel.

Five hundred marks: the price of Lena's fare to the US.

"Good," says Morel, "once the picture recovered, we have no reason to demand compensation from the authorities."

"Why not? The painting was stolen, wasn't it?"

"But, in an hour it will have reappeared."

"You know that, I know that. The authorities do not."

"But Schultze could..."

"Denounce you? So what? You are a foreign citizen, and by then you will be far from here. In any case, you can threaten them with your embassy. You'll say that *Le Figaro* and *Le Temps* will take up the story. If there is one thing these people dread, it is the foreign press. "

"You are more business minded than me, I have to admit it," says Morel, amused.

Keller looks at him sternly, and for once there is rage in his usually not very expressive eyes.

"It's not just the money," he says.

He takes a taxi home. Now that he has one thousand two hundred marks he can afford to squander thirty pfennigs. But at the entrance of the building, someone is waiting for him.

"Wassingher, my dear colleague! So, you take taxis now? How come?"

"I was in a hurry, otherwise I never do."

"But, don't you invite me to come in? I'd love to see your apartment. I bet you have valuable art works on the walls. Ha ha, don't be afraid, I'm here just to ask for your cooperation with the authorities. "

"Oh."

"Hans Schattendorf, does it ring any bell to you?"

Seeing Sasha's mystified look, he explains:

"Oberfrunck if you prefer. It's him I'm talking about. But come on, Wassingher, let's not stay here like thieves. Show me your apartment, introduce me to your sweetheart."

"But, you see, I'm in a hurry."

He takes a step towards the stairs, but Schultze blocks his way.

"Not so fast. I'm here to discuss your dealings with that gentleman."

"Listen Schultze, I have already given you your share."

"My share? As if I had any deal in your fishy businesses! No, I come on behalf of the Commissioner. He wants you to note carefully everything you remember about your meeting with Schattendorf. Very soon, maybe already today, he will call you in. What you know might be useful, and the Commissioner will reward you - you can count on a work permit. "

"A permit?" repeats Sasha incredulously.

"If you cooperate. You see, I have used my influence on the doctor. I told him that we can trust you and that you deserve help, whether you have Aryanity papers or not. After all, you were a respected professional in Babelsberg, right?"

Babelsberg. If the director of photography sent him away, it was because he had no other choice, otherwise he had kept him. He had even said that as soon as a possibility arose, he would see to it that he was hired again.

"On the other hand," goes on Schultze, "if you do not cooperate, you know already that the police is very keen on having a talk with you. You're a smart boy, I know you'll make the right decision. "

As for any illegal alien, the word "work permit" has a special aura for Sasha. It is not a document, it is much more than that. A gift, almost a divine favour.

Is it as easy as that to get on the good side of the law? he wonders.

To have the permit. To put it in the inside pocket of his jacket, take the S-Bahn to the movie studios and see the director of photography, Braillowski. To take up his work again. To rebuild what has been destroyed, to resume his life, that life that's been so abruptly interrupted. As if Hitler had never existed.

Already on his way to the rendezvous with the art dealers, Sasha had decided on the appropriate place to hand them over the canvas: at Fabriciusstrasse, a street he knows well from his Sunday walks with Lena.

It is in Charlottenburg, a quiet, patrician neighbourhood, on the antipodes, geographically and socially, of East Berlin. Here dwelt the kings of Prussia, here took the Kaiser his summer quarters, in a Baroque palace with a beautiful garden.

No "rental barracks" here, but elegant buildings. Well maintained façades in light pastel tones with white mouldings. Spacious side walks, in the shade of chestnut trees and century-old oaks. Café terraces, not mundane like those of Kurfürstendamm; quieter and more family-friendly. Unlike the streets downtown, there are almost no Nazi flags here. There has never been flags with the sickle and the hammer either. A quiet neighbourhood, on the fringes of the political struggle.

"Don't even think about that permit," says Lena as they walk towards Fabriciusstrasse. "You will never have it."

"Schultze says that sometimes they make exceptions. Aryanity is not always required."

"And what value has that guy's word?"

"That 'guy' happens to be a member of the party. He knows Dunkels who, in turn, is esteemed by Dr. Rosenberg."

"How respectfully you speak of all those gentlemen, all of a sudden."

"All I want is to stay in Berlin, get back the life we had once. It was a good life, Lena. We were happy, weren't' we?"

"You are naive, Sasha."

"And your cousin Tom, does he dream too? He, an engineer? Not exactly an utopian."

The Nazis will calm down, Tom is sure of that. They are not dumb. He mentioned Erhard Milch, a senior aviation official, but also Arnolt Bronnen, the most powerful man at Radio Berlin, both of them half Jewish.

Maybe life in the new Germany will not be so different from the old one. In the end, Sasha cares very little about politics. As long as he can live his life as he wants, it's the same to him if the name of the Chancellor is Von Schleicher or Hitler, if his party calls itself nationalist, socialist or both.

"But if you nourish those hopes, you should not take any more risks. If you intend to stay in Germany, why make plans for America?"

But he has already set the appointment with Keller and the other. And the money may prove necessary after all.

Once on Fabriciusstrasse, Sasha recognizes their car right away. A woman opens the back-door for them. The car sets off toward the north-west.

Morel unrolls the canvas. He sees the blue character on the right side, the naked woman in the centre. And Grosz' signature. He hands over a brown envelope to Sasha.

"We'll drop you off at Heiligensee," says Keller. "From there you can take the train back to town."

The young man's accent intrigues Violetta.

"Russian?" she tries. That is impossible to deny for Sasha.

They pass through a green area: the Jungfernheide. Oaks, birches. An animal gallops at full speed. A deer, maybe.

"From Moscow?" wants to know Violetta.

"From Vitebsk," lies Sasha.

"Like Marc Chagall," says Violetta. "You have great painters in your country, but today things have changed. True artists are passing through difficult times there."

"Maybe," says Sasha, who feels the urge to answer with some cultured remark, "but here, at the EDeKA , you can see things of value."

He pulls a piece of paper from his pocket. It is the photography of *The Joy is Back* that he has cut from the official catalogue.

Violetta takes a look at it.

"Interesting," she says. "But, the author can hardly be Russian. It's the gasometer exhibition you're talking about, right? The one with official art?"

Lena, to Sasha: "Stop pestering everyone with your *Joy*."

"And, what is it you like in this picture?" asks Violetta, curious.

"He knows nothing about art," says Lena, irritated with this whole business.

Sasha, hurt, remains silent.

Keller asks to see the picture.

"Ah yes," he says. "Novak. He's beginning to make a name for himself."

"It's true," says Violetta, "that his style could well be that of a Soviet painter."

"Because that's what that Novak is," Lena cannot stop herself from saying.

"Now it's you who should hold your tongue," chides her Sasha.

All remain silent for the rest of the journey. Once at Heiligensee, Keller stops the car in front of the train station. Sasha gets off first.

Lena follows, but just before getting out, she whispers to Violetta: "Look for *Celebration at the kolkhoz*, by Viktor Hermann."

"Where? Who?" asks Violetta, taken aback.

But already Sasha pulls her fiancée out by the arm. They walk up the stairs to the S-Bahn.

Morel is relieved. The painting has already cost him a thousand, not to mention Schultze's fifty. But what Navarro is going to pay surpasses largely all those sums. The first thing he will do is to telegraph the good news to Buenos Aires.

"In the meantime, where can I keep it?" he wonders.

Keller: "I would suggest my shop, but it would be safer to take it to Weyher's, a colleague. He is into classical painting, nobody will think of searching his house."

"But what about tonight? Can I bring it to the hotel?"

While they consider different possibilities, Violetta asks:

"Gaston, may I have a look at it?"

He shows her the canvas. Violetta's smile freezes, then it vanishes. Only the pupils of her eyes move, scanning the picture from top to bottom, from right to left.

32

Normally, Dunkels arrives at his office at nine o'clock, except when he comes already at eight, to check the punctuality of his employees.

But today, it's half-past seven and he's already at his post. He has bought a copy of the *Völkischer Beobachter* at the news-stand at Potsdamerplatz. He sits back in his chair and reads it absent-mindedly. At eight o'clock the employees arrive. He opens the door of his office.

"Fräulein Pressler, may I have a coffee, please?" he asks.

The secretary comes in with a tray. He grabs a piece of sugar with the tongs hanging on the handle of the sugar bowl and, releasing the pressure on it, drops the little cube into the steaming liquid. He waits a few seconds for it to dissolve, then he stirs it with the spoon. He pours a drop of cream, watches the surface of the black beverage turn dark brown and, after a second spoon stirring, shift to a shade of chestnut.

He opens yesterday's number of *Der Angriff*.

"Politics of art or the art of politics."

All art produced by the most distinguished craftsmen of the Reich, trained in the best schools, with the most eminent teachers, working in the most authentic traditions: just rubbish, declares the author of the piece. And this individual has the effrontery of attacking true artists in the same breath as he names impostors like Grosz. He is an impostor himself, usurping Oberfrunck's name. Dunkels feels a tickle of impatience, the tickle a hunter feels with his finger on the trigger and the target in the very centre of his rifle sight.

First he thought of calling *Der Angriff*. But then he judged it more dignified to show discretion. Not to splash blood on the scaffold, not to leave a mess. An ax-blow, sharp, clean. Like a surgeon, not like a butcher.

He will not denounce him publicly, he will not stage a scandal, that might prove bad for his image. He will wash the dirty linen in private. He will call the man, explain to him the risk he's taking, the weight of the club that threatens to hit him.

If he does not withdraw his candidacy, Dunkels will make everything public. Schultze will testify, Wassingher will provide the details.

But Schattendorf will save his head if he bows it. A head on which a sword of Damocles will remain forever suspended.

Why destroy him? Better to make him a decorative figure that can be used if necessary. He will have to be content with his small domain in Spandau. He will cling fiercely to it, afraid of losing even that.

He lifts the handset. He dials the number.

"Bureau of Cultural Action," answers a female voice.

"Would you care to put me through to Herr Schattendorf?" he asks in his most melodious voice. "If you are so kind."

Sasha had thought of a taxi, but settled finally for a bus. The 176 dropped him off at Potsdamerplatz, by the Bellevue Hotel. In less than five minutes, he is in front of Hildebrandsstrasse 26.

Schultze is waiting for him.

"Welcome comrade Wassingher, the Commissioner is waiting for you! Heil Hitler!"

"Sieg Heil!" echoes Sasha, but neither the tone of his voice nor the stiffness of his raised arm are as they should, judging by the frowning eyebrows of an SS officer standing there.

"Wassingher," states Dunkels, without leaving his chair. A secretary is sitting at his side, with a stenographic block on her lap.

"Tell us about your exchanges with the Head of Cultural Action," orders Dunkels.

Sasha tells him about the meeting at Reissler's, about Shadow's proposal. But he goes no further.

"Did you fulfil his request?" wants Dunkels to know.

"Excuse me Commissioner, so many things have happened these last days ..."

Dunkels chuckles.

"Well, for the moment, what you remember right now will suffice. Fräulein, type it and bring it in please. Wassingher, I have another meeting. Come back in half an hour and you will sign your statement. "

Sasha goes out on the street. His steps lead him to Potsdamerplatz, automatically. Not safe to walk here without thinking: the traffic is the city's most hectic, with dozens of bus and tram lines criss-crossing, and even if traffic lights have just been installed and a dozen policemen struggle to direct the traffic, one is well advised to keep his eyes open.

He studies the flow of vehicles and pedestrians. Two currents that circulate simultaneously on the same surface; how to make sure that they do not interfere with each other? It would be necessary, he figures instinctively, to isolate the conductors to avoid the short

335

circuit, or to coordinate an alternation of the flows. This is precisely the kind of problem they spent time solving at the Technical University.

The light turns red. He stops. In front of him, on the other side of the street, the modernist block of the Columbushaus – an ugly pile of glass and steel, judges Sasha – that contrasts with its neighbour building, the Haus Vaterland, crowned with a neo-baroque dome.

Is it safe to sign a paper? Wouldn't a verbal statement be enough for Dunkels?

He reaches Leipzigerstrasse, time to turn back. He walks past the florists' stands, stops again in front of the automatic traffic lights installed on a ten meters high tower. Five minutes later, he is back at Dunkels' office.

The commissioner beckons him to come in. Schultze is no longer there, but there is someone else in the office, a tall blond guy in his forties.

"I have the honour to introduce you to a great German artist," says Dunkels. "He has just been awarded the prize of the Fine Arts Section of Prussia for 1934."

"Thanks to your support," comments the other modestly.

"I mentioned your qualities to the Chamber, yes, nothing extraordinary about that. The rest is your own merit, Novak. The merit of your epic inspiration combined with a fine sensitivity to the deepest layers in our people's soul. "

The artist takes leave. Dunkels, satisfied, tells Sasha that Hönig, president of the Reich Chamber of Fine Arts, has just bought one of Novak's works.

"*The Joy is Back?*"

"Ah, you've seen it. Yes, and for a large sum, I can tell you that. But let's get back to our business, Wassingher: here's your statement, all you have to do is sign it."

"Commissioner," says Sasha, "is it really necessary to write it all down? I assure you that I will... "

"Come on, Wassingher, what are you afraid of? This paper has no legal value. Do you see a lawyer here, any witnesses? No, it's only to give me a clear idea of what you are going to report to the authorities when the time comes. But if you find any detail that is not accurate, we will correct it at once. Above all, don't sign anything that does not correspond to the truth!"

In exchange, Dunkels gives him a paper with his office's header. It is a formal promise to use all his influence to grant him a work and residence permit in the Reich.

If that influence allowed a plagiarist like Novak to win an important art prize, thinks Sasha, why wouldn't it be sufficient to get him a simple work permit, just an authorization to practise an honest profession?

Violetta had never heard the name, but a quick glance at the EDeKA catalogue tells her that Eberhard Novak was born in Falkenau an der Eger, Bohemia, in 1892. Vienna School of Art. Exhibitions at Linz 1931, at Zwickau 1933.

Nina Bovrik should be the right person to help her fill in some gaps. What happened to Novak between the war and the Linz exhibition, for example? All Nina knows is that Dunkels visited Zwickau's collective exhibition and went into raptures over one of Novak's works. It is important for bigwigs in the regime to have "their own" artist, and the Commissioner was delighted to hear that in Berlin no one knew Novak, that he was therefore his own discovery.

"Hitler has Ziegler," says Nina, "Göring is Peiner's patron, and now Eberhard has also his protector: Dunkels."

But where was Novak during the war?

In the Austrian army, reports Nina. Prisoner in 1916. Labour camp in Krivoy Rog, in the Ukraine.

"He spent more than ten years in Russia, he married there."

"Was he a Communist?" wants to know Violetta.

Nina shrugs.

"He lives here without being in the NSDAP, he lived in Russia without being a communist."

He married, had children, then came the civil war, the repression. He was a painter already before the war, surely he has continued to paint in the USSR. But what he painted in Russia remains in Russia.

Why did he leave the Soviets? He was in trouble: being a foreigner, of Germanic origin moreover, he became automatically suspected in Stalin's Russia.

Violetta thanks Nina and promises to call her soon. "But make sure you do it! Vittorio has something to offer you, a little job for the embassy. And you know, he has contacts in Vienna too."

Vienna. That's where Novak studied art. But there are no traces of his artistic activities there. There was the war, of course, but, before and afterwards? Still nothing. Until his 1931 exhibition in which Eberhard Novak, at thirty-nine, makes his *debut* in the world of art.

As for the other artist, the Russian, the one Novak plagiarized, it's hard to get any information about him. But browsing old Soviet catalogues, she finds some things between 1925 and 1930. They are all signed V. Hermann, except one where his first name, Viktor, appears in its entirety. The traces stop there.

"Eine Pschorr, nicht wahr?" asks the bar owner with a bottle in his hand. He opens it without waiting for Violetta's answer.

Schattendorf arrives, agitated, with drops of sweat on his forehead.

"What's the matter?" asks Violetta.

"Dunkels is after me, but if he thinks I'll give up, he'd better start thinking again."

"Is it with our prize winning painting he's threatening you? With *True Love?*"

She is delighted to see his bewilderment.

"How could you know?"

"But honey, everybody knows it in Berlin."

His confusion turns to anger.

"Just a joke," she says, and tells him about the transaction between Morel and the young Russian.

"But," he mumbles. "How can he ..."

"It's not important," she says.

"And it's your friend the merchant who has it? But, it's mine, not his."

"He paid a nice sum for it."

"Like I didn't pay myself! A thousand eggs! And where is it now?"

"It's not important, I keep telling you. Gaston is not going to exhibit it anywhere, he won't walk the streets with it under his arm. All he wants is to get it out of Germany as discreetly as possible. And you know what? He still believes it's a Grosz. "

She touches him gently. He shirks her caress.

"Dunkels knows that I tried to make that piece of junk disappear," he says.

"He's threatening you, poor thing. But you see, your dolly has something for you, something that's going to make the big bad Commissioner very very afraid."

He looks at her, his eyes empty.

"There is a painting at the EDeKA," she goes on, "signed by Eberhard Novak, which is an exact replica of *Celebration at the Kolkhoz,* which won an award at an exhibition in Dnipropetrovsk, Socialist Republic of Ukraine, in 1927. Anyone can see it, if he takes the trouble to go to the Art Library and read the volume *Here is the art of our people,* Kiev 1928. "

His expression is a compilation of utterly opposite feelings, in their most extreme registers.

"Novak, yes, I know who he is," he says. "But, Viktor Hermann?"

She tells him. The absence of all trace of the Soviet painter after 1930. The strange coincidence of his vanishing with the appearance on stage of Eberhard Novak.

The expression of his face is transformed. He looks at her ecstatically.

"You have saved me! You have been my muse, all of a sudden you become my protectress!"

"But you've helped me too, lately."

"That's nothing beside the gift you just gave me. That changes everything, now I'm sure I'll be in the Council."

"Don't be. Things can still happen."

"Listen to me: Wendtland has just told me that, out of the twenty votes, seven are mine. The scoundrel has only five, that's why it's so important for him to stop me from running: because he knows he's going to lose. But now all his threats fall flat: if he accuses me, I'll reveal this story. Novak will fall, and he will bring Dunkels with him."

How could it be otherwise? he thinks, with a feeling of victory, a victory that seemed so far away only five minutes ago.

"But, are you sure? How did he get the idea of painting the same picture twice?" he wonders.

"Go to the Library, see it for yourself. It's the same composition, the same characters, except Stalin."

"But he may simply have plagiarized it, we have no evidence that Novak and Hermann are the same person."

"Even if they are not," she says, "don't you think that seeking inspiration from a Soviet painter is serious enough?"

It sure is, thinks Schattendorf.

"Why plagiarize himself, you wonder?" asks she. "Perhaps he lacks imagination, and he never thought that anyone here could have seen that painting, exhibited long ago in a province in the depths of Russia. Maybe he's proud of that work, his greatest achievement, maybe it sums up his vision of art."

Everybody who counts in Berlin will discover, anticipates Schattendorf, that this "national" artist draws his inspiration, neither from Bavaria nor from the plains of Pomerania, not from the mighty Rhine or from the wild coasts of the Baltic Sea, but from a collective farm in Ukraine. When everyone realizes that what he portrays is not the simple life of German peasants, far from urban degeneration, but a village fair organized by the Bolsheviks under the protective eye of the Grand Master of the Communist International, then yes, he will fall, Novak. And his protector will do more than fall: he will collapse, he will break every element of his skeleton, from the upper jaw to the smallest metatarsal bone of the foot.

He is done for, Dunkels. He's dead. And all thanks to her.

"Violetta, it's not only me who will win. You will too. The world will have to recognize your value. I'll take care of it, I will not tolerate anyone not admiring you. I'll force them, I'll beat them with sticks if necessary! "

She looks fondly at him. Harry, Harry. Excessive in gloom, immoderate in joy. There are things that never change, she finds a consolation in that thought. For some odd reason, it reassures her to see her naughty boy in shape, fit for fight.

Lena and Sasha, back in their Moabit apartment. The river is nearby, on Sundays they use to sit on the banks and watch the sail boats on their way to the Havelsee.

"We'll come back one day," she consoles him.

"I will miss this neighbourhood, I will miss Berlin," he says.

"Yes, the other day you told me that you will even miss that gasometer. Maybe you'll miss your friend Schultze too?"

He makes a face.

As he was leaving the Commissioner's headquarters on Hildebrandsstrasse, Sasha had bumped into Clausen.

"Are you still here?" exclaimed the professor, surprised. "You have to leave, the police will not give you more respite and do not count on Schultze to help you a second time."

Sasha showed him the paper Dunkels had given him.

"If I get the permit, I could go back the movie studios. Not tomorrow perhaps, but in a few weeks."

Clausen put on his glasses to study the document. Then he said:

"Come with me, we'll have some coffee."

There is a bar across the street from Dunkels' office.

The professor pulled a document from his wallet. The paper has the letterhead of the Culture Commission, just like the one Dunkels gave to Sasha.

"This is an official communiqué. Do you see that signature?" asked Clausen.

It was a kind of monogram, impossible to decipher, so entangled were the lines it was made up of. Should it be read from left to right or the opposite? It could have been a verse from the Qur'an in stenographed Arabic. If it hadn't been the Commissioner's signature.

"Compare it with this one," the professor asked, pointing to the signature at the bottom of Sasha's document.

That one was easily read: R. Dunkels.

Clausen left one mark and fifty pfennigs on the table and got up.

"Throw this paper in the trash and leave the country," he concluded.

Thursday. Schattendorf is in his office, doing his best to behave as if it were a normal day, a morning like other mornings.

And until eleven o'clock, it is indeed an ordinary day. At a quarter to nine, the culture delegate from Schlosser Industries arrives. Three quarters of an hour later, a discussion with district representatives about the awarding of grants and subsidies to different associations.

At ten to eleven, his last visitor takes leave. Schattendorf tells his secretary:

"I don't take any more calls. And see to it that a telephone line is always free."

The Presidential Council of Fine Arts has been meeting since ten o'clock. They have a few topics of lesser importance to deal with, Wendtland has told him. And then, the main point of the agenda.

Dunkels is done for. Clausen has revealed everything about inventories Dunkels had tampered with and stolen paintings.

His counter-attack was feeble. He had placed all his hopes on *Nature morte*, on Schattendorf's responsibility in its disappearance, but when he received the letter with the photocopy of the Soviet volume – *Here is the art of our people* – he understood that a pact of silence was imperative.

A quarter past eleven. The phone has not rung yet. All the better, he thinks. A too quick decision would not be normal, it would even be ominous. In addition, Wendtland has probably no easy access to a telephone; the conference room is far from his usual work place.

At half-past eleven the call comes.

CONCLUSION

Nine o'clock in the morning ; breakfast in bed. Coffee and *schnecken,* instead of croissants. Coffee, *schnecken* and a freshly awakened Violetta.

The Grosz is in a safe place, the country house of a colleague of Keller. Morel has made sure that the place is dry and with the right temperature.

The day before, he had paid a visit to several of Berlin's public offices. Finally it turned out that the relevant body to submit his claim was the State Treasury of Prussia and Brandenburg.

"They will not give you a penny, do not fool yourself," Violetta warns him.

"Keller says they will. And, you're concerned too."

"Me?"

"Because the five hundred marks will be for you."

She gives him a kiss. Gaston slips a hand around her waist.

"When you hear what I have to tell you, you will not be in the mood to offer me any gifts," she says, sitting up and resting her back on the bed's headboard. "There is one thing I know, Gaston, which I've never told you."

He looks at her amused. Then he answers:

"Well, me too, I know things that I've never told you. My cousin's phone number. My shoe size. And that's not all."

Violetta sighs. She starts telling.

She begins at the end, then changes her mind and starts again from the beginning. At first, she wanted to go straight to the point, neglecting the prolegomena, but her straight line soon branches out in digressions, framed by parentheses, in turn surrounded by quotation marks. Finally, she utters:

"What I mean is: your Grosz is not a Grosz."

Morel places carefully his cup on the silver tray. Then he looks at her intensely. He rubs his eyes, opens them again, looks at her once more.

He opens his mouth, wants to say something but doesn't. He keeps staring at her.

She adds details. How the canvas made its way from her studio to the Blaue Maus, from the Maus to Frau Schramme's Paradiso, from there to a dealer who finally sold it to Keller.

His eyes are fixed on Violetta, but he does not see her. His Grosz is a Shadow. Harry Shadow is Hans Schattendorf. He struggles to grasp all the implications.

What he foresees only too clearly is Navarro's reaction. He will cancel the deal. And Galerie Morel will be in acute cash trouble. In those conditions, impossible to make any new acquisitions in Berlin.

"And that's why I struggled like a madman?" he says furiously. "To have the distinguished privilege of buying a work by your Harry Shadow? And you just watched me do it, without opening your mouth?"

"But I only discovered it yesterday! And you had already paid the Russian. But Gaston, where is the problem? Keller gave you Grosz's letter, didn't he?"

"He will, but ..."

"There are only three or four people who know the story of this painting, and they have no interest in revealing it. Your client doesn't know them and they are not aware of his existence."

"But if he ever ..."

"Does Navarro intend to exhibit the painting publicly?"

No, thinks Morel, not that one. He will hang it in his residence, in a well secluded room where there are already some Indian erotic engravings, a phallic Toltec statuette, and an anonymous oil painting with a Leda in full ecstasy and a stately swan, the size of whose male organ defies all ornithological evidence. Only his friends will have the privilege of admiring *Still Life with Three Characters*, that delightfully depraved work, from Europe's most debauched capital.

"I do not see," says Violetta, "which constellation of coincidences might cause someone down there to challenge the picture's authenticity. And if it ever happened, you can still plead innocence. It will be in Navarro's own interest to shut up. To protect his investment. And his reputation. "

Suddenly, a thought assails him:

"The whore. Do not tell me it's you ..."

She gives a naughty little laugh and covers herself with the sheet.

"And the guy on the right," she says, "is the artist himself, with a little more hair on his skull, of course."

But she's right, he has to admit. *Still life* is, for all practical purposes, a work of George Grosz.

Have all Rembrandt been painted by the master himself? What he did, like Raphael, like Titian, was to examine his disciples' work, to approve it, and to sign. And that is precisely what Grosz did: he signed his letter of authenticity.

They go out. A taxi to Alexanderplatz. The Bureau of Telegraphs. A cable. Recipient: Julio Navarro, Buenos Aires.

They walk across the square, between trams and buses. The trams move forward, one behind the other. In order to predict their coming course it is enough to observe the lines of the rails, or, if one would rather look upwards, the layout of the cables, those cables which the poles mounted on the vehicles' roof never lose contact with, at the risk of immobility for lack of power, dozens of cables that weave a spider's web over the avenue. The trams stop to let passengers alight. Those on their way up allow the others to go down, with discipline sprinkled with Berlin impatience, before rushing in through the six open doors.

"And your shady friend?" he asks. "Has he been appointed to the Chamber already?"

She puts an arm around his neck.

"Let's talk about something else, Gaston," she says as they wait for the policeman to wave them across the Dircksenstrasse.

"Something tells me they chose Dunkels instead," he says.

At the entrance of the Schaumburg Jewelery, near the Alexanderplatz' branch of Aschinger's snack bars, an old woman with a chequered handkerchief on her head is sitting on the side walk with a metal glass in front of her. She says nothing, she asks nothing, she just stares at the pavement, raising her eyes only to meet those of a lady leaving the shop with a small tastefully packed parcel in her hand.

Fifty meters further down, at the corner of Königstrasse, a horse sets foot on a stone, loses the rhythm of its trot, wobbles and collapses, slowly, heavily. The coachman jumps to the ground, puts one hand on the animal's neck, holding it by the belly with the other, and struggles furiously to help it back on its feet.

Dunkels? thinks Violetta. How could he have won? He tried to make disappear *The Joy is Back*, but it was too late, too many people had already seen it. The Führer himself had expressed his wish to acquire one of Novak's creations. And he commissioned him another painting, which will represent him, at the head of the Nazi column in front of the Feldherrnhalle in Munich, during the shooting that followed the Beer Hall Putsch. Novak will go to the Bavarian capital in person, to study the location in detail.

If a rumour arose that *The Joy is Back*, that tribute to the Führer, was a simple replica of another piece of bootlicking, the ridicule would be impossible to hold back. Harry had his finger on that trigger. For Dunkels the decision was painful but simple.

In recent months, Violetta has not dreamed. Tonight she did.

Harry and she were walking in the Grunewald forest. She doubts that he has ever set foot in that forest in real life: he finds nature depressing. They walked, like one walks only in dreams, their feet barely touching the ground. All of a sudden, as they made their way to an ice cream kiosk, Harry started to levitate, his feet gradually losing contact with the ground. He hands her fifty pfennig to buy an ice cream, but when she tries to get hold of the coin, Harry, and his hand with him, ascends ten more inches.

"Throw it down!" she shouts, and the passers-by stop to look at her. The funny thing is, they look only at Violetta; Harry and his gravitation make no impression on them. And she does not react to

349

the extraordinary in the situation either, she's not disturbed by the predicament of her friend, whose figure, smaller and smaller, ultimately melts with the clouds.

It took her a few seconds to realize that she was not in the forest, but in Morel's room. That everything had been a dream with a nightmarish after-taste, although nothing really scary actually happened. A dream, but a persistent one, unusually slow to dissipate, which continued and multiplied in other dreams, drafts of dreams, images and phrases that kept coming without respite or meaning; unraveled reveries.

She woke up, while still watching herself sleep. She sat up half-way, yet she was still lying down, her eyes closed. She breathed quietly, Violetta, sleeping peacefully, attentively observed by Violetta.

"It's five o'clock," she decided. "No, seven o'clock" "No, six."

But her watch said eight. And this time, the one who opened her eyes and the one who woke up were the same person.

"My life has no meaning" she ascertained calmly, almost unconcerned.

Berlin has been everything for her, a life elsewhere is impossible for Violetta. But Violetta is no more. It's not she who will leave Berlin. It will be another woman, a woman with scant luggage and no past.

"Are you really interested?" asks Violetta.

"Interested in what?" replies Morel, his attention monopolized by the fallen horse, which, as slowly as it had collapsed, is painfully regaining its stand-up posture.

"In who was elected to the Council."

350

"Ah, to be completely honest, I couldn't care less," he says. "All I'm interested in is Navarro, and you're right: the chances that he finds out are minimal and I can always plead innocent."

They arrive at Unter den Linden and continue towards Friedrichstrasse.

"Shall we go back to the hotel?" he proposes.

"Sir, I may have posed as a whore, but I am no nymphomaniac!"

He gives her a kiss.

"Do you love me?" she asks.

"Incessantly."

"Like you love something by Kandinsky?"

"I like you more than anything hanging there," he points to the Kronprinzenpalais, on the other side of the avenue.

"There is not much hanging there any more, they are expurgating all the collections."

He stares at the massive building. Her gaze follows his, and registers that the style of the palace is neoclassical and not baroque as she had always taken for granted, without ever giving the matter any thought.

"You'll come with me?" he asks.

"With you? To Paris?"

He will leave Germany right away, he explains, to send the canvas to Argentina from a safe place. But he'll be back in a few days.

"How many days?"

"Tomorrow I take the train to Paris. I'll be back on Friday. With a train via Hamburg arriving at five past ten to the Lehrter Bahnhof."

"Well, Mr. Morel, you tell me what to do."

A short sentence, still it takes him a few seconds to grasp its meaning.

351

"I put myself in your hands, sir", she clarifies. "Take me to Rio. Take me to Paris."

He looks at her flabbergasted, watches her speechlessly for ten seconds. Finally, he realizes:

"Schattendorf was elected to the Council."

"Yes, but how could you know?"

"It's simple, his future is assured. You're free. No reason for looking after him any more."

She had not thought of that. What she did feel was a need to cut off with her past. To erase all that had happened.

Also, she felt what frequent travellers speak about, and what she, a sedentarian, never understood: the vertigo of departure. Vertigo: what the body feels when it has lost its gravity. The first thing death takes away from us, she thinks, must be our weight. And Violetta is dead, that much is clear for her. Dead and delivered from a ballast which only served to keep Violetta motionless.

"His future is assured?" she repeats. "He won a battle, but the war will be long."

She realizes now – so many things she realizes, now that her old life is behind her – that the Novak-Hermann story was not a gift to Harry; it was a reparation. A debt has been paid. To him, but not just to him. An era is closed.

"But he has Goebbels' sympathy," says Morel. "That counts, doesn't it?"

"Do you love me?" she asks, without answering.

They are at the corner of Charlottenstrasse.

"Have they changed the traffic direction?" he wonders. "It went north-south before."

"They changed it a long time ago," she replies. "Two years at least."

"Weird," he says, frowning. His expression makes Violetta laugh.

He looks at her, earnestly.

"'If I love you?'", he repeats. "I've always found that expression pompous, pretentious. "

"Do you love me?" she insists.

Mechanically, like an obedient schoolboy who repeats a phrase to make sure he has assimilated it properly, he says:

"I love you."

"I love you," he asserts once more, so that she can hear it, but also to hear it himself. "You look so radiant today, so happy."

"I don't feel happy," she murmurs. "I'm seldom happy. Do you understand that? That I'm dark, not bright?"

"I'll still love you," he says, savoring the words' flavour. "Happy or sad".

Could that be love? " wonders Violetta.

What else should she call it ?

Some photographs are captions from German films from the 1920s and 1930s. Others, very old ones, we have found on the Internet. To our knowledge, they are free of copyright.